SPUN YARNS UNWOUND VOL. 2

A SHORT STORY SERIES

DEBBIE MUMFORD
DEB LOGAN

WDM Publishing

CONTEMPORARY STORIES FOR ALL AGES

This volume of Spun Yarns Unwound contains contemporary stories written by WDM Publishing's authors. Some are fantasy, some aren't, but they're all set in the here and now.

Deb Logan typically writes contemporary and urban fantasy for kids and teens, but four of these ten tales lean toward mystery, and two of them are definitely LitRPG.

Debbie Mumford enjoys writing contemporary stories, especially fantasy and though four are straight contemporary, the other six indulge that love.

So sit back, relax, and see what our authors think of the world today!

COPYRIGHT

Published by WDM Publishing
First published by Wild Child Publishing, June 2008
Cover and Layout copyright © 2019 by WDM Publishing
Cover design by WDM Publishing
Cover art copyright © morgueFile Free License

TEN STORIES BY DEB LOGAN

PART I

THAT LAKE HOUSE SUMMER

DEB LOGAN

AUTHOR OF *FAERY UNEXPECTED*

That Lake House Summer

SPUN YARNS

A Short Story

1

———————

Parents. Ya gotta love 'em. At least until they do something totally idiotic like taking all your carefully crafted summer plans and blowing them straight to ... well someplace even hotter than Oklahoma in July.

I mean, why in the world — this one or the next or any of the ones humanity might colonize in the next thousand years — would *anyone* think an intelligent, attractive, and eminently popular seventeen-year-old girl like me would want to spend the summer before her senior year in high school marooned in a cabin on a lake in the middle of nowhere?

Did Mom and Dad not realize I had plans? I had a cush summer job all lined up (lifeguarding at an exclusive country club pool). I had once-in-a-lifetime events scheduled (front row seats for an awesome concert with Julia, my best friend since preschool). I had a *LIFE*!

At least, I did until my parents announced we were taking a family vacation. A *mandatory* family vacation. No exceptions, no excuses.

And where were we going on this fabulous trip my younger siblings and I were being forced into? London? Paris? The Eastern

Seaboard? No. The parental units were dragging us off to a moldering old house on the shore of Keuka Lake in upstate New York.

"It's been in my family for over a century," Dad explained as we boarded the plane in Tulsa.

Great, I thought, struggling not to say anything out loud. Mom had already lectured me on the dangers of negativity. *We're probably going to have to spend the summer repairing the roof.*

"Will I be able to fish?" asked Tommy, my ten-year-old brother and the youngest of our tribe.

"Absolutely," said Dad. "We can fish off the dock any time we're not swimming."

Jessie nudged me with her sharp little elbow. "Hear that, Amanda? We can swim!"

I gave my twelve-year-old sister my best *how stupid can you be* glare. "It's a *lake,* Jessie. Of course we can swim."

We settled into the minuscule slots the airline called seats and dutifully buckled in. Jessie and I sat on one side of the narrow aisle, with Mom and Dad and Tommy across from us. Tommy had the window seat, while Dad and I — the tallest members of the family — claimed the aisles.

I sighed, fantasizing about escaping the plane just before they closed the doors and hiding out with Julia for the summer. Instead, I pulled my iPad from my backpack, switched it to airplane mode and opened an ebook file while the flight attendants secured the doors. As we taxied to the runway, I bade a silent farewell to the awesome summer I'd planned and resigned myself to the boredom of life with the rug rats: Jessie and Tommy.

2

We arrived at twilight, our rented minivan bouncing over the long, rutted drive that led from the overgrown two-lane blacktop to the lake house property. True to my expectations, the house was a nightmare. A two-story structure with peeling white paint and sagging front porch, it squatted near the lake, the red-gold light of the setting sun giving it the look of some ancient carnivore waiting to swallow us whole.

Dad parked so that the minivan's headlights lit a path to the front door. We scrambled out and stretched. After a five-hour flight and a two-hour drive, I was beyond glad to be standing on firm ground, even if said ground was in the middle of nowhere.

"Isn't it beautiful?" Mom said with a kind of hushed reverence.

I glanced at the old house and frowned, then looked at Mom. She was gazing across the lake toward the setting sun. I released my resentment long enough to take in the sight. The glowing disc of the sun slid behind dark, low hills across water that glistened like molten gold, the sky wrapped in clouds painted pink and red and orange, the edges fading into royal purple, all framed by the dark branches of two huge oak trees that grew between the house and the water.

The scene was beautiful, and I might have enjoyed it if I hadn't been aware of the lake house behind me, watching us like a hungry beast sizing up its prey. I shivered and turned from the glorious sunset, unable to resist the warning of the prickles running up and down my spine.

Dad stepped toward the porch. I grabbed his arm and he stopped, gazing at me quizzically.

"Let's not stay here," I said. "Let's go back to the state park. I'm sure we can find someplace to stay."

Dad frowned, glanced at the house and back to me. "Why? We've got a perfectly good place to stay right here." He put an arm around my shoulders and gave a quick squeeze. "Come on. You're tired and hungry. You'll feel better once we're all settled in."

I disagreed, but dutifully followed him to the front door. He was fumbling for keys when a truck swung down the drive and stopped beside the minivan. Blinded by the headlights, I put a hand up to shade my eyes and saw a figure emerge and stand silhouetted in front of the new vehicle.

"Mr. Baines?" called a young male voice.

Dad held up his hand and stepped off the porch. I followed not wanting to remain within the house's grasp.

"I'm David Baines," Dad said. "How can I help you?"

The figure stepped forward and resolved into a good-looking guy not too much older than me. He smiled and stretched out a hand to Dad.

"I'm Evan Pryce," he said as Dad accepted his hand and they shook. "My dad's the caretaker here. He was called out of town unexpectedly and asked me to come by and make sure you had food and fuel. I've got supplies in the back of the truck."

"Much appreciated, Evan," Dad said. "I hope everything's all right with your dad. I haven't see Jason since we were in our teens."

"I didn't realize you knew each other."

Evan led the way to the bed of the truck, and Dad waved us all over. "Come on everyone. Lend a hand."

Grabbing a box of lettuce, tomatoes, and other salad veggies, I followed Dad and Evan to the door. Evan steadied a box of kindling between his body and the door frame, whipped out a key and unlocked the door in a smooth motion. Shifting the box's balance he swung inside, calling, "Wait just a sec while I light the lamps."

Lamps?

Yellowish light flared and Evan reappeared carrying an old-fashioned hurricane lamp. The kind with a metal handle and frame, glass chimney and a reservoir for oil or kerosene. Seriously? This place didn't even have electricity?

I bit my lip to keep from complaining. No electricity meant no refrigerator — I glanced toward the kitchen, wondering how Mom would handle meals — but it also meant no way to recharge my iPad, which meant no music and no reading. No Internet connection meant no email commiseration with Julia. What a great summer Mom and Dad had arranged. Total isolation in a foreign part of the country with nothing to do but jump in the lake. Heck, without electricity, we'd be going to bed when the sun went down. Oh, joy! What could be more fun than this?

Once we had all our luggage and Evan's supplies inside, I finally got a decent look at the guy. Definitely not much older than me. He had the tall, lanky frame of a boy on his way to becoming a man. His hands and feet seemed too big for his body, which hadn't yet filled out, but his wavy chestnut hair and deep blue eyes were definitely attractive and he had a nice smile.

So maybe the summer had possibilities after all. Where one cute boy lived, there must be others.

While Evan primed the pump at the kitchen sink and showed Mom and Dad how to load the block ice into the icebox, I lit another lamp and explored the main floor. The front door opened into a large front room, the dark wood floor now littered with our luggage. A dark colored, dusty, overstuffed sofa hunched against one wall behind a rickety coffee table, two matching plush chairs sat across from it. A stone fireplace with a rough hewn mantle occupied the wall between the front room and the kitchen and a well-worn oak table and six chairs provided an eating area. Bookshelves lined one wall. I lifted the lamp and examined the titles. Lots of torn dust covers and books with cracked and peeling spines. I guessed these volumes hadn't been updated in my lifetime. Maybe not even in Dad's.

Between the faded wallpaper, the bedraggled furniture, and the complete lack of modern, electrical appliances, the house felt like a creature that had outlived its place in time.

Dad and Tommy lit more lamps and we all traipsed upstairs to claim our bedrooms. Make that cells. The rooms were tiny, barely big enough to hold a twin bed, and had screen doors.

I turned to Dad. "Why are there screen doors inside?"

But it was Evan who answered. "No electricity, remember? That means no air conditioning and no fans. The screen doors allow air to move freely through the house, while keeping pets, or pests, out of your bedrooms."

Mom and Dad's room was a little bigger, they had a double bed, but it too sported a screen door.

"Where's the bathroom?" asked Jessie.

Evan moved to a window at the back of the house, held up his lantern and pointed. "Right back there."

"Dad!" Jessie squealed, "Do you really expect us to stay somewhere that doesn't even have a toilet?"

"Think of it as an adventure," Dad said brightly. "I loved coming here when I was a kid."

"Good for you," I said, but so quietly that only Evan heard. He glanced sideways at me and hid a smile behind his hand.

"Don't worry," he whispered as he turned back to the stairs. "We have all the modern conveniences at my place. Even Wi-Fi."

"Want to adopt me for the summer?" I breathed. As soon as the words were out, I blushed. That had *not* sounded as flip as I'd intended.

The appraising look he gave me made me squirm. Without waiting for a reply, I moved to join Jessie and Tommy who were arguing over which room was whose.

"I'm oldest," I announced, "so I'm claiming first dibs. This one is mine." I stepped inside one of the two tiny bedrooms that looked out over the lake.

"Good choice, Amanda," Mom said, stepping in to avoid a battle. "Jessie, you take the room next to Amanda's. Tommy, you'll like this one over here," she said turning him deftly toward the little room that looked into the dark forest. "You'll be able to watch for squirrels and birds from the window, and Dad and I will be right next door."

We trooped back downstairs to find our luggage and carry it back to our respective rooms. Personally, I wondered if there'd be room in the little cell for me and my suitcase at the same time.

Before everyone could scatter to their rooms, Evan cleared his throat. "Well," he said, "it looks like you're settling in nicely, so I'll say good night. Mr. Baines, if you need anything, you have our number."

"Wait a minute," I said, suddenly struck by an alarming thought. "The house doesn't have a phone, and there's no electricity. How are we supposed to keep our cell phones charged?"

Dad grinned. "*We* won't. You're off the grid as of now, but I'll keep mine charged up in the minivan, in case of emergency."

Evan moved to the door and saluted. "Have a great stay. I'll stop by in a day or two to see if you need anything." And then he disappeared into the night.

As the sound of his truck died away, the house creaked and I imagined it exhaling in malevolent satisfaction. Another shiver ran down my spine.

"Dad, are you sure about this?" I asked. "I don't think this house likes us."

Jessie and Tommy stopped on the stairs, dropping their bags with muffled clunks. Dad stared at me, but Mom stepped forward and put a hand on my forehead.

"Are feeling well, Amanda? I know you didn't want to come, but it's not like you to be fanciful."

I shrugged away from her and faced Dad. "I'm not trying to be difficult, but this place feels haunted. I want to leave."

Something scraped across the floor above our heads, and everyone jumped. Jessie and Tommy scampered down the stairs and ran to Mom, who threw her arms about their shoulders and drew them close.

Dad moved to the stairs and peered up. "I'm sure that was just the wind," he said bracingly. "Tommy, Jessie, everything is fine. Grab your bags and lets take them upstairs. Lydia," he continued, giving Mom a meaningful glance, "speak to Amanda."

Mom nodded, and Dad and the rug rats disappeared up the stairs.

"All right, Amanda. What's this all about? I understand you're unhappy about this vacation, but there's no need to frighten the younger children."

I inhaled deeply and tried to calm the butterflies in my belly. No joy. They tumbled and whirled like they were dancing on the edge of a tornado. "Honestly, Mom," I said, my voice much steadier than my stomach, "I'm not trying to cause trouble. I just have a really bad feeling about this place." I hurried on before she could interrupt. "It wasn't so bad while Evan was here — like it was hiding its intent from him, but the minute he left I felt it again. It's like the house is alive, and it wants us gone."

Mom had been frowning until I mentioned Evan's name, then her face cleared and a smug expression quirked her lips and danced in her eyes. "Oh, I see," she said. "You feel safe when Evan's here, but don't think your father and I can protect you."

"No!" I said, raising my voice more than I'd intended. "I mean, he seems like a nice guy and all, but you're missing the point. It's not *me*, it's the *house*! It wanted him gone so it would have us to itself."

"Amanda, do you hear how ridiculous you sound? This is a house. A structure of wood and brick and stone, built by human hands. It's not alive and it's not haunted." She shook her head, picked up her bag and headed for the stairs. "Get your things. I want you unpacked before dinner."

I was severely skeptical of unpacking into the scruffy old dark wood trunk that sat at the end of my bed, but when I lifted the scarred lid I discovered several packets of lavender sachet tucked into the sections of a deep, removable tray along with a carefully lined main compartment that smelled of cedar. By the time I'd emptied my suitcase into the trunk and arranged my belongings in a sensible manner, the sweet smell of frying bacon was wafting through my screen door.

Tommy slammed out of his room across the hall and raced for the stairwell. "Bacon!" he yelled, like the little savage he is.

Jessie appeared at my door like a ghost materializing from the ether. "Come on, Amanda! Tommy will eat everything in sight if we don't get there quick."

"You know Mom won't let him eat our share," I said with a laugh, but I got to my feet, grabbed my empty suitcase and waved her toward the stairs. "But I'm starving, so I'm right behind you."

Dad and Jessie stowed the suitcases in the minivan while Tommy and I set the table. Before we knew it, we were eating our first meal at the lake house. I hated to admit it, but it was kind of cozy sitting around that scrubbed oak table by lamplight eating bacon, fried eggs, toast with real butter and sipping hot cocoa. Real hot cocoa! Not the dehydrated stuff made with hot water we always used at home. This was smooth and rich and so sweet I had to sip slowly, but oh ... so delicious!

Even though it was only 8:30 when we finished cleaning up after dinner, I was so tired I didn't even complain when Mom suggested we all head to bed.

"Great idea," Dad agreed. "It's been a long day, and we might as well start adjusting to a new schedule. With no electricity, we're going to be following the natural cycle of light and dark more closely than we do at home."

I grimaced, but kept my mouth shut. Julia was never going to believe me when I finally got to tell her about this ... *unusual* ... summer vacation.

Before I blew out the pretty little painted glass lamp beside my bed, I made sure that the flashlight Dad had given me for middle of the night excursions to the outhouse was safely under my pillow. I was exhausted, but uneasy about being alone in the dark in a house that seemed to resent me, but I'd noticed that since dinner the atmosphere had mellowed. Maybe the house was getting used to us.

I perched on the edge of my bed, bare feet firmly planted on the hardwood floor, and placed my palm flat against the wall. Closing my eyes, I sent a thought to the spirit of the house, "I'm not your enemy. I'll be careful not to hurt or damage you, if you'll give my family shelter and safety while we're here."

I know it was a stupid thing to do. Mom was right. It was a house. A building. A structure of wood and stone. It wasn't a living creature.

But I swear, as soon as I made that pact, the floor shivered beneath my feet and I heard a soft screeching like a hinge in desperate need of oil saying, "Truce."

It was probably just the wind scraping a branch across the peeling paint on the side of the house, but it calmed me. I slept deeply and peacefully, assured that the house had accepted us.

3

I'm not anxious to admit it to Mom and Dad, but I discovered myself during that month at the lake house. The absence of electronic gadgets, the isolation from all but myself, my family and a very few new friends, forced me to look inward and I found strengths and talents I would never have guessed I possessed.

We swam — a lot! — and hiked the surrounding hills. Tommy and Jessie developed a passion for fishing, and while that particular pastime held no interest whatsoever for me, I thoroughly enjoyed eating their catches. There's nothing like fresh trout sprinkled with garden-fresh herbs and baked over an open fire ... a delicacy we enjoyed often that summer.

In the evenings, we read by lamplight or worked thousand-piece puzzles on the oak table, or, my personal favorite, wrote. Mom had bought a supply of spiral notebooks, colored pencils and pens, and crayons at the general store, and we all took advantage of them. Tommy drew pictures of fish and squirrels and other rodents he observed in the woods, Jessie created mazes and flowing patterns that reminded me of Celtic knots, and I discovered a love of story telling.

My stories weren't particularly well-written, but Tommy and Jessie enjoyed listening to the ones I chose to read aloud, and Mom and Dad praised my imagination. I developed one recurring character, a little girl named Becca. I'd dream of Becca during long nights of restful sleep, and then record her adventures the next evening. Jessie was especially fond of my stories about Becca. Probably because the girls were about the same age.

Evan came by every other day or so, supposedly to check on our supplies of firewood and block ice, but I think he came to see me ... and the rug rats, of course. He swam with us, waging fierce splashing battles with Tommy and Jessie, and introduced us to the best hiking trails in the area. He also told us about the Finger Lakes, almost lecturing on the glacial activity that had created the distinctive lakes.

What he had to say was interesting, in an oddly academic sort of way, but Evan himself was more so. I studied him as he explained geologic forces to Tommy and Jessie. He loved this stuff! His face glowed as he described the movement of the ice, the grinding of the rocks, and his blue eyes darkened with intensity. He leaned forward, gesturing with his hands, as if he could make the rug rats see what he was envisioning. I was fascinated by the expressions that flitted across his face ... and by how easily I could read them.

One particularly fine day, we packed a lunch and the four of us hiked to the top of a nearby ridge. Sunlight filtered through leaves of oak, beech, and hickory as we tramped along the trail, our footsteps muffled by a thick layer of leaf duff. Jessie and Tommy darted from one side of the trail to the other, covering twice the distance Evan and I trod. Every now and then we'd stop to admire one of their discoveries, a fairy ring of mushrooms or the tiny splash of color of some late-blooming wildflower.

The trail was an easy one, the ground rising gradually, but I was still winded by the time we stepped out of the shadow of the trees onto a crag of rock at the top of the ridge. I yanked my baseball cap from my head and wiped my forehead with my sleeve, glad that I'd pulled my dark hair into a ponytail so that it was off my neck. When I finally glanced around, I stilled. The view was breathtaking. Vast forests of oak, maple, beech and hickory, with the occasional spear point of pine spread out before us with sunlight sparkling off the deep blue water of the lake.

"This is amazing, Evan," I whispered. "Thank you so much for bringing us."

"Thought you'd like it," he said with a grin. He swung his pack off his shoulders and glanced at Tommy. "Who's ready for lunch?"

With a whoop of delight, Tommy settled on a rock at Evan's feet. I swear he opened his mouth like a baby bird waiting to be fed, but Tommy denies that vehemently.

After a lunch of peanut butter and grape jelly sandwiches, Cortland apples and thirst-quenching water, Tommy and Jessie wandered off to look for interesting rocks — Tommy was determined to find an arrowhead — and flowers. Evan and I stayed on the crag, soaking up the sunshine and talking about our respective futures.

"I'm off to college in the fall," he said. "SUNY Cortland."

I stared at him blankly. "What's a sue-knee?"

He looked startled, then shook his head and said, "I forget you're not from around here. S-U-N-Y. State University of New York at Cortland."

I nodded. "I've been accepted at the University of Tulsa, but I'm not sure I want to stay that close to home. I may apply a few more places before school starts."

He peered at me from the corner of his eye while he played with a piece of dried grass. "Ever think of coming east? Cortland's a good school."

My jaw dropped. He wanted me to go to his college? Why? I mean, he had been coming around a lot, but this was one of the first times we'd ever been alone ... kind of ... Jessie and Tommy were somewhere nearby.

I closed my mouth. After all, if he was really interested in me, I didn't want to look like a complete idiot.

"Well ... um ... no," I stammered. I sucked in a deep breath and tried again. "I mean, I'd never been to New York until this summer. It seems like a nice place," I finished lamely.

He turned to face me. "You should think about it," he said, his blue eyes darkening with an intensity I'd only ever seen when he talked about geology. He leaned close to me, too close for me to continue gazing into those sapphire eyes. I closed my own, felt his warm breath whisper across my lips. He was going to kiss me. Evan Pryce was going to kiss me!

"Amanda!" Jessie's scream broke our spell. "Evan! Help!"

Evan jumped to his feet while I scrambled upright. We raced across the crag toward her voice. "Coming, Jessie," I yelled, terrified by the possibilities of what might have happened.

"It's Tommy," she cried as we skidded to a halt in front of her. "He slipped and fell and then couldn't stop himself. He went over the edge!" She pointed to a spot where the rocky ridge rounded into blue sky.

"Calm down, Jessie." Tommy's words floated up to us. "I'm fine. I'm sitting on a grassy ledge, but I can't stand up. My foot's stuck between two rocks."

My hammering heart relaxed into an almost normal rhythm and I released the breath I hadn't realized I'd been holding. I stared at Evan. "What do we do? How do we get him back?"

"Let me see where he is." Evan stretched out on his belly and crawled slowly to the place where the rock sloped over the drop-off. I followed his example, ready to grab his feet if he should start to slide.

Evan peered over the edge. "How you doing, buddy?"

"Not too bad," Tommy answered, but I could hear the fear in his voice.

"Don't worry," Evan said. "We'll have you out of there in no time."

Evan slithered back to safety and gave me a worried glance. "Jessie, I left my pack up where we had lunch. Would you go get it?" As soon as she was out of earshot he whispered, "He's safe. The ledge is stable, but his foot is caught. I'll need to go down and help him get loose."

I nodded, understanding his dilemma. "You're worried that I won't be able to get both of you back up," I said so quietly I could barely hear my own words.

"I've got rope in my pack and I'm good with knots. We'll secure it to a tree and I'll use it to guide me over the edge and down to Tommy. Once he's free, I'll assess his ankle, if he can bear weight, we shouldn't have any trouble. Actually, we shouldn't have any trouble anyway, but if something else goes wrong, do you think you can find your way home and get your dad?" He bit his lip, then added, "Better get both our dads. Mine knows his way around this kind of thing."

I closed my eyes and reviewed the trail in my mind. I hadn't paid close attention — Evan was leading and he knew where he was going, but the path had been straightforward. I could do it.

"Yes. I can get home."

"Good. If all goes well, you won't need to, but if not, take Jessie and get help. Agreed?"

"Agreed."

He leaned forward and touched his lips to mine. "I want to pick up where we were interrupted," he said with a quick grin. "Later?"

I couldn't help but smile. "Later!"

Jessie appeared with Evan's pack. He lifted an eyebrow and asked, "Do you think she's going to make a habit of that?"

I laughed aloud. "Definitely. It's her super power."

Jessie frowned. "What?"

Evan grabbed his pack from her. "Thanks, Jessie." He dug down to the bottom and pulled out a length of sturdy rope. "Now, let's find something to anchor this to."

We were in luck. The rope was long enough to tie around a stout young maple and Evan's knot work proved reliable. Within the hour both boys were safe and secure on the path.

After a brief rest, Evan found a branch to use as a walking stick and hoisted Tommy onto his back. I shouldered Evan's pack and Jessie led our procession down the trail and back to the lake house.

Mom and Dad were panicked, relieved, and grateful, all at the same time. Evan, the hero of the day, stayed for dinner and Dad even built a bonfire in the fire pit as dusk deepened.

I had a lot to think about as I fell asleep that night.

4

A few days before we were due back at the Rochester Airport for our return flight to Tulsa, Jessie disappeared.

Evan and I had been trying to find some alone time to explore the exciting new connection we seemed to be building, but between Mom and Dad's refusal to allow me to leave the lake house, and Jessie's uncanny ability to interrupt, we'd been totally thwarted. So my first thought upon hearing that Mom couldn't find her was, "Good! Maybe now Evan and I can grab a minute alone!"

Imagine my guilt when she was still missing hours later.

Evan called his dad — unlike me, *he* had a working cell phone, and a group of men gathered to search the trails near the lake house. Tommy and I donned swim suits and searched the water around and under the dock. Mom scoured the house from top to bottom, even checking the attic and crawl space which none of us had bothered with all summer.

No one found any sign of her. Jessie had simply vanished.

Exhausted by fear and guilt, I dropped into one of the overstuffed chairs in the front room and closed my eyes. As I relaxed, a shiver ran down my spine and a corresponding tremor moved through the floor boards beneath my feet. I froze, remembering my initial unease with this house. But we'd been here nearly a month, and since I'd made my pact with it that first night, I'd been at ease. Had something changed? Had the house broken our agreement and harmed Jessie?

Rage flared, coursing through my veins. If the lake house had hurt Jessie, I'd make sure it was razed and the ground beneath it salted!

As if understanding my unspoken threat, an image formed in my mind. Becca. The little girl I'd been writing stories about for the past month. One of her adventures had communicated itself to me with such intense sorrow, such soul-wrenching sadness, that I hadn't tried to write it down. I knew I didn't have the skill with words to convey her emotions, but I'd never forget that dream.

It occurred to me now that my dreams of Becca had begun almost immediately after I'd made my deal with the house. They couldn't be related, could they? Was Becca somehow tied to this house?

Was the house trying to communicate with me now? Through Becca?

"Do you know where Jessie is?" I asked the little girl in my mind.

She nodded, and once again my heart was flooded with the sad devastation of that unrecorded dream.

I jumped from my comfortable chair and raced for the kitchen, calling for Mom.

"What?" she cried. "Have you found her?"

"Not yet, but I have an idea." I pointed to a cabinet door hidden below the worktable that sat along the wall the kitchen shared with the front room, the wall that housed the fireplace in that other room. "Did you look in there?"

Mom looked blank. "No. I didn't even think of it. It's out of my line of sight."

I nodded. "But it's not out of Jessie's. Help me move the table."

The table didn't block the door, but if my dream of Becca was accurate, the door could only be opened from the outside. If I went in, I wanted Mom to have easy access to get me out.

We dragged the table to middle of the room and I scrambled to the cabinet door, praying I wasn't too late. I yanked it open and Mom held it still. I crawled inside and found my little sister, unconscious.

Pulling her out onto the kitchen floor, I glanced up at Mom. "We need to get her to a hospital."

"What's wrong?" Mom asked. "Why didn't she answer me? I've been calling her name for hours!"

"I don't know for sure," I said, "but I think it's carbon monoxide from the fireplace. It's been building up in the cabinet all month."

Dad, Evan, and Evan's dad, Jason, came through the back door, saw Jessie on the floor and the kitchen erupted in activity. Jason called 9-1-1, Evan moved to my side, and Dad scooped Jessie from the floor, saying, "What does she need?"

"Fresh air!" I yelled and we all bolted for the front door.

The emergency dispatcher recommended that we wait for the ambulance, and before I would've thought possible in such a remote location the lake house's drive was filled with flashing lights and milling people.

Jessie was given oxygen and taken to a nearby hospital, Mom and Tommy riding along with her.

The police officer, along with Dad and Jason and Evan, wanted to know how I'd found her. I couldn't very well tell them that the house and a small ghost had told me, so I just said that I noticed the cabinet and suddenly realized that its proximity to the fireplace could have been a death trap. After all, my class had studied carbon monoxide poisoning in a health unit last year.

The men went to check out the cabinet, and I followed.

Dad shone a flashlight around the enclosure and stilled. "Jason," he said quietly, "what do you remember about family legends? Didn't a little girl go missing in the '40s?"

Evan's dad frowned. "Yes. I think she was about twelve. They never found her."

Dad looked up, his expression solemn. "I think we just did."

"Her name was Becca, wasn't it?" I asked.

Jason looked startled, then thoughtful. "Yes," he said. "I believe it was. Rebecca Baines. Her parents were the last year-round residents of this house. After her disappearance, it became a vacation home. My family had worked for the Baines from time to time, so we became the caretakers." He studied me for a moment. "Have you been seeing ghosts?"

I blushed. "Not really, but I've been dreaming about Becca."

He nodded. "Every now and then a family member has sworn the house was haunted. But only family. When we rent it out to the general public, we never hear any tales. Seems Becca only wanted to talk to relations."

Dad stood and put an arm around my shoulders. "Well, I'm glad she chose to talk to you. Not only did you save your sister, but you've found a lost child. We'll give her a proper burial. Maybe that will allow her spirit to rest."

EPILOGUE

Being home in Tulsa was weird after that Keuka Lake summer. I was thrilled to have Internet access again, and being able to email and Skype with Evan was great, but the world felt noisy somehow. I missed the peace and quiet of the lake house.

Jessie recovered fully and she and I talked about her adventure in the cupboard. She'd been dreaming of Becca too. When she crawled into that cupboard, she knew she'd found the other girl, she just hadn't expected to be in danger of sharing her fate.

Evan and I were finally allowed to go on an honest-to-goodness date, and let's just say that his kiss was worth the wait! I'm prepping my application for SUNY Cortland now. A year seems like forever, but we're corresponding almost daily. By the time I get to college, I'm going to know exactly what makes Evan Pryce tick.

I already know his two main passions: geology ... and me!

PART II

AMELIA FOX: SPY IN TRAINING

DEB LOGAN

AUTHOR OF *FAERY UNEXPECTED*

Amelia Fox:
Spy In Training

SPUN YARNS
A Short Story

My name is Amelia Fox, and I'm a spy. Just like my mom.

Okay, I'm a fifteen-year-old girl, and I don't know for a fact that my mom is a spy, but come on! What else could she be? I mean, no one with a lick of intelligence — and my mom is brilliant — could possibly be content as a corporate accountant for a shoe company. I mean, really? She's got to be a spy. Traveling around the world to boring shoe conventions and factory inspections ... that's just her cover. She's actually making the world safe for truth and justice.

Just like superman. Only quieter.

So quiet in fact that she won't even admit to her family what she's up to, and our family is very small and tight. Just Mom and me and Grammie, who watches over me while Mom's off doing her thing. As Grammie always says, "It's just us girls."

Not that our family was always females only. Dad and Grandpa died together in a plane crash in the Wasatch Mountains of Utah when I was just a baby, so while I know Mom and Grammie miss them, I'm okay. I mean, it's hard to miss people you never knew.

But back to Mom being a spy, while she's never admitted

anything, I'm pretty smart, so whether she tells me or not. I know the score.

And today, my suspicions were confirmed. During my first day at my new school of all places.

2

Mercer Island Academy was designed as a stately English country manor complete with wrought iron fence enclosing the grounds. Mom dropped me off on my first morning, and I sprinted up the stone steps without a backward glance, pausing only after passing through the high front doors into the entry hall.

A pretty blonde girl dressed in the obligatory uniform of a navy, green, and black plaid skirt, white shirt and navy sweater vest, but with her shirttails hanging out, lingered just inside the front door. She clutched her backpack to her chest like a life-preserver and stared wide-eyed around the entry hall. I joined her in silent observation. Polished hardwood floors, high ceilings, and sweeping staircase. The interior walls were wood. Mahogany, just like Mom's desk at home. Several doors stood guard to the right and left of the staircase — mute sentinels guarding the school's secrets. All tightly closed. A crystal chandelier hung suspended over the center of the foyer, blocking the view up the stairs.

"It's so ... grand," whispered the pretty blonde.

"Yeah, but we're here. We belong." I tore my gaze from the crystals budding from the chandelier and smiled at her. "I'm Amelia Fox. This is my first day. I'm guessing you're new too?"

Blue eyes fastened on me and a shy smile bloomed. "Uh-huh. Paige Andrews. I'm here on a scholarship, and right now I think they made a huge mistake."

I laughed and butted her with my shoulder. "Hey. You're ahead of me. Somebody *chose* you. I'm just here 'cause Mom can afford to pay."

Paige giggled and her face lost the stressed, tight-stretched look. "Glad to meet you, Amelia. Ready to brave the ranks of Mercer Island Academy?"

"Let's do it."

We nodded to each other and marched to the conservatively clad woman who stood to the left of the stairway under a sign that read "New Students: Last Names A - L."

"Good morning, ladies. I'm Miss Wentworth, a guidance counselor here at the academy. What are your names?" She glanced at her clipboard and flipped pages until she found Paige and then me. Pulling sheets from under the clip, she handed one to each of us.

"Here are your schedules. Keep them handy until you've memorized your class assignments and locations," she instructed in clipped tones. "First, though, proceed up the stairs and to the left to the grand ballroom. Headmistress Patrick will address the school in a few minutes."

Paige and I skipped up the stairs and followed a crowd of uniform-clad kids to the ballroom. The large room was set up as an auditorium, complete with temporary stage and rows of folding chairs.

We settled into adjoining chairs and Paige grabbed my schedule to compare classes. I slipped my backpack under my seat, then peered at the pieces of paper in her hand.

"Look! We have English Lit and Algebra together," Paige said.

"Nice. Too bad we have different Social Studies teachers."

"Look at your schedule after lunch!" Paige exclaimed. "Your whole afternoon is dedicated to *Independent Study*." She glanced at me sideways. "Are you some kind of genius, or something? I've got normal classes all day."

I shrugged. "I'm smart, but I bet everyone here is. No idea what

3

Paige and I were just finishing our lunch — Chicken Alfredo with a side of peas and carrots, followed by Peach Melba for dessert — when Miss Wentworth appeared behind Paige.

"Miss Fox," she said, pinning me to my chair with a stern gaze. "Please follow me. We need to arrange your afternoon schedule."

I glanced at Paige, who gave me a wan smile, gathered my dishes onto a tray, and followed the counselor. As we passed a large metal cabinet slotted for trays, I slid the remains of my lunch into an empty slot. Just like we'd been instructed to do when we entered the cafeteria.

Miss Wentworth nodded as I joined her in the hall. "Very good, Miss Fox. You follow directions well." She led me down the main staircase to the entry hall. Pausing before one of the doors I'd noticed earlier, she chose a silver key from a keychain attached to her belt, unlocked it, and gestured me inside.

I hesitated. A locked door. Why would she take me through a locked door? Was I in trouble? I couldn't be in trouble! I hadn't been here long enough to do anything wrong.

Miss Wentworth raised an eyebrow, but remained silent.

I took a deep breath and stepped through into a mahogany

paneled hallway that smelled of lemon and beeswax. Miss Wentworth followed me and I heard the lock snick back into place. I
suppressed a shudder. Whatever was going on, I was determined to
show no fear.

Miss Wentworth's functional low heels clicked on the polished
wood floor as we approached the door at the end of the hall. I tried to
keep my rubber-soled high-tops from squeaking. My heart was
pounding so loudly I was sure the counselor could hear it, and I
wanted to keep my noise to a minimum.

As she chose a second key, this one bronze, she said, "If you
accept your schedule, you'll be issued the necessary keys."

I frowned. If I accepted my schedule? Like I had a choice?

The door swung open and I peered into a small conference room
with white walls and linoleum floors so clean they reflected the
furnishings. Plush leather seats were arranged in four rows of five, all
facing a glass and steel podium. Four additional leather chairs sat
behind the podium, facing the other twenty. Nineteen heads turned
to look at me as Miss Wentworth gestured for me to take the final seat
in the audience.

I slipped into the soft leather chair and nodded to the girl next to
me. She turned back to the podium without acknowledging my
presence.

Miss Wentworth stepped to the podium as a door opened near
the front and four additional adults entered, filing up to sit behind
her. Each adult wore a dark blue Mercer Island Academy blazer. One
man — horn-rimmed glasses, a white button-down shirt and a fussy
little bow tie — wiped the leather chair with a white handkerchief
before sitting down.

The other man — blond hair, blue eyes, white polo shirt, no facial
hair — plopped down and studied the ceiling. Which seemed odd,
since it was featureless, white acoustic tiles.

The other two female teachers were dressed identically to Miss
Wentworth. Dark blue blazers, white blouses, and pleated skirts that
fell just below the knee in the same navy, green, and black plaid that

the female students wore. Fortunately, our skirts were cut to a more fashionable length.

"Welcome, students," Miss Wentworth said, causing every eye to focus on her. "I'm sure you're all wondering about your afternoon schedules. First, let me say that while Mercer Island Academy is a fine institution of learning, specializing in preparing young people for academic success at the university level, it is also houses a rather specialized program of study accessible only to students who have been recommended by, shall we say, experts in the field."

I glanced around at the other boys and girls in the audience, wondering who they were and what we'd been recommended for.

"Mr. Smith, if you will hand out the schedules, please. Students, refrain from opening your envelopes until I give you permission."

The blond man stepped forward, accepted a stack of manila envelopes from Miss Wentworth and, checking the name on each, handed them to individual students. Most of us frowned and looked puzzled on inspecting the envelope, and when I finally received mine, I understood why.

The name on the outside was *C. Bedelia*.

My mouth fell open, but I stifled a protest. No way would I open the envelope since it clearly wasn't mine.

Miss Wentworth cleared her throat, drawing our attention back to the front of the room.

"I assure you, Mr. Smith has not made a mistake in handing you that particular envelope. You have each been recommended by someone the Mercer Island Academy trusts to be enrolled in our, uh, *unique* program of study. You have been chosen to be trained for covert operations, as spies, and as such each of you will be known by your cover, your *legend*, rather than by your true identity."

My heart went into overdrive. I *knew* it! I knew Mom was a spy, and here was the proof. She'd enrolled me in a private school and recommended me for spy training! I grinned down at the envelope and wondered who *C. Bedelia* was supposed to be and what she was going to learn this year?

"If any of you would prefer not to be involved in this program, you are free to leave the room now," Miss Wentworth continued. "Do not open your envelope. Simply leave it on your chair and exit by the door you came in through. Someone will escort your back to the office and your schedule will be updated there. You will, of course, be required to sign a non-disclosure agreement."

She paused, but no one moved.

Leave? Now? As if!

"Excellent," said Miss Wentworth. "Your training begins now. You will be given half an hour to study your schedule and memorize your legend. Do you understand, Miss Bedelia?"

A heartbeat of silence followed, then my brain caught up and I realized Miss Wentworth had asked me a question. *I was Miss Bedelia.*

"Yes, Miss Wentworth," I said in a clear voice. "I understand."

"Very good." She nodded to Mr. Horn-rimmed Glasses, who pulled a stop watch from his pocket. "Begin timing ... now!"

I ripped open my envelope with shaking fingers, more excited to be *C. Bedelia* than I'd ever been to be Amelia Fox. I yanked a sheaf of papers out and absorbed their contents.

I was Claire Bedelia, a fifteen-year-old girl from Montpelier, Vermont.

Seriously? Vermont? I was Seattle born and bred. I had no idea what a Vermonter sounded like. Would I lose credit for having the wrong accent?

No time to worry now. I only had half an hour to memorize this stuff.

My father, Gerald, was an attorney specializing in family law, my mom, Stacy, a stay-at-home mom. I smiled. Stacy. Stay-at-home. I could remember that. My ten-year-old brother, Charlie, was nuts about dinosaurs. *You have a brother. Remember that.* I was an only child in real life, so I had no experience with siblings, younger or older.

Claire was an avid soccer fan, loved horses, and dreamed of becoming a veterinarian. Gag!

I memorized details of Claire's (my) life and, with five minutes left, turned to my schedule. Mornings would remain in the larger school, picking up subjects required by the state, but my afternoons would be spent in training for covert operations.

Monday, Wednesday, and Friday afternoons would focus on Beginning Chinese, Code Breaking 101, and Self-Defense for Novices. Tuesdays and Thursdays I'd attend World Geography for Covert Forces, Introduction to Urdu, and Basic Weapons Training.

A huge grin spread across my face. This was real. I was going to learn about weapons and code breaking. I could hardly wait to get home, hug Mom, and promise never to give her attitude again for the rest of my life! This was a dream-come-true.

"Time!" called Miss Wentworth. "Mr. Jones, please collect the data and destroy it."

Horn-rimmed Glasses guy came around and we handed him our papers. I gave mine up willingly, but I noticed a couple of people still reading as the information was pulled from their grasping fingers.

"Attention please," Miss Wentworth said. The room quieted and we all stared avidly forward. "Let me explain the rules of our program. As soon as you walk through that door, you will leave your normal self behind. You will become your legend. No other student in this program will know your real name. Your schedules have been arranged so that you will not be in any non-covert classes together. However, if you should bump into one another in the hallway or encounter each other in the cafeteria, you will walk away with as few words as possible. You will not act in such a way as to raise suspicion in your civilian classmates, but you will avoid each other as completely as possible."

She waited for that command to sink in before continuing. "Also, some of you may believe that you know who recommended you for this program. Trust me; you do not. Under no circumstances will you say or do anything to cause anyone, sponsor or not, to suspect that your school day is anything other than what the civilian population of Mercer Island Academy experiences."

I shifted in my seat, suddenly uncomfortable. I really wanted to talk to Mom about all this. Evidently I wasn't the only one with issues. The room was suddenly alive with the rustle of clothes and the squeaks of distressed leather.

"This is not open to negotiation," said Miss Wentworth. "Failure to obey this rule will result in your expulsion from Mercer Island Academy. Not just the covert program, the academy in general. Do I make myself clear?"

We murmured our assent, and the room fell silent.

"At the end of this school year, if your sponsor is in a position to do so, he or she may choose to reveal himself or herself to you. However, please understand, that the decision is your sponsor's ... and his or hers alone. You may never be told who recommended you. Learn to live with not knowing."

For the rest of the afternoon we solidified our legends by introducing ourselves to each other and reciting our new identities. Finally, in the last half-hour of the school day, we were assigned to pods. Each of the five adults would be mentoring four students. My pod, code name: sea lions, would be under Miss Wentworth's watchful eye.

Before we were dismissed for the day, Miss Wentworth issued our keys. "Silver for the entry hall door," she said, "bronze for the door to this room. Tomorrow you'll be escorted into the classroom and laboratory section. Plan to arrive early. You'll need time for orientation. Any questions?"

I raised my hand. "Just one. Why keys? Wouldn't cards and card readers be simpler?"

She nodded. "They would. They would also be less secure. You see, while you might think that these locks could be picked easily, you'd be mistaken. The keys are of different metals for a reason. The lock mechanism reads the chemical composition of the key as well as whether or not the teeth fit the tumblers. Anyone attempting to use a copy would find themselves in trouble in very short order."

"Wow," said the other girl in our pod, code name: Nancy.

"Wow, indeed," agreed Miss Wentworth. "Now, guard your keys. They're coded to you, so if a set shows up in someone else's possession, we'll know who the careless party was."

Four heads nodded solemnly.

"Very good. You've had a long first day. Mark, Nancy, Sheldon, and Claire, I'm looking forward to training you. Go home. Sleep well. Commit nothing to paper or pixels, and remember who you are at all times during the day tomorrow."

"Thank you, Miss Wentworth," I said, and using my bronze key for the first time, slipped into the mahogany paneled hall.

4
_____

That was the beginning of the hardest and best school year of my life.

Every morning I arrived at school as Amelia Fox, best friend of Paige Andrews. After lunch, Paige ran down a hall to chemistry while her best friend Amelia disappeared to a carrel in a special section of the research library to study the mathematical theorems involved in population health. A topic no sane teenager would want quiz me on.

In reality, I used my silver key to step through a door in the entry hall, morphing from Seattleite Amelia into Claire Bedelia, a Vermont girl who adored her little brother and carried his picture with her everywhere.

As the year progressed, our pod began to speak Chinese during our weekly sessions with Miss Wentworth. On rare occasions she would switch to Urdu and anyone who didn't follow the transition was sentenced to remedial classes after school.

Weapons training was a mixed bag. I'd never be a whiz with bow and arrow, but give me a Sig Sauer pistol and I could break it down, clean it, and put it back together fully loaded with the safety on faster than anyone else in my class. I was even a decent shot.

But code breaking was my favorite class. My brain understood codes. I could look at a coded transcript and literally see the letters and numbers rearrange themselves before my eyes.

Evidently, this was expected.

"Your sponsor told us to expect you to be a natural at code breaking," Mr. Jones said after I'd aced a particularly difficult exam. "And I must say, you haven't disappointed. I'm very pleased with your work, Miss Bedelia."

"Thank you, sir."

While not a class, as such, we also learned highly effective methods of memorization, because nothing we were working on was allowed to leave our section. No papers. No computers, laptops, tablets, or cell phones. Claire Bedelia did not exist beyond the door with the silver key and neither did her studies.

One interesting sidelight of this restriction was that as I became an ace at recollection, I worked on expanding my retentive capacity by gathering intelligence on my fellow students. First I found the members of my pod and surreptitiously learned their real names and personal data. Nothing written, of course, and nothing obvious. Even Paige, who spent nearly every minute of my non-covert day by my side, never noticed me observing classmates.

Like code breaking, intelligence gathering came as naturally as breathing.

By the end of the school year, I could have told Miss Wentworth anything she wanted to know about any member of my covert pod. Of course, I didn't. If she wanted the information, she'd have to ask. I'd already decided that next year, I'd set my sights on learning about the upperclassmen. So far, I'd only caught the occasional glimpse of an older covert ops student, but next year, they'd be on my radar.

And so, as my first successful year of spy training ended, I looked forward to finally having a long talk with Mom. I could hardly wait to tell her everything I'd learned and to hear a little bit about what she actually did. Not the boring balance sheets and stock reports that were her legend, but the exotic places she'd been, the important intelligence she'd gathered.

Because I knew my mom was a spy, just like I was becoming, and I

5

—————

When the last bell rang on the final day of school I bounded out to the car, too excited for words. Mom and I could finally talk!

Only Mom wasn't behind the wheel of our midnight blue Mercedes coupe. Grammie was driving. I shelved my disappointment, climbed into the front passenger seat, and asked, "Where's Mom?"

Grammie watched me buckle up before answering. "She had that convention in Geneva, remember? Her flight left at noon." She flipped on her turn signal and moved slowly, carefully into traffic.

"I remember," I said with a sigh, "but I thought she was leaving tomorrow."

"That was the plan until her administrative assistant called with an updated schedule."

"Oh. Okay."

"So, how was your last day?" Grammie asked. "In fact, I haven't heard enough about your whole year. Now that it's over, I want to hear everything." The car slid to a stop at a traffic light and Grammie and I looked at each other.

No, I thought. *It couldn't be!*

Grammie chuckled. "Had you fooled, didn't I? You thought your mother sponsored you."

"Seriously?" I asked. "It was you?" My heart plummeted, taking my mood with it. "Mom didn't think I was good enough?"

The light changed, but Grammie didn't move the car forward. "Oh, sweetie!" she said, as a horn blared from the car behind us. "Just a sec."

Grammie pulled across the intersection and into a convenience store parking lot. She killed the motor, then turned to face me.

"Amelia Fox, your mother loves you with all her heart. If she'd been able or had known anything about this program, she would've recommended you in a heartbeat."

I blinked back the tears that had been threatening to fall and stared at Grammie. "What do you mean, 'if she'd known'?"

Grammie beamed. "Sweetheart, your mom isn't a spy, has never been a spy. She didn't have what it took and your grandfather and I knew that. We never recommended her for training."

"You and Grandpa?" I asked. This couldn't be true. But how else would she know about the training program, about my needing a recommendation? "Y...you were spies?"

"Indeed we were," she said, nodding exuberantly. "Two of the best. And you father was a CIA analyst. He wasn't a field operative, was never interested in that aspect, but he finished the training and could break code faster than anyone else in the service." She smiled at me. "Pretty sure you take after him in that department."

My mind whirled. Mom was a civilian, but Grammie and Grandpa and my dad had all been spies. Code breaking was in my blood ... just not from whom I expected.

"So, Mom doesn't know anything about the covert operations department at Mercer Island Academy?"

Grammie shook her head. "Not a blessed thing, and we're going to keep it that way, aren't we?"

I thought about my plans for the upperclassmen next year, and how I'd be expelled if I told a civilian about my studies. I loved my mom, but I loved my training too.

"She won't hear it from me," I promised.

"Good girl," said Grammie, "but now that you know I sponsored you, you can tell me all about your adventures. I'd love to hear who's teaching you and what kind of assignments you're being given."

I breathed out a happy sigh and nodded. I could hardly wait to tell her!

EPILOGUE

Okay, so I was wrong. My mom's not a spy.

But my grandmother is, and I'm a spy-in-training.

Now that I have a confidant to share my successes and failures with, I really excited for my next year of training to begin. But for right now, Grammie and I have a lot of catching up to do before Mom gets home from Geneva!

Can life get any better?

I can hardly wait to find out!

PART III

ANGELIC VOICES

DEB LOGAN

AUTHOR OF *FAERY UNEXPECTED*

ANGELIC VOICES

SPUN YARNS

A Short Story

1

Susie Emerson sucks. I can't believe I ever admired her. Mrs. Davis gave that descant solo to me. My voice was supposed to lilt over the rest of the choir, float to the rafters above the sanctuary, maybe even soar right up to heaven and please God with its sweetness. Until Mrs. Davis reassigned the descant to Susie.

If Susie's mother wasn't the Director of Music at Valley Christian Church, I'd trap Susie in the alley and tear her hair out. Actually, I'd be doing her a favor. That fine, white-blonde, wispy stuff hardly qualifies as hair. If I pulled it all out by the roots, some decent, dark, thick curls might have a chance to grow.

Yeah, I know. Violence is never the answer, but it sure felt good to think about.

"Deanne Lawyer!" Mrs. Davis' voice cracked over my head like a whip and forced my thoughts away from Susie's destruction.

"Yes, ma'am?"

"I asked you to trade places with Susie. I want you to lead the soprano section." She turned to face the other girls as I switched seats with Susie. Mrs. Davis missed the smirk Susie aimed at me, but I didn't.

You are SO toast. I settled into her vacated chair. Your own mother won't recognize you when I'm finished.

I plotted as I sang the melody line to our portion of the Easter cantata. Honestly, the soprano part was so predictable, even the eight-year-olds should be able to sing it without sheet music or my strong voice to lead. In spite of the ease of the part, I still heard Heidi waver off- key, so I turned my head and aimed my clear, perfect- pitch voice in her direction. She pulled into the key and held her own.

What to do about Susie? I wanted my descant back, but couldn't fault her execution of that soaring counterpoint. If only, I'd had some warning about her backstabbing. I could've held my own in a fair fight, but when Susie Emerson, my fourteen-year-old idol, pulled in close to me and sang right in my ear...well...it'd take a stronger vocalist than I was at the moment to stand up to Susie's voice and sight read at the same time.

Unfortunately, the same tactics wouldn't work for me. My voice could blow the wax out of your ears, but Susie wasn't sight reading. Like I said, her mom was the Director of Music. Susie had been studying that piece since before Mrs. Davis settled on it. She might've even talked her mom into insisting Mrs. Davis choose it. Score one for 'Sucky' Susie.

The soprano section sounded like a single voice by the time Mrs. Davis released us for the day. I ran to find my parents and did such a great imitation of a happy twelve-year-old Mom didn't even narrow her eyes. Mom's amazing. She always knows when I'm plotting something. Maybe she's psychic. Or, maybe she just knows kids.

I'm the youngest of six, which has some definite disadvantages — experienced parents being a major one. Some of my friends get away with the dopiest stuff just because their parents don't know any better...yet. Mom's on a personal crusade to educate the adults in my sphere of influence. She's determined to ruin all possibility of fun in my universe.

Anyway, I had her fooled for the moment. I giggled and teased Roger, my fifteen-year-old brother, all the way home, secretly longing to escape to my room to determine Susie's doom.

I worried the problem that whole week — I can be a real bulldog when I get my teeth in something — but didn't come up with a single usable tactic. After all, I wanted to live to sing that descant, and if Mom caught me doing anything really bad, life would end.

Then, Sunday morning, while my other four brothers piled into the van that masqueraded as our family car, Roger handed me the answer.

"Listen, squirt," he said. "I know you're friends with Susie Emerson," Yeah, right. "so you might want to warn her. Jason Billings is a nasty piece of work."

I let my eyes go wide in little-sister innocence. "What's Jason got to do with Susie?"

"Word is they're meeting in the hall behind the baptistery between services." He stopped, reconsidered, and changed direction. I love watching Roger think; psychics need not apply. "Well, warn her not to go. I'd hate to see a friend of yours get hurt."

I kept all understanding off my face as I allowed my I-don't-have-a-clue expression to morph into my whatever-you-say-oh-godlike-brother smile. "Okay, I'll tell her."

Roger smoothed back his blue-black hair and climbed to his assigned seat. I stifled my desire to leap in the air and do back flips, and instead stepped daintily to my spot behind Mom.

"Everyone ready?" Dad asked.

Oh, yeah, this is going to be a GREAT Sunday.

2

I think the pastor's sermon centered on "Love Your Enemies," but I wouldn't swear to it. I didn't hear much since my obsession with catching Susie where she shouldn't be filled my brain.

When the service ended, I escaped Mom's chaperonage by racing to walk with Angie Cooper and her mom. Mom approved of Mrs. Cooper.

"Oh, no," I said, infusing mortified horror into my voice.

"What is it, dear?" asked Mrs. Cooper.

"I forgot my offering for the starving children in India! I have to go find Roger. He'll know what to do."

"Do you need me to come with you?" she asked, as I wove through the parents herding children to Sunday School.

"No, thank you," I called over my shoulder. "I know where he is."

Free of supervision, I turned down an unused corridor and raced for the warren of halls behind the baptistery and choir loft. Yes! Deserted hall — now, where to hide?

I just managed to pull my camera-phone from my pocket, step behind the baptistery door and leave it open a crack before my quarry arrived.

Susie slithered down the hall from the office wing and Jason sauntered in from the sanctuary. They met right in front of my narrow line of sight. Oh boy, did they meet! I've seen lots of kisses at the movies, but I'd never seen one like that. I swear, the air around my head tingled and the pit of my stomach did weird twisty things.

I aimed my camera-phone through the crack and got an eye-popping picture. I started to put it away, but the electricity in the air kicked up a notch. I aimed without looking and snapped a second shot, just to be on the safe side.

"Oh. My. God!" I couldn't help myself. I yanked the door open and stepped into the hall. I knew I should be quiet, but Jason's hands...well, his hands jerked away from where they had no business being, so maybe yelling wasn't such a bad thing.

"Deanne!" Susie's face turned brighter red than the baptistery curtains. "What do you think you're doing?"

"What am I doing? Well, I'm sure not sucking face in the hall with a creep like Jason!"

The creep growled and stepped toward me.

"Don't even think about it," I said. "Remember Dave, Harry, Gabe, Phil, and Roger?" I ticked my brothers' names off on my fingers as I chanted them. Okay, so being the youngest of six has its uses, too.

Jason scowled, turned and strode back toward the sanctuary. Leaving me and Susie. Alone. In a deserted hall.

The older girl glared at me. "What do you want, punk?"

"I want you to screw up the descant so badly Mrs. Davis has to give it back to me."

Susie laughed. "Right. Like that's going to happen."

She curled her upper lip in a nasty sneer and said, "What? You think you're going to tell my mom about this? It's your word against mine, and everyone knows you're a jealous little prig."

"Maybe," I said, "but I've got evidence." I held the phone up where she could see the picture. Considering I hadn't aimed, it showed a very clear image of just what Jason's hands shouldn't have been doing.

Susie blanched and lunged for the camera.

I jerked it away and said, "Don't. Unless you want me to hit the

3

On Easter Sunday, I sang the descant perfectly. The rest of the choir sang great, too. Even Susie. I have to admit, that girl has a great set of pipes. The Director of the Adult Choir, Mr. Jordan, found me after his choir members put away their music and hung up their flowing white robes.

"Well, Miss Lawyer," he said, his eyes twinkling behind inch-thick glasses, "that was quite a performance. You'll be a fine addition to the adult choir in a few years."

"Thank you, sir." I pasted a sweet smile on my face and tried to calm my flip-flopping heart. Mr. Jordan liked my descant!

He looked over my shoulder, smiled broadly, and patted me on the top of my head. Can you imagine? He patted my head like I was a dog. Or worse, yet, a baby.

"Excuse me, my dear. I see Miss Emerson getting ready to leave." He stepped away from me, still talking. "It's time to move her out of the children's choir. We could use a strong voice like hers in the soprano section."

I gaped after him as he wove through the milling choir members to Susie. I didn't need to be close to see triumph light her face. My spirit sank. Susie won after all. I moped toward the door on the opposite side of the room. I touched the metal doorknob and it hit me like an electric shock. Susie was gone. I would be the reigning Queen of the Choir.

My smile reappeared and I ran to find my parents. I had to tell them about Mr. Jordan's compliment!

PART IV

MOM'S HELPER

DEB LOGAN
AUTHOR OF *THUNDERBIRD*

MOM'S HELPER
A "Read-to-Me" Story

1

Benjamin looked up when his Irish Setter stopped digging; he watched the dog turn his slender snout toward the house. The big dog always heard Mom before Benjamin did. Benjamin listened really hard, but he didn't hear anything.

He wished he had ears like Rusty's.

He stretched out grimy fingers and stroked the long, silky hair on Rusty's ear, then felt his own naked one. How could Rusty hear so much better when his ears were clogged with hair? Benjamin puzzled over this problem until he heard his mom's voice.

"Benjamin! Benjamin David, where are you?"

"Here, Mom." The sturdy little boy scrambled to his feet and ran around the corner of the house.

"What were you doing around there?" Mom's voice was tired. She was always tired these days. Tired and sad.

"Nuffin'." He scuffed the dirt with the toe of his red sneaker. "Helpin' Rusty."

The big red dog bounded up and danced on the cement at Mom's feet. She smiled at his antics and her shoulders dropped a fraction of an inch. "What did Rusty need help with?"

Benjamin heard the shift in Mom's tone and grinned up at her. "We're playin' with dirt. It's soft and squishy, and Rusty likes it a lot!"

Mom sighed and shook her head. "You're going to need a good scrubbing before dinner. Oh well, never mind that now. You and Rusty have fun, but stay where I can see you from the window."

"Okay, Mom." He turned to run across the sparse grass, Rusty trailing at his heels.

Benjamin didn't like this new backyard. There wasn't anything to do in it. Not like his old yard. That one had a swing set, a real pool and a trampoline. Benjamin liked the trampoline best. He and his dad had lots of fun jumping on it.

Dad.

He didn't want to think about Dad. He wanted to play with Rusty.

Benjamin looked around. Where did Rusty go?

He moved down the fence line until he could see the side yard, but still be seen from the kitchen window.

There he was!

Rusty had returned to the hole he was digging in the cool, brown earth.

Benjamin hesitated. He wanted to go help Rusty dig, but he wanted to obey his mom, too.

The hot sun beating down on his blond head made the decision for him. There wasn't any shade in the part of the yard the window could see. All the shade was over there with Rusty and the hole.

Besides, he was Mom's Helper. He needed to take care of Rusty.

Benjamin helped Mom as much as he could. She was so sad since Dad...

No. He wasn't going to think about that.

Mom needed him to keep an eye on Rusty.

His decision made, Benjamin ran across the yard to the growing mound of dirt next to the fence. Rusty looked up as he arrived and wagged his tail happily.

Benjamin settled himself on the ground and began arranging the soft, cool earth in neat little piles. Some he squished together in his hands, making lopsided balls. Some he pushed into hills and valleys and drew roads through with his fingers.

He wished he had one of his trucks to drive on the roads, but he didn't want to get up and go inside. If he did, Mom would probably make him wash for dinner.

Road construction absorbed his attention so completely that he didn't notice when Rusty stopped digging and started wriggling.

Not until it was too late.

He heard a happy bark and looked up to find Rusty staring at him from the other side of the fence.

"Rusty! What are you doing out there?" Benjamin watched in horror as Rusty pranced toward the street.

"Rusty! Come back here!"

The big dog stopped, looked back at Benjamin and wagged his tail. Benjamin saw him wink, and knew Rusty wasn't coming back.

He should go get Mom. Mom would know what to do.

But Mom was so sad ... if Rusty ran away, she would be even more unhappy.

Benjamin looked from the dog to the house and then at the hole. He could do it. He could get through that hole and bring Rusty home.

Mom wouldn't know Rusty tried to run away. Mom wouldn't have something new to be sad about.

He was Mom's Helper. He could do this.

2

Benjamin laid down on his belly and squirmed across the cool dirt. When his head reached the fence he pushed it so close to the ground his left ear filled with grit ... but his head went under!

He kept squirming.

Once, he raised his shoulder a little too high and felt the fence scratch his skin, but it didn't hurt much. He pressed his shoulder closer to the earth and kept wriggling.

Rusty danced back to the fence, cheering him on with happy little yips.

Finally, he was through the hole. He stood up, brushed some of the dirt off his jeans and T-shirt and looked at his dog.

"That was very bad, Rusty," he scolded. "You get right back in our yard."

But Rusty had other ideas.

The big red dog dropped to a crouch, then bounded up to lick Benjamin in the face. Before Benjamin could recover, Rusty took off down the sidewalk.

Benjamin wiped his face on his shirt, looked once more at his home, then ran after the happy dog.

Catching Rusty was an adventure.

Benjamin had never been out of his yard without an adult before. He felt very grown-up as he ran down the street after the red dog.

When he came to the first corner, he stopped. Rusty paused on the other side, watching to see what he would do.

Benjamin remembered what he'd learned about crossing streets. He looked first one way, and then the other.

He didn't see any cars at all. Carefully, he stepped into the street. Still no cars.

He dashed across, hoping to catch Rusty's collar. But the long-legged animal loped away before he got to the other side.

This game of run-and-wait lasted a long time, until they came to a busy street.

Benjamin struggled to keep up, to keep the dog in sight. He groaned as Rusty pranced into a knot of people just as the traffic light changed.

Before Benjamin could reach them, they'd crossed the street; traffic flowed across his path again.

Rusty sat on the far corner, his tail beating a lively rhythm on the sidewalk.

Benjamin looked around. He knew this place. This was the corner where Mom always stopped and waited for the red hand to turn to a white person before she jogged across the street, pushing Benjamin in the oversized stroller.

He looked at the traffic light. He saw a red hand. He waited.

Soon the traffic stopped and the light changed to the white man.

Benjamin stepped off the curb and, keeping his eyes on Rusty, ran across the street.

The cars moving past at his side scared him. His knees felt weak and wobbly, but he kept moving toward his dog.

Rusty seemed to understand Benjamin's fear. He sat patiently, waiting for Benjamin to catch up.

When Benjamin stepped onto the sidewalk, he threw himself at the big red dog and hugged him tightly. Reassuring warmth flowed from the dog to the boy.

He did it!
He caught Rusty.
He helped Mom.
Now he just had to take Rusty home.

3

Benjamin studied the street. He knew where he was, but he didn't know how to get home.

Rusty knew, but Benjamin couldn't trust Rusty to go straight home. He grabbed Rusty's collar and moved away from the busy corner.

He spied a wooden bench beside a store window and led Rusty to it. His knees still wobbled slightly as he climbed onto the bench.

"We have to go home, Rusty," he said, staring firmly into the dog's liquid brown eyes. "Mom's getting dinner ready."

Rusty rested his chin on Benjamin's lap. His eyes looked mournful.

"It's okay. You don't have to be sad. You didn't mean to run away." Benjamin stroked the dog's silky head.

He needed to think.

He couldn't follow Rusty home. Rusty might not go straight home.

He wasn't sure he could find the way back by himself. He needed help.

Dad always said if he got lost in the forest, he should hug a tree 'til Dad found him. But there weren't any trees here, and Dad...

No. He wasn't going to think about Dad.

Mom said he should never go anywhere with a stranger, so he couldn't ask a grown-up.

Wait a minute!

There was one grown-up he could ask.

Mom always said, "Policemen are our friends."

That was the answer. Benjamin needed to find a policeman.

He stood up and walked back to the corner, still holding Rusty's collar. The Irish Setter, tired of the game of chase, seemed content to stay close to Benjamin's side.

Benjamin looked down the street the way he'd come. He didn't see any policemen.

He looked the other direction. No one that way either.

He turned around and looked at the store window next to the bench. There were yellow curtains in the window, and lots of white letters on the glass.

Benjamin recognized the letters, but he didn't know what B- A- K- E- R- Y- spelled.

He thought about his problem for a minute, and decided that if he didn't go anywhere with them, it would be okay to ask a stranger to call the police for him.

He marched up to the store and right in the open door.

"Here, now," said a loud voice, "you can't bring that dog in here! Shoo... outside with you." A huge woman dressed all in white rolled toward him. She shook a flour-covered finger at him.

Benjamin froze; he held Rusty's collar with both hands. His wide blue eyes filled with tears. He was tired of helping Mom.

He wanted to go home.

The woman came closer and knelt in front of Benjamin. She must have seen the tears, because she didn't sound angry anymore.

"What's the matter, little fellow?" she asked, her voice much softer now. "Are you and your dog lost?"

Benjamin nodded. "Rusty and me need a policeman, please."

Mom would be proud; Benjamin remembered his manners.

The woman smiled. "That's a very sensible request, young man."

She took Benjamin's grubby little hand and led him to a table near the front door.

"I guess you and Rusty better sit here while you wait." She pointed her finger at Rusty. "You, sit!"

Rusty sat, then laid down at Benjamin's feet.

The woman looked surprised, and pleased.

"I'll be right back," she said as she bustled behind a counter filled with breads, cakes and cookies.

Feeling safer now, Benjamin noticed how sweet the air smelled. The sight and smell of food reminded him that he hadn't eaten yet.

He was really tired.

His legs twitched from running. His stomach growled and twisted, and his eyelids kept trying to close.

Helping Mom was hard work.

He stretched one foot out to touch Rusty, and laid his head and arms on the table.

4

When Chloe walked into the bakery, she thought her heart would burst with relief. There he was, her baby, safe and sound. She drank in the sight of her grimy little boy asleep at the café table with his big red dog stretched at his feet.

She turned to the police officer who accompanied her. "Yes, that's him. That's my son, Benjamin."

"I knew the minute the call came in that it had to be your boy." The officer smiled. "I'm still amazed he got this far. Two miles is a long way for a four-year-old to travel."

Chloe nodded. "Rusty must've been on his way to the dog park. I'm just glad they stopped here."

She turned and walked to the counter. "Thank you so much for giving him a place to wait, and for calling the police," she said to the bakery owner. "If anything had happened to him," her voice caught, and she paused a moment before continuing. "My husband died a few months ago. When I lost my house, too, I thought I'd lost everything."

She turned to look at her sleeping child. "I was wrong. My world is sturdy and healthy, and very tired at the moment." She turned back and gave the woman a tearful smile.

"My pleasure, ma'am, and I must say, he's a good little fellow." She gave Chloe an answering grin. "Even if he did bring a dog into my bakery."

"Yes," said Chloe, "Benjamin's a good boy. His dad used to call him 'Mom's Helper.'"

EPILOGUE

The next day Benjamin helped Mom put a big rock in the hole where Rusty had escaped.

"If you see Rusty digging near the fence again," Mom said, shading her eyes with one hand, "what should you do?"

"I'll tell you and we'll find another big rock," Benjamin said with a grin.

"Perfect," said Mom. "That will be the best way for you to be my helper."

Benjamin hugged Mom, then patted Rusty on the head and said, "C'mon, Rusty. Let's race to the house!

PART V

DEIRDRE'S DRAGON

DEB LOGAN

AUTHOR OF *FAERY UNEXPECTED*

DEIRDRE'S DRAGON

A "READ-TO-ME" STORY

1
——————

Deirdre rubbed her eyes, and then stared open-mouthed at the dragon squished onto the window seat. He was shiny, golden, and too big to be believed.

The dragon oozed off the cushion onto the hardwood floor. He yawned and stretched, reminding Deirdre of a really big (make that gigantic!) cat.

She stood perfectly still, heart pounding so hard her fingers and toes felt like they might explode. She wondered if the dragon was hungry, but mostly she wondered what dragons ate.

"Caviar," the dragon rumbled, licking his lips. "You know, little black fish eggs, but I'll settle for peanut butter and jelly on rye."

"You, uhh, you talked! Where did you come from? Wait a minute. I didn't say that out loud." Words gushed from Deirdre's mouth. She was standing in the library of Gran's Scottish mansion talking to a dragon, and all she could do was ask stupid questions.

"Of course I talk," said the dragon, "and I hear your thoughts, too." He lifted his lip in what Deirdre hoped was a dragon smile. "As to where I came from, why, you called me."

"I did? I didn't mean to. I mean, I'm sure you're a very nice dragon and all..." her words trailed off. She took a deep breath and tried again. "How did I call you?"

"You touched that silver medal, and on your twelfth birthday, too." A wisp of smoke escaped his nostrils.

Deirdre hoped he didn't belch up a flame. With all these books, she'd be toast in a heartbeat! Oh, yeah, the medal. She glanced at the ornament clutched in her sweaty palm. The bright disk boasted a tiny picture of a dragon in mid-flight.

"I am bound to the females of your bloodline," the dragon continued, "but you must be twelve before I'm allowed to show myself." He lowered his head and looked straight into her eyes. "Happy birthday, Deirdre."

"Thank you." Mom would be pleased. Even with her mind in a whirl, Deirdre remembered her manners. Mom. Aha! "Does my mother know about you?"

"Of course." He turned his jewel-bright eyes away from Deirdre and glanced around the room. "She's heard all your Gran's stories, just as you have."

"No!" Deirdre cried, stamping her foot. "That's not what I mean, and you know it." She decided to be more specific. "Does my mother think you're real? Has she ever talked to you?"

The dragon ambled to the hearth and curled up in front of the extinct fire. "No." He yawned and nestled his triangular head onto his front feet. Claws flashed, and then retracted, rescuing the hearthrug from certain destruction.

"Why not?"

"The enchantment skips a generation. You won't be ready to give me up when your daughter turns twelve." His eyes sparkled, laughter dancing in their depths. "But when your granddaughter comes of age, well, that will be another bowl of caviar."

"Well ... what if I don't have a daughter? Or a granddaughter?"

His head jerked up, his eyes round as saucers. "No granddaughter? But you have to have a granddaughter!"

"No, I don't," Deirdre said, her heart skipped a beat. Arguing with a dragon might be dangerous, but this was important. "Mom says I can be anything I want." She planted her fists squarely on her hips and stared up into the dragon's glittering eyes. "Dad says so, too. I'm going to be an astronaut and discover new planets."

The dragon stared at her. His huge eyes whirled, and the spiky tip of his golden tail beat a rapid rhythm on the hearthrug. "Maybe you could have a daughter before you go exploring?"

She relaxed a little and considered his suggestion. "Maybe, but I might be too busy training. You might have to wait until I get back from my new planet."

He looked so disappointed. She wanted to ease the sting. "Maybe I'll name my first planet after you. Say, what is your name?"

He stood proudly on all four feet, wings furled tightly against his back and made a noise that sounded like chewing up rocks and gargling the slurry.

"Oh." She cleared her throat -- it hurt just listening to that name – and said, "well, maybe I'd better just take you along when I go exploring." She paused, thought about that terrible noise, and asked, "I don't suppose you have a nickname?"

He grinned his toothy grin and said, "You may call me Roddy."

Voices in the hall interrupted them. Deirdre turned from the dragon to stare at the closed door. A moment later, it burst open and Dad stepped into the room.

"Hi, Dad," she said, stuffing the medal into the back pocket of her jeans. She glanced over her shoulder at Roddy.

The majestic beast was gone. In his place lay Gran's favorite toy -- the dragon she'd told all her stories about.

2

_____

Late that night, Deirdre snuggled under the covers of the huge bed in Gran's guest room. The old mansion whispered and creaked around her. Another night she might have been frightened, but not tonight.

Tonight Roddy lay stretched across the length of the bedroom floor. His huge bulk protected her from the unaccustomed night sounds.

"What if Mom comes in?" she whispered.

"She'll see a toy on the floor," he replied. "Go to sleep, Deirdre, you're safe with me."

She closed her eyes and thought about home. What was she going to do with a dragon in Denver?

"Have the time of your life," came the nearly silent answer. "We'll have wonderful adventures. Just wait and see."

PART VI

SALT WATER

Deb Logan

Salt Water

A *Siren Tales* Short Story

CHAPTER 1

Families. They're all weird in their own special ways. Take mine for example: very small — just me and Dad; with one major phobia — salt water. But I was about to break free of the family taboo. I couldn't wait!

I settled my backpack on my shoulders, slipped into the crowded, narrow aisle of the economy section of the 737 airplane, and followed Emma toward the exit. The air was stale, heavy with competing perfumes and the smell of tightly packed people. My stomach jumped and rumbled, partly with excitement, but mainly from hunger. My bacon and egg breakfast had been hours ago and the meager cup of apple juice on the flight had only made me hungrier.

People ahead of me jostled around in the tight space retrieving carry-on bags and cases from white plastic overhead bins. I watched in amazement as rolling carts were jerked from the compartments and lowered to the aisle, often missing other passengers' heads by inches. Slowly the line ahead of me settled and shuffled forward.

I'd never flown before. I'd heard friends talk about the crowded conditions on flights, but I'd never imagined this. Total cattle car!

Still, I couldn't believe my luck. When my best friend in the whole world, Emma Walker, had invited me to come with her family to Portland, Oregon, I thought I'd died and gone to heaven! Then reality rushed in and killed the happy glow. Dad would never allow it.

I'd spent my whole life in Wichita, Kansas, as far from salt water as Mom and Dad could manage and still live in the continental United States. I knew all about wheat farming and cattle ranching, but I'd only seen the ocean in television shows and movies.

Mom's phobia of salt water was over the top. I never knew why; she wouldn't talk about it. I supposed Dad knew, but his lips were sealed too. Maybe she was attacked by a shark as a child. At this point, I'd never know. She died in a car accident when I was ten.

After Dad and I recovered from the shock of our loss, I thought maybe he'd relent on the family phobia. Maybe we could drive down to Corpus Christi, Texas like my friends' families and I could swim in the Gulf of Mexico. But no. Dad continued Mom's vendetta against the sea.

To my complete amazement, Dad said yes to the trip west with the Walkers. Go figure.

Emma and I followed her parents through Portland International Airport, taking in the cool inlaid mosaic floors and smooth stone seats carved to resemble seals and salmon. Almost made me wish I was still young enough to make the adults stop so I could climb and slide. But I maintained my fifteen-year-old dignity and just gazed at everything with jaw-dropping wonder.

What Dad didn't realize — because I hadn't been stupid enough to tell him — was that Emma's great-aunt owned a vacation home in Cannon Beach, Oregon, and that was our final destination. I was finally going to see the ocean. Not just the Gulf of Mexico, but the full-blown, honest-to-God Pacific Ocean!

My heart beat wildly with anticipation and I couldn't have wiped the stupid grin off my face if I'd tried.

CHAPTER 2

On the trip from Portland to Cannon Beach, Mr. Walker drove Great-aunt Sarah's Lincoln Town Car, while the elderly woman sat in the passenger seat and directed. Mrs. Walker rode in back with me and Emma. Lovely scenery unfurled beyond my window, so unlike the flat plains of Kansas. Mount Hood stood sentinel behind us while we drove through the lushly green rolling hills of Oregon's wine country.

As we neared the coastal range the highway became a tunnel through forests of tall timber. Great-aunt Sarah provided a running commentary on the plant life: Sitka spruce, Western Red Cedar, and big-leaf maple, not to mention the undergrowth of Oregon grape, wild raspberry, and unbelievable ferns.

The forest had begun to thin when I noticed the smell. Salt! I rolled down my window and was immediately buffeted by moisture-laden wind.

"Maris!" Emma howled. "What are you doing? Put that window back up."

I closed my eyes and inhaled deeply. "That's it, isn't it?" I asked, ignoring Emma and savoring the smell. "That's the ocean."

"Whatever are you talking about, dear?" asked Great-aunt Sarah.

"We're miles from the coast. I can't see so much as a glimmer of the Pacific yet."

I shook my head, eyes still tight shut. "Not sight. Scent. I can smell it."

The wind continued to howl past my open window, but the people in the car were oddly silent. As though everyone but me held their breath.

Finally, Mrs. Walker broke the spell. "Well, I don't know whether it's the ocean or not, but the air certainly smells different from Wichita. Why don't you roll that window back up, Maris?"

I opened my eyes, realized that Emma and her mom were both being whipped by the wind, and pressed the button to raise my window. "Sorry," I mumbled and inhaled the enticing aroma one last time as the window sealed closed. The air in the car settled, though it now felt stale and dead, the bewitching moisture and odors having been conditioned away.

Very soon now I'd have my first view of the Pacific. Excitement thrummed in my blood, drying my mouth and heating my skin. I could hardly wait to escape the confines of the car and dive into the waves.

I've always been a natural in water, my swimming teachers quipped that I was part fish. I'd been on swim teams forever. My high school coach called me his secret weapon. But I'd never swum in open, unfiltered, un-chlorinated water. The sea-salt in the air excited a part of me I hadn't known existed, ignited a fire in my blood, and throbbed in my temples.

Mr. Walker guided the car over a final rise and I saw it, shimmering on the horizon. The ocean! Sparkling in sunlight like an enchanted kingdom. A soft, sweet song whispered through my mind. I shook my head, but the melody remained. A phrase floated to the surface: siren song. The sea was calling me home.

I shook my head again, dropped my gaze from the enchanting view, and turned to Emma. "Do you hear anything?"

She met my gaze with a puzzled expression. "Like what?"

I shrugged. "I dunno. A song maybe? Or wind chimes?"

Emma cocked her head, listening. "Nope." She studied my face, a small frown creasing her brow. "Are you feeling okay? You're kinda flushed."

"I'm fine," I said, a bit too quickly. "It's probably just wind-burn from opening the window like a dork."

She grinned. "Don't worry. I was a complete goof the first time we came out to Cannon Beach. The ocean is just so totally un-Kansas."

"Tell me about it," I said with a glance out the front window. "I haven't even reached it and I'm totally off-balance."

CHAPTER 3

I danced with excitement as we settled into Great-aunt Sarah's beach home. Perched on a cliff above the shore, the cottage's silvery-grey shingle siding and moss-covered roof looked at home against the backdrop of blue sky, grey-blue water and roiling, foaming breakers.

The tiny bedroom I was to share with Emma boasted pine paneling and two narrow built-in beds, one on either side of an over-sized window with an ocean view. A small table hunched before the window, onto which Emma promptly deposited her suitcase. I plopped mine on the floor and stood gazing at the constantly moving water, transfixed.

"It's tight, I know," Emma said, breaking my reverie, "but we won't be in here much. This is just for sleeping."

I nodded, my gaze never leaving the ebb and flow of the mesmer-izing waves. "It's perfect. How soon can we go to the beach?"

Emma laughed and opened the bedroom door. "The car's unloaded and we're as unpacked as we're gonna get. Let's go now."

Pulling my attention from the fascinating water, I glanced at her. "Where are you going? Aren't we going to change?"

She cocked her head and stared at me. "What? You want to swim?

I thought we'd just walk along the beach."

A slow flush rose up my neck and I worked not to turn my gaze back to the ever-changing water. That enticing melody still whispered in the back of my mind, calling me home.

I held my breath and reminded myself that home was in Kansas ... with Dad.

Just as Emma's expression tightened with concern, I blurted, "Let's put on our suits and cover-ups. That way, if the urge strikes, we can jump in the water."

"Sure," Emma said with a shrug. She closed the door and we rifled through our luggage, extracted our suits and stripped down.

Emma pulled on a very skimpy two-piece in blazing red which looked great against her well-tanned skin. Em worked hard on that tan, spending hours in the local tanning salon. With her dark hair pulled up and threaded through the back of a red ball cap and her lacy white cover-up, she looked like a model for a tropical paradise.

Me, not so much. The only daughter of a single dad, the only swimsuits I owned were of the one-piece swim team variety. Still, I wasn't here to show off my curves (or lack thereof), I was focused on getting wet. Good thing, too. My red-haired, freckle-faced, fish-belly white-skinned self was no competition for Em in the sexy-beach-bunny department.

I yanked my royal blue suit on, grabbed my dad's old button-front shirt — white with blue pinstripes, my version of a cover-up — and headed for the door.

"Don't you want a hat?" Emma asked. "I've got an extra."

I considered. "Nah. My hair's too short to get tangled by the wind, and I'd probably manage to lose it. Let's go."

We made it as far as the living room, where Great-aunt Sarah stopped us.

She sat in a dark brown overstuffed chair, her feet resting on a black vinyl footstool. The house smelled a bit musty, having been closed for several weeks, but the room was pleasantly cozy. Oval braided rag rugs dotted the pine floors while framed maps and pictures of boats and ocean vistas accented pine-paneled walls. Like her chair, the rest of the furniture was well-worn, but serviceable. The jewel of the room, the thing that drew my eye and held it, was a wide picture window framing a stunning view of Haystack Rock, rising like a sentinel from the surrounding waves.

Great-aunt Sarah launched into a well-rehearsed speech about the dangers of the ocean. How we must be aware and vigilant. Sneaker waves. Undertow. Logs. Anything deposited on the beach by the water could be snatched back again at a moment's notice.

I heard her warnings. They registered in my mind, but my attention was caught again by the shifting tides, by the quiet song whispering to my soul.

Finally, she released us.

"We'll be careful, Great-aunt Sarah," Emma called as we stepped onto the deck that protruded from the cottage and hung above the cliff.

I followed Emma to a set of steps cut into the cliff side and we scrambled down to the beach. The sand was soft and warm beneath my feet, deep enough to be difficult to walk in until we reached the packed sand that had been hardened by wave action.

Emma turned to skirt the water's edge and headed toward Haystack Rock. She strode along on dry packed sand, well away from the dark, water-soaked areas where waves danced back and forth.

Not me. I headed straight for the water. Haystack Rock looked interesting, but not nearly as beguiling as the foaming white water. Now that I was on the beach, with the moisture-laden air in my lungs, the smell of salt flaring my nostrils, and my own personal siren song lilting in time with the roaring surf, I couldn't hold back. Not another instant.

I ran into the waves. Felt the sea foam sizzle against my ankles, the wet sand slide from beneath my feet as the retreating waves pulled the loose top layer back into the depths.

Emma shouted my name, and I had just enough presence of mind to yank off my cover-up, toss it toward her, and remind her that I was a very strong swimmer before I ran forward and plunged headlong into an oncoming breaker.

Bliss! Inexplicable joy flooded my soul. I stretched out and pulled my body through the roiling water until I reached the calm beyond the breaking waves. I swam on, falling out of the standard strokes my swim coaches had drilled into me and changing to an undulating motion that drove me through the water. The shelf of beach dropped away and deeper water beckoned. I dived, unconcerned for air or water temperature or pressure.

Fish of all shapes and sizes swam with me and past me. The water darkened as I descended away from the light. Minutes passed as I explored my new kingdom, delighted and amazed by the quiet, the utter peace, the buoyancy of body, mind, and spirit.

Slowly my rational mind took hold.

You're too deep, it cried. *You'll drown. Swim to the surface. Now!*

But another bit of my being, a piece long buried, disagreed. *Be at ease. You're home. This is where you belong. See how your feet and hands have changed? So have your throat and lungs.*

I hung suspended far beneath the surface and examined my body. The new voice, the long-buried bit of myself was right. I had changed. The salt water had altered my anatomy. My feet were now long and slender, the toes splayed widely with webbing joining them. I had grown my own flippers! My hands were similarly changed.

No wonder I had been able to propel myself so quickly through the waves.

As long as I ignored the panicked, purely human part of my mind, I felt no need to surface. No need for additional air.

I felt my neck with webbed fingers. Nope. I hadn't grown gills. How was I not oxygen deprived? Was I oxygen deprived? Was this feeling of peace the euphoria of an oxygen-starved brain? Was I dying right now, but too relaxed to recognize my peril?

My swirling thoughts were interrupted by a nudge in my back and a happy presence in my mind.

Welcome, cousin! Where is your pod?

I sculled around and found myself facing the long nose and sleek body of a bottle-nosed dolphin.

Cousin? I thought and was astounded to see the dolphin nod in agreement. *We can communicate?*

Of course, cousin, she answered. I didn't know how, but I knew her gender. Knew that she was right. We were cousins of a sort. Both air-breathing mammals of the deep ocean.

Where is your pod? she asked again. *Are you lost?*

I don't have a pod, I said. *I've never been here before. As to lost, I think I can find my way back to shore.*

To shore? Why would you go there? You look healthy enough. Surely you don't intend to beach yourself?

Frantic concern colored her thoughts, and I realized that to her beaching was a form of suicide. I hurried to explain. *No. No. I'm well and I mean myself no harm. It's just that I've never been in the ocean before. I live on land with my father.*

She swam around me and I resisted the temptation to follow her movement. She needed to examine me from all angles.

What is this odd skin on your body?

It's a swimming suit, I said. *People put them on to swim. We don't go naked where others might see us.*

But there are no people here.

I didn't know I'd be coming here when I got dressed.

You truly have no pod? No one to teach you?

No. My father is far away. Inland. I came here with friends.

And suddenly I remembered Emma and her family. They would be frantic! They'd think I'd been swept out to sea and drowned.

I turned to my companion. *I must go back. My friends will be worried about me.*

I will swim with you to shore, at least as close as I dare.

Thank you.

I am Neela. I will watch for you, she said. *When you come again, I will teach you.*

I paused in my stroke and hung in the water again.

I would like that, Neela, I said. *I'm Maris.* I hesitated, and then blurted my question. *Do you know what I am?*

She swam forward and nudged me gently in my middle. *Of course,*

CHAPTER 4

Neela accompanied me back to the place where the ocean floor rose nearly to the surface. The wave action was boisterous as the surf broke upon the beach. She nudged me a final time and wished me safety upon the land.

I let the waves carry me to shore and then fought the outgoing current to find my feet. What would happen when I left the water with webbed feet and hands? Would Emma and her family consider me a monster? Would they abandon me here on the Oregon coast, half a continent from my father?

I rose dripping from the waves, my hands tingling as they met the air, the last droplets of salt water returning to the ocean. I held them before my face and found that I had human proportions again. Normal sized palms and fingers. Not a bit of webbing to be seen.

Stepping from the water to the damp packed sand, the same tingling raced across my feet and ankles and I knew my secret would be safe as long as I swam alone. I walked forward a few paces and dropped to the sand, shielding my eyes from the too bright sun of the late July afternoon. I'd grown accustomed to the dimness of the deep.

Too bad I couldn't shield my ears as well. The water had been so quiet. Even my conversation with Neela had been more thought than sound. Now waves roared, pounding the sand, gulls cried as they wheeled in the air above me, and children screamed in delight, running back and forth, playing tag with the surf.

And then a particularly shrill scream cut through the air and made me jump to my feet.

"Maris!"

I shaded my eyes with a hand and stared in the direction of the yell. Emma ran to me, trailed by her mother and father and a couple of hunky guys in wetsuits carrying bright orange flotation buoys.

Emma was breathless when she reached me, her ball cap askew and her lacy cover-up hanging off one shoulder. She grabbed me, hugged me so hard I thought my ribs might crack, then pushed me away and glared at me.

"Where have you been?" she demanded. "I've never been so scared in my life! I was sure you'd drowned. What happened? Why were you gone so long?"

"Slow down, Em. Jeez," I said. "Give me a chance to say something."

Her parents and the guys, undoubtedly some kind of life guards, caught up and I found myself surrounded.

"Are you hurt, Maris?" asked Mrs. Walker while Mr. Walker and the guys looked me over from head to toe.

"I'm fine," I said, a flush creeping up my neck at the intense scrutiny. "I was just swimming."

"Maris!" Em said, her voice higher and louder than usual. "You've been gone over an hour. And you didn't surface after you dived into that wave. I watched. I never saw you come up."

"Jeez, Em. Who knew you were so paranoid? Of course I surfaced. I'm standing right here, aren't I? You must've just missed me in all that foam. I mean, it's not like I can breathe under water, or anything."

A guilty twinge made my cheeks burn even hotter at the half truth, but what was I supposed to say? I mean, there I was, standing on the beach looking perfectly normal. How crazy would they think me if I told them I'd developed flippers in the water and an out-of-this world lung capacity? And no way did I want to try to explain about Neela.

Mr. Walker turned to the hunks in wetsuits. "Thank you for your quick reaction time, but it looks like we've had a false alarm."

The older guy — he was probably in college — smiled and held out a hand to Mr. Walker. "No problem, sir. We're just glad everything turned out okay." He nodded to me and said, "As for you, miss, we'd recommend that you not swim alone in the future. These waters can be treacherous. The buddy system is best."

"Thank you," I said, dropping my gaze. "I'm sorry I worried everyone."

The guys strode off, and Mrs. Walker draped an arm across my shoulders, gently steering me toward the cottage. "When I think of what might have happened," she said with a shudder. "I can't imagine calling your father and telling him we'd lost his daughter to a sneaker wave at the Oregon coast."

Dad. He had a lot of explaining to do, but I wasn't sure if I was ready to face that particular conversation just yet.

Later that night, I rested on my narrow bed and listened to Emma's even breathing mingled with the song of the surf. What was I going to do? Could I just go back to Wichita at the end of the Walker's vacation? Forget what had happened to me in the wild Pacific waters? Forget what I was and what I could do?

No. I couldn't go back. I couldn't pretend not to be a creature of the sea. I'd felt so at home in the ocean. So ... right.

But what about Dad?

I nearly gagged on a new emotion. It flowed up from my belly in an overwhelming wave and clogged my throat so that I choked. My blood fired and my face flamed in the darkened room. I was so angry my blood pounded my temples and made my head ache.

Mom and Dad knew what I was, and they'd kept it from me. They'd kept me away from salt water all my life because they'd known what would happen when I came in contact with it. They should've told me. One of them should've warned me.

The pounding receded and my thoughts calmed. Of course, I

wasn't blameless. I'd known I was coming to the beach and I hadn't told Dad. Hadn't given him the opportunity to warn me.

Well, of course I hadn't! If I'd told him we were headed to the Oregon coast, he wouldn't have let me come.

My thoughts circled back to Dad keeping my true nature a secret from me. He had no right!

I'd have to call him tomorrow. Fifteen was too young to just say, "Nope. Not getting on that plane. Not going back to Kansas." I could disappear into the ocean, let everyone believe I'd drowned, but that wasn't right. Emma didn't deserve that grief; her parents didn't deserve the guilt.

I had to have it out with Dad.

But right now, I needed sleep. I turned over in the narrow bed and let the sound of the surf wash over me. I imagined myself in the quiet depths, with Neela at my side and allowed the cool calmness to buoy my soul ... and slept.

CHAPTER 5

Cannon Beach is a lovely, upscale seaside community that burgeons to many-times its off-season population during the summer months. We were in the height of tourist season and all the streets and shops teemed with people. Emma and her parents decided to brave the crowds to see the sights of the little town the next morning. I begged off.

"I'm fine," I said as we ate a leisurely breakfast on the deck. Somehow the ocean breeze made everything taste better. Of course, warm cinnamon rolls dripping with butter, fresh squeezed orange juice and hot, aromatic coffee would be awesome almost anywhere. "I just don't feel like shopping. Besides, I need to call my dad."

"Don't worry, Amelia," said Great-aunt Sarah. "I'll be here. Maris and I will keep each other company once she finishes her call."

Emma looked disappointed. "I wanted to show you my favorite kite shop. Maybe rent a three-wheel bike for a ride on the beach."

"Maybe we can check that out after lunch? I really need to talk to Dad this morning."

"Okay," she said, brightening. "I challenge you to a kite flying contest this afternoon."

"Deal," I said.

With the Walkers out of the house and Great-aunt Sarah reading in the living room, I grabbed my cell phone and closed myself in the bedroom. I wondered briefly if I should take this conversation down on the beach — I really didn't want to be overheard, but decided that the bedroom was secure enough. It wasn't like Great-aunt Sarah would be listening at the door, and between the wind and surf, Dad and I might not be able to hear each other if I went outside.

I sat on my bed and stared at Dad's name on my phone for a moment, then took a deep breath and punched connect.

The phone rang.

And Dad answered. "Hello, pumpkin. How's my girl?"

I heard the smile in his voice and my heart melted. Whatever he'd kept from me, he'd thought he'd been protecting me.

"Hi, Dad," I said with more warmth than I'd felt only a moment before. "Have you got a minute. I need to talk to you."

"I've always got time for you, pumpkin. Is anything wrong?"

I closed my eyes, took a deep breath, and confessed. "Dad, we're not in Portland. Emma's great-aunt has a beach house…"

"Tell me you're not at the beach, Maris," Dad interrupted, his voice pleading. "Please, Maris. Tell me you haven't touched salt water."

A sob caught in my throat and choked me. "I'm sorry, Dad," I whispered. Then my eyes popped open and anger throbbed at my temples. "Why didn't you tell me?" I cried. "I had a right to know. I shouldn't have learned what I am from a passing *dolphin*!"

"Oh, honey," Dad moaned.

My anger ebbed as quickly as it had surged. I slumped back against my pillow and sighed. "Tell me everything, Dad."

"I'm so sorry, sweetheart. I suppose your mother would've told you by now, but I didn't know what to do, how to explain. When she died, I just kept doing what we'd always done. I kept you away from the sea."

"But why?"

"God. I wish I was there. I wish I could see your face."

"I don't know," I muttered. "It might be better this way."

Dad's breath caught in an audible gasp. "Pumpkin, you know I love you?"

"Just tell me the truth, please." My voice broke on that last word and I swallowed a sob.

"Alright," he said in a dejected tone. "This is going to sound like someone else's story. You've never known..."

"Dad!"

"Okay." A sound whistled through the phone as he drew a deep breath. "I grew up on the east coast. Sailing was my passion. When I was a young man, I decided to sail around the world. I spent months plotting my course, deciding where to make port and take on supplies, where I would stop and take a break from the loneliness. I planned an entire year's adventure."

"I never knew you sailed," I said in spite of myself.

He laughed, though it sounded a bit grim. "Well, your mother and I tried very hard to bury our past."

"I don't understand."

"I know." He paused a moment and then continued. "Anyway, I ran into a raging storm in a deserted part of the Pacific, far from land. My ship sank. I was drowning in storm-tossed water. Had no idea which way was up and even if I'd known, I had nowhere to go.

"Then someone grabbed me and hauled me to the surface. Your mother saved me. She swam with me to a deserted island, and then later, we made our way to an inhabited one."

"Wow," I said, amazed at Dad's close call.

"Yes, it's an unbelievable tale, which is why we kept it to ourselves," he said. "We fell in love of course, and settled in Hawaii. I worked for a local sight-seeing company, taking tourists out on a sailing ship and letting them snorkel around on a nice, safe, little sand bar. Your mother lived with me, but would disappear for days at a time into the ocean.

"At first I worried when she disappeared, but she always came home, so I simply accepted that I loved a siren and our lives would never be what you'd call normal."

"So how come I've never heard any of this?" I demanded. "Why do we live in Kansas? Why aren't we still in Hawaii?" I took a deep breath and wailed, "Why the secrecy?"

"Because of you," Dad said simply.

"What?"

"When she discovered she was pregnant, Aline was frantic. She didn't know what you would be, whether you'd be a siren or a human or something in between. She couldn't risk you being called to the sea and then drowning because your body wasn't properly equipped."

"You mean..."

"It was your mother's decision to move inland. She gave up the sea to protect you and I honored her sacrifice, probably kept honoring it too long."

Silence had never sounded so loud.

"I wish she'd told me," I whispered. "I have so many questions."

"I know, pumpkin," he said quietly. "I know."

CHAPTER 6

After Dad and I said good-bye, I curled into a ball and wallowed in self-pity for a bit. I mean, my mother wasn't human and my dad was a ship-wrecked sailor. Heck, when it came right down to it, I wasn't even human. My entire life had been nothing but lies and deception.

How was I going to face Emma? How could I go back to being a teenage girl from Wichita, Kansas?

"This is so stupid," I said to the empty room. I jumped off the bed, grabbed a fresh swimsuit from my suitcase and quickly changed clothes. "I'm going for a swim, and nobody's going to stop me."

I stalked from my room ready to face down Great-aunt Sarah, and found her dozing in her chair. Careful not to disturb her, I slipped out of the cottage and skipped down the stairs. Without another thought, I ran into the surf and plunged headlong into an oncoming wave. At least this time, no one would be watching to see whether or not I surfaced.

After pushing through the wild breakers, I swam with the undulating motion that now felt as natural as walking. Before long I felt a presence and turned to find a seal swimming toward me.

You are Maris, he said. *I am Screed. Neela told our herd about you. Come, I'll take you to her.*

Thank you, Screed.

I followed him through deep blue water. Sunlight filtered down in shimmering shafts and fish darted away. I wondered why until I remembered that seals eat fish.

I spent a relaxing few hours swimming with Neela, Screed and their many relatives. They taught me a lot about my new reality. How to time my dives, which fish to follow and which to avoid, how to hide from predators, and how to locate pods of dolphins and herds of seals.

At last I noticed that the sun was past its zenith and remembered my promise to fly kites with Emma in the afternoon. I said my farewells to the dolphin pod and raced Screed back to shore.

As I surfaced in the waves just below Great-aunt Sarah's cottage, I heard shrill screams. My immediate thought was that Emma couldn't have been worried about me this time. She hadn't even known I'd gone swimming! But then meaning penetrated and I realized that a distraught mother was screaming for help for her son.

I looked around, saw a small boy being tossed in the waves and then disappear beneath the translucent foam.

Without thinking, I plunged back into the waves and swam to the place I'd seen him disappear. I searched the currents sweeping out to sea and saw his limp body caught in an undertow.

I raced the current, glad for the strength and speed of my new, improved body. I reached the child, tugged him free of the current's grasp and sped to the surface, praying he'd breathe once his face was in the air.

He didn't.

Screed joined me, sniffing the unconscious child. *How can I help?*

I need something solid to push against, I said. *I have to get the water out of his lungs.*

Screed held the child in his flippers and rolled onto his back so that the child rested on his chest. I moved beside them and attempted

CPR. Thank heavens the school swim team insisted that all members learn first aid!

Unsure that my efforts would be successful — after all, CPR wasn't designed to be performed at sea with a seal as a backboard — I gave it my best shot, and after a few pushes, the little boy spit up a quantity of water and then gasped in a deep breath, though his eyes remained closed.

Thank you, Screed. This child owes you his life.

Screed shoved the little boy into my arms, barked happily, and sped away.

Cupping the boy's chin in my webbed hands to keep his head above water, I swam back to shore, hoping my hands and feet would transform before anyone noticed anything odd.

I needn't have worried. Everyone was so focused on the little boy, they barely noticed me. By the time the mother turned to give me a tearful smile, I was just another dripping-wet teenage girl.

Emma was very impressed when she heard about my ocean save.

"It was no big deal," I said quietly. "I told you. I'm a strong swimmer."

EPILOGUE

The rest of our seaside vacation was enjoyed by all. No one worried about my long swims anymore, and I was happy to join in family activities on the land.

I talked to Dad daily and we developed a plan. Once I got home to Wichita, we were moving to Hawaii. Dad had already contacted several old friends, and had a job waiting. I'd miss my friends of course, but Emma was already dancing with excitement about visiting me in Hawaii.

My adventure at Cannon Beach had changed my life forever, but it was a change I could live with. In fact, I was looking forward to getting to know the dolphins, whales, and Hawaiian Monk seals off the Maui coast.

PART VII

SIREN SURF

Deb Logan

Siren Surf
A *Siren Tales* Short Story

PROLOGUE

What a difference a year makes!

Last year I thought I was a perfectly normal teenage girl. I lived in Wichita, Kansas and had never even seen an ocean. I'd definitely never been near salt water.

Now I live in Hawaii with my dad and swim in the Pacific Ocean every single day. And... I know the truth.

I'm not a human girl.

I'm a siren. A creature of the sea.

Kind of like a mermaid, but without a tail or scales or gills. When I swim in salt water, my body transforms. My hands and feet elongate and my toes and fingers become webbed. And my lung capacity goes off the charts! I don't breathe water, I just hardly need to breathe.

Well, to be honest, I'm only half-siren.

My mom rescued my dad when his small sailing vessel went down in a storm far out to sea. She was a siren; he was a human. They fell in love, moved to Hawaii, and lived happily ever after.

Until I came along.

Mom didn't know whether I'd have enough siren blood to transform, but she was sure I'd be drawn to the sea, so she convinced Dad to move inland to protect me. At least until I was old enough to understand the dangers and let Mom test me, slowly and safely, to see if I could handle myself in salt water.

Unfortunately, Mom died in a car accident before she got around to testing my abilities — or telling me what I am.

Poor Dad didn't know what to do. He was grieving for his lost love, didn't have a clue how to explain everything, and had no way to test me. So he just kept doing what he'd always done: kept me in Wichita, as far from salt water as he could manage.

That kind of worked. Until I told a little fib.

Okay. It was a full-blown lie. I admit it. I deceived my father.

My best friend in the whole world, Emma Walker, was going to the Oregon coast on vacation, and her family invited me to join them. Since we were flying to Portland, Oregon, I kind of *forgot* to mention to Dad that Portland wasn't our final destination.

I mean, really!

I knew he wouldn't let me go if he knew we were headed to the coast, so I just let him assume....

It was wrong; I shouldn't have done it.

But because I did, I finally learned the truth.

Fortunately, I lived to tell the tale.

After Dad and I had it out over the phone, we started making plans to move to Maui.

So here I am, a siren's daughter living in paradise and exploring the Pacific Ocean on a daily basis with my friends: bottlenose dolphins, Hawaiian monk seals, sea turtles, and the occasional humpback whale calf.

Life is good.

1

Even in paradise, a teenage girl has to go to school.

Bummer.

Especially when said girl is new to Hawaii, has no friends, and isn't even fully human. I'd much rather spend my time in the water, or even helping Dad wrangle tourists on one of Captain Bill's snorkeling cruises. But Dad insists I need my education.

I repeat, bummer.

So on Monday of the second week of August, I dragged myself out of bed, pulled on my best khaki walking shorts, the only blue polo shirt I owned that wasn't emblazoned with Captain Bill's logo, and stuffed my bare feet into a respectable pair of leather sandals, as opposed to the ratty flip-flops I usually wore down to the beach. Shuffling dispiritedly into the kitchen, I poured myself a glass of POG — a juicy blend of passionfruit, orange, and guava that I'd decided was the next best thing to ambrosia— and popped a couple pieces of bread in the toaster.

"Got everything you need?" Dad asked as he emerged from his bedroom.

We'd been really lucky to score a two-bedroom condominium just a block from the beach. It wasn't as roomy as our house in Wichita, but our building had two elevators and a coin-op laundry, and the seven acre complex boasted a water feature with a koi pond, swing sets for the littlest residents, and swimming pool and half-size basketball court for everyone else.

Why anyone would want a swimming pool when the ocean was less than a block away was beyond me, but it was a feature the sales rep had stressed while trying to reel Dad into a contract. Not that the guy had needed to work too hard to land us. The condo had everything we needed: two bedrooms, a kitchen, a bath, and easy access to the ocean. Anything else was a bonus. Nice, but unnecessary.

I sipped my POG and shrugged. "Everything but my freedom."

Dad laughed and tousled my short red hair. My human genes came straight from him. I'd inherited his red hair, gray-green eyes, and pale, freckled complexion. I looked nothing like my mother, who had been an exotic, dark-haired beauty. But there was no doubt I was her daughter. Not once I stepped into salt water!

"Come on now," Dad said, a slight wheedle to his tone. "It's not that bad. You always liked school in Wichita."

My toast popped up at that moment, so I turned away from him and flipped the hot slices of perfectly browned bread onto a plate. "In Wichita I knew everyone," I said, glad he couldn't see my face. "Here my only friends are bottlenose dolphins and Hawaiian monk seals."

Dad stepped to my side and draped an arm across my shoulders while I buttered my toast. "You'll make friends, Maris. In a month you'll feel like you've lived here forever."

I slipped out of his embrace, moved to the refrigerator and grabbed a jar of orange marmalade. "I guess," I said, slathering my buttered toast with the rich orange jam, "but that doesn't make today any easier."

Dad poured a cup of coffee from the pot that had just finished perking and followed me to the little glass-topped table on our lanai. We set our food on the table, plopped into its matching stackable metal chairs, and drank in the ocean view from our little second floor balcony. I inhaled the warm, balmy air, heavy with the delicious tang of salt water, and closed my eyes.

It was worth it.

Every uncomfortable moment in the day to come was worth it to live here instead of Wichita.

I turned to Dad and smiled. "I'll be fine, Dad," I admitted. "I'm just nervous. Sure, I have friends in Wichita, but here..." I paused and waved toward the ocean. "Here I know who and what I am and I can indulge my love of salt water every single day."

Dad nodded, but his expression was solemn, almost mournful. "Your mother would be so proud." He glanced out to sea. "I wish she were here. I wish she could teach you all the things you need to know."

I dropped the last bite of toast on my plate, pushed back my chair, and moved around the little table to hug Dad. "So do I," I said quietly, emotion thickening my voice, "but we're doing fine. You brought me here, Dad. You dropped everything and brought me to paradise. I'll figure out what I need to know. The dolphins and the seals have helped me a lot already."

Dad kissed the top of my head, and we separated. We both wiped our eyes, and then he smiled at me. "We're doing fine," he agreed, "but now you need to get moving. You don't want to be late for your first day at Kahalawai High."

I laughed. "You're right. The new girl should definitely not get off on the wrong foot on her very first day."

2

My first day at Kahalawai High turned out to be a no-brainer. Dad dropped me off at the administration office, where I met my counselor, got checked in, and received my class schedule. I was also given a map which, considering this school has twelve permanent buildings and a whole bunch of temporary ones, was actually a necessity.

Who ever heard of a high school with a 75 acre campus?

Anyway I managed to find all of my classes, following the map from building to building until the final bell rang at just after 2:00 p.m.

That's when my day *really* started.

I'd heard some kids in class talking about meeting after school at Kanaha Beach. I'd been here long enough to know that the beach wasn't far from either Kahalawai High or my apartment, but I hadn't brought a swimsuit to school, so I needed to go home first. I didn't know anyone well enough to ask for a ride, so I walked the mile and a half home as fast as my sandal-clad feet would carry me.

Once back in my apartment, I dropped my backpack, left Dad a note— just in case— and quickly changed into my favorite blue floral swimsuit and ratty flip-flops. Now, I could've walked to the beach, it was only a couple of miles, but I swim a lot faster than I walk so it only made sense that I should take the water route over to Kanaha Beach. I raced across Kahalui Beach Road to my own personal water access. Not that my ocean access was anything special— just a rocky strip between the street and the ocean— but that was all I needed. Leaving my flip-flops beside a convenient rock, I stepped into the water, waded out a few feet, then slipped beneath the surface.

The Salt Water Effect, my own personal name for the phenomenon, began as soon as I stepped into the ocean. My feet became long and slender, the toes splaying widely and webbing stretching between them. When I dove beneath the surface, my hands underwent a similar change, but that wasn't the really cool part. That belonged to my lungs. I didn't grow gills; I'm not a fish, but like the seals and dolphins who had befriended me, my lung capacity expanded off the charts. I hadn't really pushed myself yet, but I'd found that I could stay underwater as along as thirty minutes without a problem. And I had no idea how deep I could dive. Hadn't tested that either, and wouldn't until I had human back-up.

Or better yet, found another siren.

Seals and dolphins are great swimming partners, and I knew my friends wouldn't let me drown, but neither would they be able to provide CPR if I needed it. Nope, testing my limits wasn't on my list of 'must-do' accomplishments.

But I could swim near the surface for hours, and that was all I had in mind for today.

I swam out past the breakers and made my way east along the shore until I saw a bunch of folks snorkeling and body surfing just beyond a wide strip of white sand beach backed by the green canopy of heliotrope and milo trees. Kanaha Beach park was a picture perfect spot for a late summer afternoon gathering of teenage water lovers.

I made my way past snorkelers too intent on the fishy inhabitants of the Pacific to notice a girl whose flippers weren't plastic, and stepped out of the water in an area too rocky to be appealing to the masses. Choosing a convenient rock, I sat and waited for my body to return to its non-Salt-Water-Effect status.

The change didn't take long. In less time than most people spend washing them, my hands had returned to what I still thought of as normal. Taking a deep breath and hoping the drum roll of my pulse couldn't be heard on the outside, I walked over to join a group of ten or twelve kids I'd seen at Kahalawai High earlier that day.

Talk about sticking out like a sore thumb! Most of the kids had gorgeous, sun-kissed brown skin and straight black hair. The guys and gals in the group of European ancestry were also evenly suntanned from living under the tropical Hawaiian sun.

Me? Even after two months of cavorting in the Pacific and helping out on Captain Bill's island cruises, my skin was still fishy-belly pale, though I was sporting more and larger freckles than I'd had in Kansas.

And my hair? Far from the shiny, lustrous, straight black of the native Hawaiians, mine was red and naturally curly to the point of frizziness. At least at the moment it was slicked back from my face due to my underwater swim, though short tendrils at my temples were beginning to spring back into curls.

Whatever.

I am who I am... and I'm a lot more than what the kids on the beach could see.

As I approached the group, one dark-haired, perfectly tanned girl looked up, smiled and waved. I angled my steps to join her.

"Hi," I said, trying to infuse my voice with confidence. "I'm Maris. Maris Grainger."

"Anita Mukai," she said, holding out her hand. "I saw you in chemistry this morning. You're new to Kahului, aren't you?"

I nodded, shaking her hand firmly. "My dad and I moved here from the mainland a couple of months ago."

She smiled and turned to the others. "Hey, everyone, say hello to Maris. She's new to the islands."

Suddenly I was the center of attention. Everyone wanted to know who I was, where I'd come from, whether or not I liked Maui, and most importantly, could I surf?

I answered questions, shook hands, smiled, and tried desperately to remember names. The kids were all so friendly! Everyone was anxious to help the haole— someone like me who hadn't been born in the islands— find her way around.

When they learned I'd been on the swim team in Kansas, but had no idea how to surf, Daniel Garcia grabbed a board with one arm and my hand with the other and would've pulled me straight into the water if it hadn't been for Anita.

"Slow down, Daniel," Anita said with a laugh. "Maris hasn't said she wants to learn to surf." Turning to me, she cocked her head and raised an eyebrow. "Do you?"

My face flamed, a less than desirable trait I'd lived with my whole life. When I'm embarrassed or unsure, my face informs the world. Professional poker player is definitely NOT a career option.

I stammered a bit and finally managed to say, "No... at least... not right now."

Truth was, I'd love to learn to surf, I just wasn't sure how that would be possible. I mean, the Salt Water Effect would announce my difference to anyone who spent time with me in the Pacific. I was already the new girl; I wasn't anxious to become known as the not-quite-human girl, too.

Daniel's shoulders drooped, he dropped my hand and glanced at his bare feet, which he shuffled in the warm white sand. "Sorry, Maris," he mumbled.

I smiled and punched him lightly on the shoulder. "No problem. Maybe another time."

He looked up at that and flashed a brilliant smile. "Any time!"

With that, the group broke up. Daniel and Jason Okamoto ran into the surf with their boards, then paddled out to catch a breaker. The waves weren't high today, but they didn't care. Surfing was surfing, even if some of it was just body surfing.

Several of the others grabbed masks and fins and swam out

beyond the breakers to snorkel, but Anita and a few other girls remained on the sand.

"You look like you could stand to catch a few rays," Anita said, gesturing to my pale skin. "Do you have a good lotion? One that will let you tan while protecting you from sunburn?"

I shrugged. "I'm lucky, I guess. Even here in the tropics, I don't burn, but I don't tan either. I just get more freckles."

Amy Lindsey, another girl of European descent, nodded. "One of my cousins has that problem. I always tease her that maybe someday her freckles will all run together... then she'll have a nice even tan."

Everyone laughed. "I can always hope," I said when I'd stifled my giggles. I didn't have a towel to spread out on the sand, but Jenny Yamamoto had an extra. She seemed a little surprised at my lack of beach necessities, but handed it over with a smile.

We spent a relaxing afternoon sunning, swimming, surfing, and snorkeling. And if any of my new friends noticed that I never so much as put a toe in the water, they chose not to comment. When it was time to leave, I walked the others to their cars, but declined to accept a ride home.

"No worries," I said. "I live nearby. I'll walk."

With calls of "see you tomorrow," we parted company, and as soon as my new friends were out of sight, I returned to the Pacific to let the Salt Water Effect take hold and swim home.

Tomorrow would be a better day. I had friends now.

3

By the time October rolled around, I was well established at Kahalawai High. Anita and Amy had become my best friends, and Jenny accepted me easily into her circle as well. I still missed Emma, but she and i talked on the phone often and occasionally managed a video chat. Plus I had the wonders of the Pacific to keep me occupied.

The pod of bottlenose dolphin I often swam with introduced me to humpback whales, sea lions, and the awesome sea turtles who inhabited the waters and reefs near my home. But best of all was my discovery of a colony of selkies who lived on the Forbidden Island of Ni'ihau.

I knew intellectually that such creatures must exist— I mean, I'm half siren after all!— but I'm not sure I ever expected to meet one. Having a friend like Serena who could swim with me as a seal and then remove her sealskin and lounge on a beach with me as a teenage girl... well, let's just say it was very liberating!

And then there were the boys.

We left Wichita before I really had a chance to date. I mean, sure, a whole group of us would go out for pizza and a movie, but I was only fifteen when I discovered exactly who and what I am. After that,

I was too focused on the move Dad and I were about to make to seriously consider any of the guys I knew as dating material.

But now I'm sixteen.

And living in paradise.

And I know who I am.

And... well... BOYS!

I know, I know. The Salt Water Effect complicates things, but as long as I stay out of the Pacific I can dream of dating. And I know some seriously hunky, athletically built guys! I mean, just about everybody surfs here, and surfing is an extreme sport. It takes muscles and coordination and good lungs and... let's just say the surfer guys are built!

Three guys in particular had caught my eye and any one of them could cause me to go all tongue tied if I wasn't prepared to chat. Kyle Lee, Jason Okamoto, and... Daniel Garcia.

Yep. The guy who'd nearly dragged me into the ocean when we first met had turned into a major heart throb for me. Danny was in several of my classes, and once we got past the embarrassed stage, I discovered he was smart, fun to hang with, and had a great sense of humor. Plus, it was a major rush to watch him surf. Danny didn't just have fun with a surf board, he was good.

So when the gang invited me to tag along to Ho'okipa Beach to watch the surfers do their thing, I was thrilled.

Dad, of course, gave me the third degree.

"How many kids are going?" he asked, frowning as he buttered a slice of toast Wednesday morning before our planned outing on Saturday.

I did a quick head count in my mind before I answered. "Ten. Anita, Jenny, Amy, me, and Fiona," I said, ticking each name off on a finger, "plus Danny, Kyle, Jason, Billy, and Adam."

"How will you get there?"

I bit into my own toast, chewed quickly and swallowed. "Honestly, Dad, it's only about twenty miles up the coast. I could swim it easily."

He glared at me and didn't say a word.

"Fine. We're taking three vehicles to accommodate everyone and all of the boards. I'll probably ride with Anita."

Dad considered. "From what I hear, there are some dangerous waves in that area. You won't try to surf, will you?"

I really wanted to roll my eyes, but controlled myself. "You know perfectly well I won't get in the water. The Salt Water Effect, remember?"

He shrugged, but nodded. "Don't your friends think it's odd that you don't swim or anything?"

My turn to shrug, and chug a mouthful of POG. "Probably, but they don't bug me about it."

"Okay," Dad said after taking a swig of coffee. "I know you're in no danger in the water, no matter what the waves are like. Just make sure whoever is driving is good behind the wheel. If you're not comfortable, if they've been drinking or anything, swim home. Or call me and I'll come get you."

This time I did roll my eyes. "Dad, my friends don't drink or do drugs. They get their kicks from catching waves."

He nodded. "Good enough. I'll be working a snorkeling cruise to Molokini on Saturday, but call me if you need me."

I grabbed my backpack, hugged him, and headed to school. "Don't worry, Dad. Everything will be fine."

Famous last words.

4

Saturday dawned clear and gorgeous. Let's be honest. *Every* day dawns clear and gorgeous here.

I jumped out of bed, raced to dress in my new favorite swimsuit, a deep purple tankini with an awesome color shift design, shorts, T-shirt, and flip-flops, and packed my swim bag with the essentials, towels, sun lotion, bottled water, sunglasses, and a floppy hat. When everything was ready, I carried it all out to the kitchen, toasted a bagel and smeared it with cream cheese.

Dad was just finishing his coffee, and told me to have fun as he grabbed his car keys and headed to Maalaea Harbor and his job with Captain Bill's Island Cruises.

I'd just finished chugging my POG and rinsing off my dishes when a car horn honked. Opening the door, I stepped out, waved at Anita before grabbing my things and heading out for the day.

Anita's car was loaded with three surf boards, me, and Amy. Billy was also driving. He had Jenny, Fiona, and Kyle. Danny and Jason were bringing the other six boards. Nine boards and ten people. Everyone would be surfing but me.

Ho'okipa Beach boasts some of the best surfing on Maui. Depending on where you paddle out, you can catch nice normal waves all the way to monsters. Most of the gang was planning to stay in the main flow, with a few of the more adventurous guys thinking about surfing the Point or even the Pavilions.

I didn't expect anyone to risk the Jaws. That's where the legendary swells can occur, and even the pros have to be towed in rather than paddling out to catch a wave. We didn't expect any tremendously huge waves today, but it was moving on toward winter, so anything was possible.

Once everyone was in the water, paddling out to ride their waves, I moved down to a deserted patch and slipped into the water. I wanted to be part of the action, I just didn't want anyone to catch me at it.

Diving down into deep water, I swam with my undulating stroke out well past the breakers where I could keep an eye on my friends, but not be seen. They'd be watching the waves, not staring out to sea for a single red-haired female.

It was a glorious day to be alive. Clear blue skies, hot yellow sun, just enough wind to provide decent waves, and a sea turtle circling my webbed feet. Every now and then, when it looked like some of my group would be taking a break, I'd head in, give the Salt Water Effect time to dissipate, and then race back to our beach towels. No one wondered at my wet hair, they just assumed I'd taken a dip in one of the safe-for-swimming areas.

We enjoyed a picnic lunch of turkey and cheese sandwiches, grapes, and cold, bottled water while everyone replayed their morning rides.

"You really need to let me teach you, Maris," Danny said around a mouthful of grapes. "You're missing all the fun."

I shook my head. "Are you kidding? I'm having a blast watching you guys ride."

He shrugged. "Whatever. If you change your mind, you don't have to start here. We could do your initial lessons back at Kanaha Beach."

Amy batted his shoulder. "Leave her alone, Daniel. Not everyone has to surf."

Danny ducked his head. "Okay. Okay." Then he grinned at me. "But I'm available. Just sayin'."

My heart skipped a beat and my face flamed, so I grabbed a bottle of water and chugged it, using the motion to turn away. He hadn't meant it the way I wanted to take it. Not like he was available to date. Just that he was willing to teach me to surf. That was all.

Wasn't it?

After lunch, we all took a nap in the sun. There's nothing like reclining on a beach towel under a hot Hawaiian sun with a floppy hat over your face to make you feel like all is right with the world. Except maybe when the guy you have a crush on flops down beside you and offers to rub lotion on your shoulders!

I peeked out from under my hat to find Danny sitting in the sand beside my towel.

"Need anything?" he asked. "I'd be happy to add some more lotion... to your back... I mean..." He stopped, his cheeks flaming, and dropped his gaze. "I mean, if you're interested, I'd..."

"I'm interested," I said, sitting up and meeting his gaze, "but not in suntan lotion... or surfing."

His Adam's apple bobbed, and he stared at me with those gorgeous brown eyes in his awesomely handsome brown face. Slowly he nodded. "What about a movie and a pizza tomorrow night?"

I blushed, but grinned. "That sounds perfect."

He jumped to his feet and yelled, his arms spread wide. "I asked... and she agreed!"

Our friends sat up, laughing at him.

"Of course she did," Anita said as she turned over and laid back down.

"About time," said Jason, and threw an empty water bottle at Danny.

Danny hopped around, grinning like a maniac, and I grinned too. Suddenly, he grabbed his board and raced for the water. "Later!" he called and used his excess energy to paddle out to sea.

Everyone else returned to dozing in the sun.

But not me. I watched Danny's progress, frowning. I didn't like the angle he was taking. If he kept that up, he'd be swept out toward the killer waves at the Jaws.

He was too excited about asking me out. He wasn't paying attention to the currents.

Ignoring who might be watching, I ran for the water and dove as soon as the land dropped away. Danny was an excellent surfer, but I wasn't taking any chances. Not now that he'd asked me out!

Of course, I'd never risk losing any of my friends just to protect my secret, but Danny...

Danny was special.

As I'd feared, the currents were sweeping Danny and his board into dangerous waters. I dove deep beneath the waves and fought the current as only a creature of the sea can. I kept pace with him, and when a monstrous wave flipped him from his board into the swirling rage of the undersea chop, I was there to pull him to the surface, far beyond the wild breakers.

He gasped deeply, pulling as much air as he could into oxygen starved lungs, pushed the hair from his eyes and stared at me.

"How... what? Did you just pull me up from the wash? How did you do that? What are you even doing out here?"

"I thought you were in trouble," said, not meeting his eyes. "I'm a really strong swimmer."

He shook his head, his eyes narrowed against the sun. "No way. If I couldn't handle that wave with a board, there's no way you swam through it."

We were both bobbing and sculling to stay in place in the relative calm of the water beyond the breakers. I pushed my hair out of my eyes, and Danny grabbed my hand, staring at the webbing between my fingers with disbelief.

I cursed myself.

Why had I done that? Why had I raised my hand out of the sheltering water? Had I been trying to sabotage myself?

Whatever. The damage was done now.

I wrenched my hand away from him and said quietly and in a

menacing tone, "Tell anyone, and I'll just say you hit your head on your board. You're hallucinating. No one will believe you."

His eyes widened and his face paled, but he didn't say anything.

Something nipped at my webbed feet, and I sank beneath the surface. A sea turtle nudged my shin and a bottlenose dolphin drew up beside me in concern. Using the telepathy I'd established with my fellow creatures of the sea, they asked if I required assistance. I held out my hands and stroked the dolphin's sleek side and the turtle's wrinkled neck, assuring them that I was fine. The dolphin nodded upward at Danny, was I sure?

Danny, though still on the surface, had dipped his face beneath the water and was watching us.

I'm fine, I said into our link. *He's a friend. You can go if you wish.*

At least, I hoped Danny was still my friend.

The dolphin and the turtle swam away, and I returned to the surface.

Danny stared at me, solemnly, but without fear. "Let's head to shore," he said. "We need to talk."

I nodded my agreement, and towed him perpendicular to the shore until we arrived at a place where the waves were manageable. Then, after giving him fair warning, I pulled him into the depths and towed him through the breakers' chop until we surfaced in a calm swimming area.

Walking out of the water, I saw our friends down the beach, dragging Danny's board out of the water and searching the waves for some sign of him.

I nodded toward them. "Not now," I said. "We need to let everyone know you survived." I gave him a meaningful glance. "Think of a story while we walk. I just went for a quick dip. What's your excuse?"

Everyone was astounded by Danny's survival. Amazed that he'd gotten away from an undertow that had ripped his board away from his leash. When all were convinced that he'd suffered no ill effects, the group decided it was time to pack up and head home.

While we were loading the cars, Danny caught my arm and gazed at my hand. Shaking his head, he said, "I saw what I saw."

I wrenched my hand away, but refused to look at him. "My apartment as soon as you and Jason finish unloading." I gave him my address and stalked away to help Anita and Amy.

5

There's nothing worse than waiting for a friend to disown you.

Dad was still at work when I got home, so I put my things away, washed the salt water from my face and hands, and set out a plate of oatmeal cookies and a pitcher of lemonade on the table on the lanai. I didn't really expect Danny's visit to make it to refreshments, but I needed to do something besides sit and wait for the axe to fall.

When the knock finally sounded on the front door, I squared my shoulders, pushed my hair away from my face, and opened the door to the guy who had *almost* been my boyfriend. To my surprise, he held out a bouquet of pink plumerias, white tuberoses and red carnations.

"I never thanked you for saving my life," he said, pushing the flowers into my hands. "Thank you."

Tears welled in my eyes, threatening to overflow and stream down my face. I blinked as rapidly as I could, and taking the bouquet, stepped away from the door.

"Thanks," I said. "Let's sit on the lanai." I gestured to the little patio and turned to find a vase for the flowers. When I carried the bouquet to the table, I found Danny munching a cookie and staring out at the Pacific Ocean across the street.

"So what happened out there today?" he asked, gesturing toward the water with the half-eaten oatmeal cookie.

And just like that, the moment of truth had arrived.

"I'm, uh, not entirely human," I said as quickly as I could force the words out.

He nodded. "I kinda figured that. So what are you?"

I stared at him. This wasn't at all what I'd expected. He was so calm. I'd expected him to rant, to yell. I'd even wondered if I'd be safe trying to talk to him without my dad present. And here he was, calmly eating a cookie and asking for information.

Weird.

"I'm a siren," I said.

He cocked his head and raised an eyebrow. "A siren? Really? Aren't you kind of red-haired and freckly to be one of the legendary sea creature who lures sailors to their deaths?"

I glared at him for a second, and then relaxed and smiled. "Maybe, but I'm still a siren. Or at least, I'm half a siren."

He'd started to pour a glass of lemonade, but stopped when I said that. "Half a siren? And you're from Kansas?" He finished filling the glass, handed it to me, and poured another for himself.

And just like that I poured out my whole story to him, including the fact that everything I knew about being a siren had come from dolphins and seals.

"Wow," he said, when I finished. "If I hadn't seen your hands and watched you talking to a dolphin and a sea turtle, I'd never believe it. You look perfectly normal now."

I nodded. "It's the Salt Water Effect."

"The what?"

"The Salt Water Effect. If I'd never stepped into salt water, I'd never have known what I was. That's why we lived in Kansas. To protect me, in case being half a siren wasn't enough to let me survive in salt water. Can't get much further from the ocean than Wichita, Kansas."

His gaze softened. "I'm sorry about your mom."

I nodded. "Me too. I have a million questions, and no one to answer them."

"I bet."

I squirmed in my chair, and finally met his gaze. "Are you going to tell?"

His eyes widened and his eyebrows rose. "What? Of course not!" He picked up his glass and sipped his lemonade. "I mean, first off, who'd believe me? But more importantly, you're my friend, and you saved my life. I owe you."

I lowered my gaze and fiddled with my glass. "I don't want you to *owe* me. I want you to keep my secret because you like me and wouldn't want to hurt me."

"Look at me, please," he said, and I raised my gaze to meet his.

"I do owe you, but I also like you and I definitely wouldn't want to hurt you. I'll keep your secret," he said, and held out his hand. "Friends?"

I accepted his hand and we shook. "Friends."

"So," he said, his cheeks going a bit red, "are we still on for pizza and a movie tomorrow?"

I grinned. "You bet!"

EPILOGUE

So here I am, a red-haired, freckle-faced teenage siren living in paradise. I swim in the Pacific Ocean almost every day with bottlenose dolphins, Hawaiian monk seals, sea turtles, and the occasional selkie. But I also go to Kahalawai High School where I have good friends and a certain very special guy who not only knows my secret, but still wants to date me.

Danny and I have progressed from pizza and movies to surfing lessons. Since I no longer have to hide the Salt Water Effect from him, I'm fulfilling my dream of learning to surf... and Danny Garcia is an excellent teacher.

Dad was amazed and alarmed to learn that someone else knew about my heritage, but he's gotten to know Danny and agrees that he's trustworthy. Mind you, he did threaten Danny's life if anything bad should happen to me. A conversation that left Danny a bit unnerved.

But since our greatest danger exists when we're surfing, I'm not too worried. Danny's an excellent surfer... and I'm an even better siren.

Life is good.

PART VIII

FLUTTERBIES AND FRENCH TOAST

DEB LOGAN

BESTSELLING AUTHOR OF *THUNDERBIRD*

FLUTTERBIES
AND
FRENCH TOAST

THE *CHANGELING* ORIGIN STORY

1

Jennifer patted her expanding abdomen and smiled.

She was so lucky.

Not only had she and Rick both survived intense cases of the viral pandemic that had swept the planet seven years ago, but they'd found each other, fallen in love, and married. And now their first child was on the way. In a mere three months, they'd meet the amazing little person their love had created.

She couldn't wait!

But today she was on her way to a friend's house for what she considered a class in Motherhood 101... a play date with a group of toddlers and their moms, all of whom were also pandemic survivors. The young women had formed a bond as they recuperated from the virus in the busy New York City hospital and had pledged to stay in touch when the world returned to normal.

No matter what.

Now most of them were busy young mothers, and Jennifer was about to join their ranks.

She'd dressed with care that morning, still enjoying the novelty of elastic-front maternity pants and a flowing top in pastel pinks, greens, and blues. Her more knowledgeable friends had warned her that her feet would swell in the final months, but her favorite royal blue ballet flats still fit perfectly.

Sliding behind the wheel of her red Audi sedan wasn't as easy as it used to be. She'd had to move the seat back a bit and change the angle of the steering wheel to accommodate her baby bulge. Jennifer wasn't a tall woman, so finding a comfortable seat position while maintaining her ability to reach the accelerator and the brake was a challenge. But she'd figured it out. No way was she going to sit home alone just because she was pregnant and short!

Arriving at Danielle's stately brownstone home in Queens, Jennifer scored a parking spot less than a block away. Walking— or should she say waddling?— the short distance left her winded, and she paused a moment to catch her breath and ease her back before grasping the wrought iron railing and hauling her bulk up the steps to the front door.

She didn't even have to ring. Trudy opened the door before Jennifer managed to step onto the landing.

"Jennifer! So glad you could make it. Come on in. Danielle is busy getting snacks for the little ones, so I'm on door duty."

Trudy, a tall, slim blonde, ushered Jennifer into the living room. "Find this woman a chair," she called gaily to a room bursting with young women and toddlers. "She looks like she's about ready to pop!"

"Oh, she does not!"

"Jennifer you look wonderful."

"Here, honey, come sit by me."

Before she'd managed to say a word, Jennifer was settled in an overstuffed armchair.

Trudy waved and smiled and returned to the front door, her five-year-old son Tyler trailing along behind.

Danielle's home was happy chaos. Babies crawled on her immaculately polished hardwood floors or rested on small quilts waving hands and feet in the air and cooing happily. Toddlers cruised the furniture, plopping unexpectedly onto well-padded bottoms, and pre-schoolers raced from living room to dining room to kitchen and back again.

And all of them squealed continuously... some delighted, some angry at having a toy snatched from their grasp, and others simply overstimulated by the noise and movement.

Moms alternately cuddled, scolded, and laughed, depending on the needs of the moment.

The very mercurial moment.

Jennifer relaxed into her chair, stroking her baby bulge. Soon she'd be one of those moms, and her baby would be adding his or her voice to the chaos. She smiled. Pandemonium for the pandemic survivors.

Life was good, and she was blessed.

Suddenly a scream broke over the ambient noise. A high-pitched, terrified, *adult* scream. Everyone, from smallest infant to scolding mom, froze. All movement and sound ceased. The little ones too startled to cry, the moms on alert. All eyes turned toward the front door.

Trudy screamed again, a wordless inchoate expression of terror, and dropped to the floor beside her son. The little boy convulsed on Danielle's spotless hardwood floor. His sneaker clad heels drummed against the wood; his eyes stared upward, glazed and fixated; sweat beaded his forehead.

The hush of surprise ended as abruptly as it had begun. Children wailed, mothers rushed to scoop their offspring into their arms, and Jennifer grabbed her purse, yanked out her cell phone and called 9-1-1.

2

In the weeks that followed Trudy's son's death, Jennifer's world flipped into unreality.

Again.

Little Tyler wasn't the only child stricken, but all of the fallen had two things in common: they succumbed on or near their fifth birthday, and one or both of their parents were pandemic survivors.

Some, like Trudy's Tyler, died. Others fell into a coma, but awakened a day or two later. Whole and healthy and... changed.

The young survivors exhibited strange and inexplicable powers.

Dangerous powers.

News agencies reported fatalities on a daily basis, and the numbers grew exponentially as more and more five-year-olds survived their ordeal. For though the little ones now controlled unimaginable power, they were still only children. They acted with the thoughtlessness of any five-year-old, and were completely oblivious to the potentially deadly consequences of their actions.

And unlike their normal counterparts, they had no adults to guide and discipline them.

Their parents tried, and too often died in the process. The

changelings' families simply had no clue what their children had become or how to help them understand and master their... gifts.

Jennifer and Rick watched the news with horror, knowing that the baby still safely cocooned in Jennifer's womb would be a changeling. How could it not? They were both pandemic survivors... and their survival was on record. When Jennifer entered the hospital to give birth, they would lose their child.

Jennifer had been in constant contact with her group of friends. All were shocked and grieved by Trudy's loss, but one by one all of the other young mothers suffered losses of their own as government officials tracked down pandemic survivors and confiscated their children.

Age no longer mattered. Enough five-year-olds had changed that world leaders were taking no chances. All children of pandemic survivors were removed to state facilities where their growth, development, and mutations could be monitored and studied.

A cure would be found and families reunited.

Eventually.

It was hoped.

Finally, a night came when Rick and Jennifer could no longer delay making a decision. Jennifer was the last of her group. Everyone else, parent or not, had been contacted. There was no way she could hide her pregnancy at this late date. She would be taken into custody until she had given birth. They both knew it.

"We have to leave," Rick said quietly, but with a grim determination Jennifer had never seen before. "Tonight. Tomorrow may be too late."

Jennifer hugged her baby bulge protectively as her heart-rate spiked and adrenaline flooded her system. "Where will we go? How will we survive?"

"Pack a bag," he said, seeming to ignore her questions. "One for you and one for the baby. We can't take everything, but we'll take what we can. I wish we had a van instead of the sedan, but I'll pack tight."

Tears filled her eyes, but her mouth was dry as sand. She swallowed, and asked again, "Where, Rick? Where can we go? Everyone knows we're survivors, and everyone is terrified of changelings. Who will risk helping us?"

"No one," he said grimly, "and we won't ask. We're going to disappear." He grabbed her hand and pulled her into the bedroom. Opening a closet, he yanked out every suitcase, gym bag, and duffle he could find. "Pack!"

Jennifer nodded and got to work. Beside her, Rick rifled through drawers and threw clothes into a duffle. He explained as he sorted the necessary from the nice.

"My grandparents owned a piece of land in Montana. Somewhere between Missoula and Great Falls. I've got the address programmed into my phone. It's just a vacation cabin, but it's still in the family and no one has used it in years. I doubt anyone but me remembers it exists."

He zipped the duffle closed and chivvied her to the nursery.

Her beautiful, perfectly appointed nursery. She had everything she could possibly need to care for her baby in that pretty little room with its fresh pale green paint and clean white trim. A sturdy oak crib, matching changing table, and the sweet little chest of drawers with decals of baby animals decorating the front. All a waste. Her baby would never sleep in that beautiful crib.

Rick pulled a collapsible travel bed encased in a sturdy vinyl bag from the closet. "Good thing Danielle gave you this when Amy outgrew it. We're going to need it."

The sight of the portable play yard with its attachable bassinet and changing tray calmed her. She'd have a miniature version of her nursery after all. Steeling herself, she packed everything she could fit into a suitcase or a box. Her baby was not going to be stolen from her, but he or she wasn't going to suffer privation either. Not if she could help it.

Rick worked steadily through the evening and night, packing the car as tightly as he could. At last, they were ready to begin their cross-country trek. With a final glance at the now denuded nursery,

Jennifer flicked off the lights, locked the door, and left everything not packed in the car behind.

As she settled into the Audi's passenger seat and clicked her seat belt around her swollen middle, she sighed. She'd survived before. She would survive again. She had Rick and their baby, and that was all she needed. They'd figure everything else out as they went along.

Including how to survive a changeling's fifth birthday.

3

Emily Ann was a beautiful child with a personality as sunny as her gold-blonde hair. She was the light of Jennifer and Rick's lives, and loving her and raising her was worth every sacrifice they'd made in the last five years.

The first year had been the hardest. Rick's grandparents' cabin had been in a sad state of disrepair, but he'd found capable hands to help him restore it in the nearby community of Granite Park. Fortunately, they'd also found a midwife willing to deliver the baby at home.

They'd worked hard and now had a comfortable little homestead, complete with chickens, a cow, and an abundant garden. The young couple might have started out as city folk, but they'd had strong incentive to make their new life work, and having Emily Ann in their lives... well she was worth all the changes.

But the time for Em's change was approaching. Fast. They could only pray they'd learned enough to help her... and that they'd given her strong enough genes to allow her to survive.

On a sunny July morning, Jennifer escorted Emily Ann to the vegetable garden. She had weeding to do. The sun warmed her back as she knelt on a paver between the rows of carrots and summer squash, heightening the scent of the marigolds planted along the garden's edge as a form of natural pest control. Bees buzzed among the sunflowers, and birdsong filled the gentle breeze.

"Remember," Jennifer told her daughter as she weeded the carrots, "one of these days you're going to feel a little bit sick. When that happens, you tell Mommy or Daddy right away. Okay?"

"'Kay," Emily Ann said, watching wide-eyed as a caterpillar crept along a paving stone.

Jennifer glanced at her daughter and, noting Emily's concentration, asked, "What've you found?"

"A c'piller. It's fat and fuzzy."

Jennifer nodded. "That's good. It means it's nice and healthy and will spin a good cocoon." She smiled and pulled off her gardening glove to ruffle her daughter's bright gold hair. "Do you remember what happens to caterpillars?"

Emily nodded. "They turn into flutterbies."

"Butterflies," Jennifer corrected absently. She'd just realized... that caterpillar was a perfect analogy for her daughter. Emily was about to go into a coma, a cocoon of sorts, and when she emerged— for she would emerge; Jennifer refused to believe the change would kill her precious daughter— she'd be changed as well. Not a butterfly, but a new and powerful form of human.

Rick and Jennifer had done their best to prepare for Emily's transformation. They loved their daughter completely and made sure she knew it to the core of her being, but they were not indulgent. They had done their best to instill a sense of caution in their little girl, a realization that danger existed and that she needed to obey when they asked.

They couldn't guess what powers Emily would possess when she woke from her coma, but they prayed she'd trust them enough to let them guide her, to help her make good choices as she explored her new reality.

Time would tell if they'd done enough.

4

Emily's fifth birthday dawned clear and bright. Jennifer had stayed up late baking and decorating a cake for her daughter's special day, but she still rose with the sun. The change was coming, she could feel it, and she didn't want to miss a moment of the time she had left with her daughter.

When first Rick and then Emily stumbled sleepily into the kitchen, the air was thick with the scents of coffee, warm bread, and bacon.

Emily's eyes widened when she saw her mom sliding slices of French toast onto plates. "Yum!" she crowed, scrambling to her place at the table.

Rick smiled. "Happy birthday, kiddo." He hugged her, then held her at arm's length. "Teeth brushed? Face and hands washed?"

Her face fell. She glanced from her dad to the French toast and back, shaking her head.

"Well, hurry up," he said, giving her a little push toward the bathroom. "I promise, no one will eat a bite 'til you get back."

She smiled and raced from the room.

"That was well done," Jennifer commented as she finished plating their breakfast.

"I thought so," Rick quipped, pouring milk into his daughter's glass before picking up his own cup of coffee.

A crash from the bathroom caused him to drop the cup. Its shattered pieces lay ignored on the floor as Rick and Jennifer ran to their daughter.

Emily convulsed on the white tile of the bathroom floor, her eyes closed, a sheen of sweat coating her brow. Rick and Jennifer knelt on either side of her and waited, not daring to touch her. When her body quieted, Rick carried her to her room and placed her gently on her bed. Jennifer wiped her face with a cool cloth and checked her for bumps or bruises.

"She has a knot on the back of her head," she said, probing the area with gentle fingers, "but there's no bleeding. I'm sure it'll be fine when she wakes up."

"If she wakes up," Rick said, his voice bleak; his face pale with shock.

"Don't even think that," Jennifer snapped. "Of course she'll wake up. She's strong and healthy and she has the gene from both of us." She glared at him. "She'll wake up!"

He sighed and sank to the floor beside his little girl's bed. "You're right. She's going to be fine," he said, infusing confidence into his voice. Then lowering his eyes to his daughter's pale face, he whispered, "She has to be."

Jennifer sat down beside him, closed her eyes, and rested her head on his shoulder. "She has to be," she agreed, "or all of this will have been for nothing."

He put his arm around her shoulders and pulled her close. "It wasn't for nothing," he murmured. "We've had her for five years."

She nodded, tears streaming down her cheeks. "And they were happy years. Not like my friends' babies who were stolen and raised like lab rats."

He kissed the top of her head. "If nothing else, we gave her... and ourselves... five good years."

"There'll be more," she whispered, holding him tightly. "There have to be more."

And so they sat on the floor beside their child's bed, their celebratory breakfast forgotten, as they waited and prayed for fate to allow their little butterfly to emerge from her coma cocoon.

Emily Ann woke to a wondrous new world. Colors brighter than anything she'd ever imagined danced in the sunlight streaming through her bedroom window. As she watched, the colors merged into shapes, the shapes into tiny people.

Tiny people with wings!

When they realized her eyes were open, the tiny people fluttered over to hang suspended above her face. Just like the mobile she'd loved when she was little. She giggled. A mobile of tiny flying people!

Something stirred on the floor beside her bed. She turned her head and saw Mom and Dad getting to their knees. Why were Mom and Dad on their knees by her bed?

She frowned.

Why was she in bed? She was supposed to be brushing her teeth and washing her face so she could have French toast!

"Flutterbies," she murmured, "and French toast."

Her mom grabbed her dad around the neck and screamed, "She's awake!"

Dad's eyes got all round and huge and he said, "She can't be. It's too soon."

And the flutterbies fluttered around her head making sweet little tinkling noises, kind of like the glass wind chimes Dad bought for Mom and hung out in the garden.

Then Mom and Dad were both hugging her and kissing her and getting her all wet with tears. She liked it for a while, but then she wanted them to...

STOP!

And just like that Mom and Dad froze.

But the flutterbies buzzed around her head. She frowned. What did they want? If only she could...

UNDERSTAND!

Suddenly their buzzing made sense. They were talking to her, telling her things she needed to know, but there were too many of them. She needed just...

ONE!

All but one of the flutterbies drifted to the ceiling, quietly. The one who was left floated right in front of her nose and spoke in a high-pitched, but perfectly understandable voice.

"Release your parents, little one," the flutterby said. "They're in danger. They can't breathe while they're frozen."

Emily Ann's eyes widened in surprise. "I'm hurting Mom and Dad?" she asked.

The flutterby nodded. "I know you didn't mean to, you just woke up," she said.

The flutterby was a girl! Just like Emily Ann! Well... maybe not *just* like.

"Think, little one," the flutterby girl said, "think about how much you love them and how you want them to be safe and happy." She paused for a moment, cocked her head and asked, "You do love them, don't you?"

"Of course I do," Emily Ann said. Then she closed her eyes and thought about Mom and Dad and her birthday breakfast and how much fun they would have today. After all... flutterbies and French toast!

Mom and Dad sat down with a thump. One on each side of her

bed. They took deep breaths and stared at her, then each other, then her again.

"What happened?" Mom finally asked, in an odd, wheezy kind of voice.

Emily Ann scrambled out of bed, hugged Mom, then ran around to the other side and hugged Dad. Glancing at the flutterby girl, she said very carefully and not in that you-must-mind-me kind of voice, "You were hugging me too tight, so I asked you to stop, but the flutterby told me I was hurting you and that I had to remember that I loved you."

She raced to her bedroom door, stopped and grinned at her parents. "I do love you," she said, "and I love French toast, so now I'm going to brush my teeth and wash my face so I can have some!"

And she scampered down the hall.

6

Rick and Jennifer stared at each other across their daughter's empty bed.

"Flutterbies?" they asked in unison.

After a moment, they stood, brushed themselves off, and went to the kitchen to salvage Emily Ann's birthday breakfast. They still didn't have a clue what had happened, but their precious daughter was alive and well... and the two of them had survived their first encounter with her newly awakened power.

And whatever else the flutterbies might be, it seemed they were capable of helping Emily Ann navigate her new reality... and Jennifer and Rick were willing to accept any help they could get.

They just might be the luckiest people on the planet! Their changeling daughter had survived and emerged from her coma in record time. Their family was safe and happy and healthy, and they had years and years ahead to love each other and learn about changelings... and maybe even flutterbies.

Life was good.

PART IX

EMMA: A FEYLAND DRYAD

DEB
LOGAN

AUTHOR OF
FAERY UNEXPECTED

EMMA:
A FEYLAND DRYAD

FROM ANTHEA SHARP'S WORLD OF FEYLAND

1

―――――

I held my breath as Uncle Jim lowered the helmet onto my head and adjusted the interface to the grav chair he'd designed specifically for me. He maintained a steady stream of explanations as he worked, while I fought to focus on his words, to stay grounded in reality, to not allow my hopes to soar too high. If the interface didn't perform as he expected, I didn't want to fall too far. I released my breath and concentrated on what he was actually saying ... not what I desperately wanted to hear.

"All right, Emma," he said, hands dropping to his sides. "I want you to relax. When you're ready to begin, think very clearly *Enter Feyland*. When you want to quit, think *Leave Feyland*. Do you understand?"

I blinked twice. My version of yes, and prayed that this new brainchild of Uncle Jim's would work. I tried to relax. It should work. Why wouldn't it? After all, my uncle was the famous James Carter, chief designer of the hottest full-D immersive game on the market.

"Good. I'm switching the interface on ... now."

Uncle Jim looked almost as nervous as I felt. His light brown hair was a mess—he kept running his fingers through it and tugging the longer bits on top until they stood nearly straight—and his thick glasses sat slightly askew on the bridge of his nose. Right now he'd make a great mad scientist in a sci-fi vid. A wave of fondness washed over me. He'd always been kind to me, had worked to understand me, and now I watched as he turned the dial that could change my life forever.

He smiled. "Now it's all up to you, Emma."

I closed my eyes, held my hopes and fears tight, and thought, *Enter Feyland.* A black shield slid into place over my eyes, isolating me from the sunny conservatory where I spent my days. A large gold *F* outlined in flames appeared and hauntingly lovely music filled the air. Golden words replaced the *F* and my adventure began.

WELCOME TO FEYLAND
A VirtuMax Production

A welcome screen replaced the title and as the screen changed, the words morphed from gold to scarlet before turning to ash and seeming to blow away. This was better than watching vids with my dad. This was all-encompassing. I was there. I could almost feel the breeze and smell the ash. The game hadn't even started and already it rocked!

As Uncle Jim had explained, my first task was to create a character. After reading through the list of classes, I chose a dryad. My sense of humor might be warped, but I found a certain poetic fitness in playing a character whose main defense would be to turn into a tree and become immobile.

Trumpets blared and the screen flared with golden light. Dizzying disorientation seized me and my stomach lurched as if my chair had suddenly dropped several feet. I closed my eyes and willed myself to calmness. I was no stranger to unpleasant surprises. I could handle this.

Taking a deep breath, I opened my eyes.

I was standing in a woodland clearing, surrounded by white-barked trees. Shock froze me in place, my reality shattered by those three words: *I was standing!*

Not sitting. Not reclining. Not supported by anyone or anything. I was standing in a clearing, on my own two feet, as if it were the most natural thing in the world. As if I were the normal girl I'd always dreamed of being. As if I'd just awakened from a hideous nightmare to find myself here, in this peaceful wooded glade, surrounded by white-barked trees with silvery leaves, under a clear blue sky, with soft moss beneath my leather-booted feet and encircled by a ring of mushrooms.

Laughter bubbled up inside. I wanted to jump for joy! I'd read that phrase a thousand times, but never expected to feel the impulse. Could I actually do it? Could I step over those mushrooms? Their jaunty red caps sprinkled with white spots encouraged me to try.

"Go ahead," they seemed to say. "You can do it. You can do anything. This is Feyland!"

Gathering my courage, I did what all the doctors had said I'd never do. I took a step, and after that, another, and suddenly I was running and jumping and twirling and waving my arms with abandon. I was alive! My body was fully functional!

I laughed and cried and danced and celebrated the enormous gift Uncle Jim had given me. The blessed man had no idea what I felt. How could he? How could anyone whose body behaved the way it was supposed to understand how I felt?

Exhausted by joy, I flopped onto the mossy greenness and rolled, unconcerned about staining my comfortable brown tunic and deep green tights. I closed my eyes and breathed in the goodness of the glade. A cool breeze kissed my face and ruffled my short dark hair. The air smelled of growing things. Rich dark soil, fragrant flowers, and mossy grass bruised by my frantic exertions.

What a perfect day!

As my heart rate settled, I heard a movement. Booted feet on soft earth? Opening my eyes, I sat up and glanced around. A young man, boy really, probably a teen like myself, leaned against one of the white-barked trees at the edge of the clearing.

He was dressed in a loose linen shirt with a dark brown vest laced across his chest and matching brown pants. His hair was golden brown and when he smiled at me, it was like the sun emerging from behind a cloud.

"Hello," he said. "You're new here, aren't you?"

I nodded and scrambled to my feet (to my feet! All by myself!), brushing leaves and grass from my clothing and trying to contain the giddy laughter that still wanted to bubble over.

"I've been watching you," he said, and I swear his eyes actually twinkled. "You seem happy to be here."

"I am," I answered. "This is amazing. I never want to *Leave Feyland*."

And just like that, my adventure ended. The shield retracted and I found myself blinking at Dad and Uncle Jim. Back in the real world ... where I was so terribly afflicted with spastic quadriplegia that I couldn't speak or even sit in a grav chair without straps to hold my body erect.

2

I wanted to scream, to rage at the injustice of that simple phrase pulling me back to a reality I didn't want to acknowledge.

Uncle Jim must have recognized the anger and disappointment on my face. He knelt before my grav chair, and placing his hands on mine where they were strapped in place said, "It's okay, Emma. I can see you have something to say. Let's try the interface's other function."

I frowned. The interface had another function? Something other than allowing me to play the full-D game that Uncle Jim and his company had developed?

"I know it's hard," Uncle Jim continued, "but I want you to relax. Be calm."

When my breathing regulated and my face relaxed as much as it ever did, he nodded.

"Good girl. Now, compose your thoughts. When you're ready, think *Activate Speech Mode*, then think what you'd like to say. When you want your thoughts to be private again, think *Deactivate*. Understand?"

I blinked twice.

He grinned and held crossed fingers up where I could see them. "Good luck!"

I closed my eyes, thought about all the things I wanted to say. All the things I'd waited my entire life to express, but not now. Now I just needed to tell Dad and Uncle Jim about the interface ... and the magic of Feyland.

Concentrating with my whole being, I thought, *Activate Speech Mode*, and then, *Does this work?*

An oddly mechanical female voice shouted the words.

Dad stumbled forward and dropped to his knees in front of my grav chair. His fingers trembled as he stroked my cheek. "I hear you, baby. I hear you!" Tears brimmed in his eyes and he turned to Uncle Jim. "Thank you, Jim. I can't ..."

Uncle Jim put a hand on Dad's shoulder. "There's no need, Kent. I'm just so pleased it's working."

They both looked at me.

I'd have grinned if I could. Instead I thought, *Feyland is amazing, Uncle Jim! Dad, you wouldn't believe it. Everything works there. My body works! I can stand and walk and run ... and I can talk. It's ... it's like a dream come true!*

The voice, my pseudo-voice, had a mechanical twang, but the volume regulated now that I knew it worked and wasn't pushing the thoughts with quite that initial intensity. The voice also sped up and increased in pitch in response to my emotions ... and it was nearly instantaneous. A real-time echo of my thoughts. I deactivated it so I could think while I waited for their response.

Uncle Jim beamed. "Emma, that's wonderful." He paused, a little frown creasing his brow. "But why did you come back so soon if everything functioned correctly? Jennet can spend hours in that game."

Jennet. Uncle Jim's daughter. My cousin. The girl who was everything I should've been if life had been kinder. Even though she was only two years older than me, the differences between us were huge. Jennet was perfect, while my difficult and traumatic birth left me with a severe form of Cerebral Palsy. We should've been best buds. We'd grown up together. Our mothers had been sisters and for most of our lives we'd lived only a few miles apart ... but it's hard to get to know someone when you can't communicate. Now though ... maybe we could become real friends at last. Even beyond family ties, we had a lot in common. We'd both lost our mothers a few years ago. We were both motherless girls with overworked, overburdened fathers. Too bad Uncle Jim's work with VirtuMax had caused them to move to Crestview a while back.

But I could think about my family issues later. Right now, I had more pressing matters to discuss. A chill ran through me. I never imagined the word *discuss* would apply to me!

I activated my speech mode and explained what had happened. "Could you please change the exit phrase, Uncle Jim? I was having a great time, and I'd just met another player. We were talking when I said, 'I never want to leave Feyland,' and suddenly the game ended and the interface brought me back here."

Uncle Jim's face cleared and he laughed aloud. "Of course! I can fix that right now. What would you like it to be? Obviously it needs to be something you can remember easily, but not something that you're likely to say in casual conversation." He grinned and straightened his glasses. "I evidently failed on that last bit."

Dad changed position so he was sitting on the floor by my grav chair instead of kneeling. "I can't believe I can hear you, Emma. After all this time, you can actually tell us what you want." He leaned back on his hands, a thoughtful expression on his face.

"What about *Deactivate Feyland*?" Uncle Jim asked. "That way both of your 'stop program' thoughts will be similar."

Dad nodded. "I like that. What do you think, Emma?"

I wished I could nod, too. Of course, I wished I could do a thousand things that my body was incapable of. Right now, I needed to focus on the amazing gift I'd been given. "I can remember that, and I can't imagine that phrase coming up in conversation."

Uncle Jim stepped to the laptop computer that he'd connected to the interface and began typing. "I'll fix that right now, Emma, and then I'll leave you and your dad alone so you can talk." He glanced up and smiled. "You can continue your game after you've had a chance to catch up."

"Thank you, Uncle Jim," I said, savoring my ability to speak. "For everything!"

3

Two hours later, I reentered Feyland.

Once again I stood inside a ring of red-capped mushrooms with cheerful white spots, in a forest clearing surrounded by white-barked trees with silver leaves. The sun shone from high in the prettiest blue sky I had ever seen and a light breeze played with the ends of my hair. I hopped over the mushrooms, grinning, and twirled. Feyland might be an illusion, but it was one my mind welcomed. I was free! From my chair and the restrictions of my damaged body.

I glanced around the glade and spotted a path leading into the woods. Time to really begin the game. I picked up the oak staff that was part of my costume and fingered the tender twigs and budding leaves that adorned its crown. Magic was awesome. It gave me working arms and legs and let a staff that should be dead wood sprout greenery. How cool was this place?

I marched across the clearing to the mouth of the path, stepped onto its pebbled surface and called, "Watch out, Feyland. I'm a dryad and my name is Emma ... and I'm free at last!"

My heart beat with joy as I skipped down the path, living staff in hand. I almost started singing—just because I could—but the birdsong and the breeze rustling through the leaves was too pretty to compete with.

I'd just settled down to a quick walk when the path widened into another clearing. Instead of a circle of mushrooms, this one held a low slung cottage of white-washed stone and a thatched roof. Window boxes of bright red flowers hung below each of the two windows. A Dutch door stood between them, with the upper portion open. A large oak tree stood beside and just behind the cottage, its wide canopy shading the small dwelling.

Stepping into the clearing, I stopped and leaned against my staff, enjoying the peace of the glade. What a charming place to live! I tried to imagine what kind of person lived in such an idyllic cottage. This was Feyland, so the inhabitant would undoubtedly be some race of faerie. Perhaps a dryad? The oak tree certainly seemed to be protecting the place. But I didn't think dryads lived in houses. An elf?

Before I could speculate further, a gnarled old man appeared at the door. His face was as wrinkled as a raisin, and nearly the same deep purple color. The top of his head was bald, but white hair streamed from a half circle that ran around his scalp from ear to ear. Bushy white eyebrows and a luxurious mustache that flowed into a full beard completed his hairy appearance.

He eyed me from head to toe then met my gaze. "Who are you and why are you disturbing the quiet of my glade?" he asked in a rather belligerent tone.

"I, uh, I'm a dryad," I said, not quite sure how to answer. "I'm just out for a walk and the path led me here."

"Just out for a walk, heh?" He looked me over again and scowled. "Well, if you want to cross my glade, you'll have to pay my fee. If not, you can just turn around and go back the way you came."

Hmm. This must be the first quest in the game. Since I didn't really want to return to my grav chair in the conservatory, I really had little choice.

"What is your fee, good sir?"

"There's a stream just beyond my oak tree. Bring me a fish for my supper and I'll give you a token that will allow you safe passage through the Forest of Fear."

The Forest of Fear? That sounded ominous. Safe passage would definitely be a good item to add to my inventory. I glanced at the massive tree. I hadn't seen any sign of a stream and I hadn't heard the gurgle of flowing water. Maybe it was a bug in the game, but a system so intricate that it could make a quadriplegic girl believe she was walking ought to be able to handle a little thing like the sound of running water. Was this funny looking little man lying to me?

And that wasn't even the main question. If I managed to find the stream, what would I do? I didn't have any idea how to catch a fish! I mean, I'd listened to enough audiobooks to know people used fishing poles, or rods and reels, but I didn't have any of that stuff. I looked at my staff. Could I use it for a fishing pole? Maybe, but what about a hook and a line? Could I catch one with my bare hands? I'd heard of folks who could, but I usually couldn't use my hands for anything, so I certainly didn't have any experience with such things.

Still, what did it matter? I'd come to Feyland to play a game, so play I would.

"I accept your offer, good sir." A soft chime sounded. Interesting. I hoped that was a good sign. "I'll return with your fish as soon as I can."

"See that you do," he said with a sniff, and disappeared into his home.

I walked past the cottage toward the spreading oak. With every step, the sound of water grew stronger. At first it was a barely detectable gurgle, but by the time I reached the tree, the stream fairly sang. My steps quickened. I could hardly wait to see it, for its melody sang of splashing rivulets, of currents crashing into rocks and then swirling past. It sang of joy and freedom, and my heart sang with it!

My feet skipped across the meadow between the oak and the stream, and I laughed with joy at my unfettered movement. I under-stood the water's song because my heart was singing the same one.

I ran along the bank until I came to a young willow overhanging the stream. Once upon a time the current had cut into the bank just beside its roots and then swirled away. Now the willow shaded a deep, quiet pool. A good-sized rock guarded the stream bank, and I sat, trailing my fingers in the water. The movement created soft ripples in the cool, dark water, distorting my reflection.

As the ripples dissipated, another reflection appeared in the water. A golden haired youth. I turned to see the boy I'd met earlier standing a few feet behind me.

"You came back," he said, smiling. And just like earlier, that smile made the day seem brighter, like the sun had ratcheted up a few notches. "You left so suddenly, I wasn't sure you would."

My cheeks heated with a blush. "Yes," I said. "That was a mistake. A glitch in my interface. I didn't mean to disappear."

"I'm glad. Your words certainly didn't seem to match your actions!" He grinned, and then his expression sobered. "Will the *glitch* happen again?"

How odd. He almost stumbled over the word glitch. As if he'd never heard it before. As if he didn't understand what it meant.

"No. My uncle fixed the problem. I'm all set now." His expression cleared and he dropped to the grass beside my rock. "I'm new to Feyland," I continued, "but I don't recognize your costume. What class player are you?"

He glanced away, picked up a pebble and tossed it into the quiet water. The movement caught my attention and we both watched the ripples as they moved outward, only to be lost in the froth of current in the center of the stream.

"I'm a faerie knight," he said. "A member of the Bright Court."

I continued to watch the water as it splashed and swirled in the dappled sunlight. Joy personified.

"A faerie knight? I don't remember that being an option. Do you suppose we're playing different versions of the game?"

"No," he said quietly, his voice so low his words were almost drowned by the noise of the stream. "It is not an option for humans ... and I am not playing a game. At least, not the kind you imagine."

My heart pounded so hard my vision turned gray around the

edges. I didn't understand. Something was wrong with what he'd just said. Should I leave? Should I think my safe words and flee the game?

Probably.

But he hadn't done anything to threaten me, and I wanted to understand. If I could.

I turned away from the sparkling water and studied him. Same golden brown hair. Same linen shirt with dark brown vest and pants. He was the same boy I'd met earlier. I hadn't felt threatened then, and I didn't now. Only his words were strange.

"I don't understand," I said, and he turned his attention back to me. Our gazes met and locked. His eyes fascinated me, green with interesting little flecks of orange. I could get lost studying those eyes, forget all about my questions and concerns. I closed my eyes and shook my head. When I opened them again, I concentrated on his hair instead, the way it waved across his forehead and curled around his ears.

Good lord! What was it with this guy? Even his hair was mesmerizing!

I licked my lips and dropped my gaze to my own hands. "What do you mean, 'it's not an option for humans'? You're human, aren't you?"

He gave a little bark of laughter and I glanced up again.

"No. I am not human, but you are safe with me, child of man. I knew what you were the moment I saw you. You think you are playing a game, but you have stumbled into my realm. The true Realm of Faerie."

My eyes widened and my pulse rate soared. "But...but...that's not possible! Faerie doesn't exist!"

His smile was a little sad now. "Oh, I assure you it is and it does. Others have stumbled across the threshold before you, little one. We, all of us who live in the realm, have standing orders to bring any humans we find before the Bright King."

"And the little raisin man who sent me to this stream? Does he have those orders too?"

My knight nodded. "He sent you here and alerted me." He paused, studying my face, his own creased with a frown. "But ... I cannot say why, but I find myself reluctant to take you to the king. There is something about you that is different from other humans who have wandered into Faerie. Something sad and joyous, innocent and ancient, all at the same time. You perplex me, little human." He stopped again and then asked, "Will you gift me with your name?"

Alarm bells rang in my brain. I'd heard lots of fairy tales. I'd lived vicariously through the quests and magical encounters recorded in books. I'd always believed them to be fiction, stories conjured from the imaginations of their writers, but now.... Now I didn't know what to think.

But one of the recurring themes in such fantasies is that names have power. And here was a self-professed faerie knight, a guy who claimed not to be human, asking me to trust him with my name, my essence.

"You first," I said, though how I expected to know if he told the truth, I'll never know.

"In your tongue, my name would be Brendan, but my true name is Bréanainn."

His name sounded something like "Bree-nin," but pronounced like the breeze whispering through the silver leaves of the white-barked trees.

"Thanks," I said, "but I think I'll stick with Brendan. My name is Emma." There. I'd told him the truth, but not all of it. He didn't need to know my full name.

He rose to his knees before the rock where I sat, took my hand, and bent to kiss it. "It is my very great honor to know you, Emma." Without releasing my hand, he raised his eyes and met my gaze. "Know this, if it is within my power to do so, I will protect you as you journey through Faerie."

My jaw dropped. If the old tales were true, faeries didn't lie. They might withhold information or they might lead you to jump to the wrong conclusion, but they didn't tell outright lies. If he really was a faerie, if this wasn't just another bit of programming in the game, Brendan had just pledged to protect me.

A giddiness to rival discovering that my body worked rose up and nearly swamped me. I smiled so broadly my cheeks hurt.

When my emotions were semi under control, I thanked him, at least, as much as I dared. That's another bit of fairy lore: faeries don't go in for thanks. "I don't really know what's going on, but I understand what you just said. I'm honored, Brendan."

He nodded and sat back, leaning on his palms. "I hope that someday you will explain the inconsistencies I sense in you," he said. "You fascinate me, Emma ... who pretends to be a dryad in a game that is not a game."

I laughed aloud, stood and spun around. I spent enough time sitting in my grav chair in the conservatory. I wanted to run and jump and dance while I had a body that could do all those things!

"Do I really have to catch a fish for the little raisin guy?" I asked.

Brendan grinned. "Not if you do not wish to, milady. And you should know, the *little raisin guy* is one of our best gatekeepers. He is a tomten who followed the Vikings from their lands to ours and finally found his way to Faerie. The Bright Court is now his home."

"So," I said, "the Bright Court takes in strangers and wanderers?" A thought so daring I wasn't sure I should allow it to take root pushed its way into my mind. Could I? Would I dare? Should I even wonder if it would be possible for me to become part of Brendan's Bright Court? It would mean leaving the human world behind, but that wouldn't be so bad. I mean, it wouldn't exactly be a loss to leave my grav chair and my hospital bed and my poor, damaged, quadriplegic body behind. But it would also mean leaving Dad ... and good people who cared about me, like Uncle Jim.

Besides, I didn't know enough about this place yet to even consider such a question. Better to file it away, somewhere deep and dark, where it wouldn't tempt me to ask. Right now, I should just enjoy the game and Brendan's friendship, and glory in the gift Uncle Jim had given me.

Brendan and I danced to the music of stream and birdsong, away from the water and back up into the meadow. We laughed and twirled and leapt and ran until we fell into an exhausted heap among the sweet green grass and fragrant wildflowers.

I was still catching my breath when Brendan jumped to standing and froze.

"What?" I asked, alarmed, but he waved me to silence as he scanned the horizon.

The next thing I knew, he'd pulled me to my feet. "Your game gives you specific powers, does it not?"

I nodded. "I have something called Wasp Sting and Thorn Bite," I said, "and I can turn into an oak for short periods of time."

"That should suffice," he said, still scanning the sky.

"Brendan, what's wrong?"

"The Wild Hunt is coming. Our friend the tomten must have alerted the court to your presence."

"What should I do?" I asked, fear making my voice shrill. "Should I leave?"

"That might be best."

I took a deep breath and reached for the calm I always held in reserve for hospital visits and painful tests. When I felt centered, I said, "Deactivate Feyland."

Nothing happened.

I didn't return to my grav chair in the conservatory. I was still in a grassy meadow sprinkled with wildflowers staring at Brendan.

He tipped his head and cocked an eyebrow at me. "Why do you remain?"

"It didn't work. What do I do now?" Even I could hear the sound of pounding hooves and pack dogs barking.

"They will arrive in mere moments. The Horned One's magic must have trapped you here. Quickly, become a tree."

Oh, wow! Just like that, do something I'd never tried before. I scolded myself for not having used all of my items at least once, so that I knew what they'd do.

No time for if-onlys. I had to act.

I checked my inventory, chose Be An Oak, and activated the item.

My arms and legs snapped together as my body became the trunk of a tree. My hair stood on end, the strands separating and lengthening, reaching for the sky and blossoming into a canopy of limbs, twigs and glossy green leaves. My toes stretched into the meadow's soil, lengthening and digging, becoming roots that held me firmly in place. My face melted into bark, and while I couldn't exactly see, I perceived all that happened around me.

I was immobile, locked inside a protective barrier of wood and leaf, unable to communicate with Brendan.

Entirely too much like the Emma I'd left behind in the real world.

Panic swamped me, but I fought through it. I'd lived this way my entire life. Only today had I truly been able to communicate in the real world and dance and play in Feyland. I could bear this. I knew this. And, most importantly, I knew this self-imposed immobility would end.

Just like I knew that my silence had ended at home.

Uncle Jim had given me a miracle. I still couldn't dance and play at home, but thanks to the interface, I'd never be a prisoner in my own skull again.

I could endure being a tree in Feyland, and I could endure spastic quadriplegia at home. The interface had freed me.

Brendan's voice filtered through my fevered thoughts. "They come. Do nothing until I say it is safe."

I rustled my leaves in acknowledgement.

Brendan sat at my base, leaning against my trunk. He whistled merrily and was soon surrounded by a pack of milling, snuffling dogs with evil red eyes. A dozen riders on black horses drew up before him. The leader chilled my sap. A massive figure with a dark face and antlers sharp as knives.

"Bréanainn, knight of the Bright Court," said the Horned One. "We seek a mortal who has dared to enter our realm."

Brendan stood and inclined his head. "Lord of the Wild Hunt, good fortune to you."

"Do you know aught of whom we seek?"

"I saw a mortal maiden at the faerie ring this morning," Brendan said, perfectly truthfully, "but she disappeared before I could detain her and drag her to my liege."

The Horned One's steed pawed the earth just beyond the reach of my roots.

"She is not here," he stated.

Brendan gazed around the meadow. "I see no mortal maid."

"Indeed." The Horned One studied Brendan for a moment. "Ride on," he commanded his huntsmen. "We'll seek elsewhere for the human." And with that both pack and riders surged away, riding not across the meadow, but into the sky where they disappeared among the clouds.

Brendan waited for a long moment before turning to my tree. "Return to your natural form, Emma. You are safe now."

I released the oak spell and transformed into my Feyland self.

Brendan caught me when I stumbled and would have fallen. He hugged me tight, then held me at arms length. "Your spell should work now, little one. It would be best for you to return to the mortal realm."

I nodded my agreement, still a bit sluggish from my stint as a tree.

"Dare I hope that you will come again?" he asked.

"Oh, yes," I answered with a smile. "I'll definitely be back." My smile faded. "But how will you know when I come? How will we find each other?"

He pulled a golden chain from beneath his shirt and unclasped it. "Please," he said. "Accept my token. As long as you wear this talisman, I shall find you. Anywhere. Even in the mortal realm, though I have never sought to enter that fell land."

He placed the chain around my neck and I touched the filigreed pendant that dangled from it before tucking it inside my tunic.

"I'll wear it always."

"Lest you be alarmed," he said with a smile, and again it seemed like the day brightened, "be aware that this talisman will manifest only in the Realm of Faerie. You will not see it in the human world, or even in the game you think you play, but unless you remove it here, it will remain with you and will mark you so that I may find you."

I nodded. "I understand." I didn't, not really, but I could see that Brendan believed his words, so I accepted his belief.

He raised my hand to his lips and kissed my knuckle. "Safe travels, Lady Emma."

I smiled, embarrassed, but incredibly happy. "And to you, Sir Brendan." Withdrawing my hand from his, I murmured, "Deactivate Feyland."

4

Dad and Uncle Jim and Jennet and I sat in the conservatory where I could use Uncle Jim's special grav chair and interface which allowed me to speak. We'd finished dinner —a rather tedious affair for me since I couldn't communicate and my nurse had to feed me — and were discussing Feyland. I raved about the game, praising the interface and Uncle Jim's amazing work. Jennet looked at me a little strangely from time to time, but it was so nice to be able to talk to her at long last that I didn't worry about it.

Finally, Dad and Uncle Jim went to the library so Uncle Jim could use Dad's computer to show him the screenie version of Feyland. Dad was so excited about me being able to use the game that he was thinking about buying a Full-D gaming system for himself so we could play together.

That sounded great to me. I wanted Dad to see me as my Feyland self, and I wanted to introduce him to Brendan. Dad wouldn't have to know that Brendan wasn't just another teenager playing a game. Some things were better left unsaid, and I knew Brendan would understand. Faeries are masters of illusion.

Jennet scooted her chair closer to me and said, "Did, uhm, anything unusual happen to you while you were in-game?"

"Unusual?" I asked, hoping my computer voice sounded innocent. "Like what?"

"Well," she said, glancing around to make sure we were still alone. "I couldn't help but notice a certain, well, *glow* about you. I mean, I know you're excited by how realistic the game is, and how it allows you to walk and talk and everything, but still..." She paused, licked her lips, and then blurted, "You just seem, I don't know, different."

I blinked. First she asked if anything unusual had happened in the game, and then she noticed a difference about me, a *glow*? Could it have anything to do with Brendan's talisman?

"Well," I said. "I made a friend. A boy." If I'd been capable of blushing, I'm sure I would've turned bright red.

"A boy, huh?" She smiled, relief evident in her expression. How odd. "What character class was he playing?"

"That was kind of strange," I said, watching my cousin for a reaction. Jennet was an expert on Feyland. If there was such a thing as the Realm of Faerie, I was willing to bet she knew about it. "He said he was a faerie knight, but I didn't see that classification when I chose to be a dryad. Do more choices open up when you get to the higher levels?"

Jennet's face paled, and even though she quickly clasped her hands, I noticed a slight trembling.

"No," she said quietly. "The character classes don't change." She licked her lips again and then asked, "What else did he say?"

"Well, he told me he wasn't human and that he was part of some court, and was supposed to take stray humans to see the king." Jennet's face went paler still, but I kept going. "Honestly, I didn't know what to think, except that he seemed to believe what he was saying. Was it all just part of the game, Jennet?"

My cousin shook her head, took a deep breath and exhaled slowly, her eyes closed. When she opened them, her color looked better. "No, it's not part of the game. Not at all. The Realm of Faerie is very real, Emma, and it can be dangerous. If your new friend told you he's a faerie knight, he probably is."

I blinked, gathering my thoughts before willing my mechanical voice to speak. "I guess I should tell you about the talisman, then."

Jennet narrowed her eyes. "What talisman?"

"The necklace. He gave me a necklace and said it would mark me ... that as long as I wore it, he'd be able to find me. Anywhere. Even here."

"Oh, Emma." Jennet closed her eyes and almost moaned. "Tell me you didn't accept it."

For the millionth time, I wished I could move my head, wished I could nod my agreement. But of course, even if I could move, I wouldn't have been able to do that. I *had* accepted the necklace.

"No," I said, my new voice firmer and more confident than I felt. "I accepted it. I'd show it to you, but he said I wouldn't be able to see it in this world ... or even in the game."

She reached forward and touched my cheek, staring straight into my eyes. "Promise me you won't go back into the game without me. You can't risk finding yourself back in Faerie without backup."

I hesitated. I wanted to visit Feyland again as soon as possible, even with everything Jennet had said. I'd been frightened when the Wild Hunt appeared, but I'd never felt threatened by Brendan. I really wanted to see him again. But Jennet definitely seemed to understand things I didn't and much as I wanted to experience a fully functional body again, I wasn't interested in endangering myself.

Unfortunately, Jennet and her dad were just visiting. Her Full-D system was at her home in Crestview. I had no idea how long they intended to stay. How long was she asking me to wait?

My cousin seemed to read my mind.

"I know I'm asking a lot," Jennet said, gazing so intently into my eyes that I wondered if she really could read my mind. "I can't imagine what it must be like to finally be free of that chair, to be able to move on your own and talk without assistance. I'm sure you want to go back into the game as soon as possible."

She laid her hand, her strong capable hand, over my withered one and stroked my fingers. I couldn't feel her touch, but I saw the movement and read the compassion in her eyes.

"We don't know each other as well as we should, Emma," she said quietly. "Stuff has always come between us." Her eyes flicked from the bands holding my upper body in place to the grav chair and back to my face. "But I need you to trust me in this. Faerie is a dangerous place. There are things I need to tell you, stuff I need to explain, and it'll be easier if we're in-game when I do it. Will you wait for me, Emma?"

I blinked twice, then remembered I could speak. "I do trust you, Jennet. Your dad has given me a miracle. I can wait a few days to experience more."

She nodded. "Thank you, Emma. I'll call as soon as we're home and we can meet in Feyland." She grinned and her eyes sparkled with excitement. "I can't wait to see your dryad character and to have some real girl time, just the two of us. It's going to be mag, playing the game together!"

5

The next few days were the longest of my life.

Okay. That's not true. I'd endured much longer hospital stays, including ones that had centered on horrifically painful testing. I was no stranger to discomfort. But this wasn't about pain. This was about excitement and anticipation. I longed to return to Feyland, to the freedom I enjoyed there. But I'd promised Jennet I'd wait, so wait I did.

I had long conversations with Dad, my nurse, my physical therapist, anyone who would stand still long enough to hear about the wonders of Feyland and how awesome my uncle was to have made it possible for me to play and, no less importantly, to talk! But I resisted the urge to enter the game alone.

Finally. FINALLY, Jennet called and Dad gave me the time she'd arranged for us to meet in-game. I stared at the clock across the conservatory, and the instant the second hand hit the appointed time, I thought, *Enter Feyland!*

When the opening screens cleared, I stood inside the ring of mushrooms in a familiar clearing surrounded by white-barked trees with silver leaves, and Jennet stood just outside the circle. At least I thought it was Jennet. She looked a little imposing in her long, blue

Spellweaver robes, her blonde hair covered by the hood, and leaning on a mage staff.

We stared at each other for a moment, each coming to terms with the changes in the other's appearance. Jennet broke our self-imposed silence.

"Oh my god, Emma! Is that really you?"

I grinned and twirled around inside the circle of mushrooms. "It's me," I cried, "and I can stand and walk and run and dance ... and talk with my own mouth and vocal chords! Isn't this the best?"

Her eyes brimmed with tears. "You're beautiful," she whispered. "I mean, you are in the real world too," she wiped her cheeks as a few tears escaped, "but ...."

"Yeah, I know," my own voice sounded a bit husky, "it's hard to see past the facial tics and grimaces that I can't control and all the straps and stuff holding me in place."

"Oh, Emma!" She stepped across the mushrooms and pulled me into a tight hug. "Your dad is going to flip when he sees you here. You're absolutely glowing with joy."

We parted and both of us wiped our eyes. I sniffled a bit, then sucked in a breath, and marshaling my emotions, asked, "So what was so important that we had to talk in Feyland?"

Jennet dabbed her eyes one last time with the sleeve of her robe, straightened and said, "Right. Warnings first, then we can play. First up, take a good look around. Do you see anything different this time? Anything that doesn't look the same as the times you entered the game alone?"

"Besides you being here?"

She cocked an eyebrow at me with a *Well, duh* expression on her face.

I grinned, ducked my head and immediately noticed a difference. "The mushrooms," I cried. "They're brown!"

"They haven't been before?"

"No. Both the other times I landed in a circle of red mushrooms with little white spots."

She nodded and released the breath she'd been holding. "Okay.

That's your trigger. When you play the game on your own, if the mushrooms are red and white, leave immediately and try again later. If they're brown, like these, it's safe to play."

"Seriously?"

"Seriously. The circle of red caps indicates that you've landed in Faerie instead of Feyland."

Jennet stepped out of the circle of innocent brown mushrooms and I followed. "That's a relief," she said.

"What is?"

"That the mushroom circle holds true. When you went straight to Faerie on both your first two attempts at the game, I was afraid you'd stumbled across a thin spot we weren't aware of."

"Who's 'we' and what's a thin spot?"

"We're the Feyguard. We've been appointed by the Old Ones to guard the borders between our world and the Realm of Faerie and rescue humans who stumble across unaware."

"Like me."

"Exactly like you," Jennet said with a nod. "But no one else has ever been marked so that they could be traced into our world. That talisman you accepted really worries me."

I touched the place Brendan's talisman rested. Even though I couldn't see it, I knew it was there. "He said I was special," I said, half to myself. I looked up at Jennet. "Do you think he meant it?"

"You are special, Emma," she said, her voice full of ... I wasn't sure what, but I thought it might be respect. Not something I'd had much experience with. "In so many ways." She gave me a one-armed hug, and said, "What can you tell me about your friend?"

"Well, he told me his name..."

"He *WHAT*?" Jennet yelped.

"Yeah," I said with a smile. "I've read enough fairy tales to know that's significant too."

While we talked, we strolled along a path strewn with tiny white flowers, beneath the arching branches of those lovely white-barked trees. Their silver leaves rustled in the breeze, reminding me of the bamboo wind chimes that hung in our garden at home. I told Jennet everything that had happened in my first two visits to Feyland, or rather, as I now knew, to the Realm of Faerie. The only thing I left out was Brendan's name. He'd given that to *me*. If he wanted Jennet to know it, he'd have to tell her himself. She seemed to understand. At least, she didn't press me on that point.

"And he pledged to protect you?" she asked, a puzzled frown on her pretty face.

I nodded. "I trust him, Jennet," I said quietly as we stepped into a clearing that led down to a little stream. Very little. Barely more than a trickle of water.

My eyes widened in surprise and I grabbed Jennet's arm. "There he is!"

Her head whipped up and she gazed at the trees behind us. "He can't be. We're not in Faerie. We're in the game. I was very careful!"

I pointed, and she turned to look toward the rivulet.

Brendan stood just beyond the trickle of water that barely qualified as a stream. A soft heat-haze shimmered around him as he raised a hand, palm out, in greeting.

"Oh!" Jennet exclaimed, as I practically ran to meet him. "Emma! Stop!" she cried. "Don't cross the running water."

I stopped just short of the stream. It was so narrow and shallow that it wasn't much of a barrier, but if Jennet didn't want me to cross, I wouldn't.

"I'm so glad to see you," I said to Brendan. "I wondered if you'd come."

"It is hard for me to enter your game," he said. "It is part of the mortal realm and therefore foreign to me. I cannot stay but a moment. I haven't the strength."

Jennet approached cautiously.

I nodded toward her. "This is my cousin," I told him. "I've been telling her about our adventures, but I haven't mentioned names." I laughed, a bit nervously. "It makes introductions a little awkward."

He smiled and bowed to Jennet. "I recognize you, Guardian," he said. "You need have no fear. I mean your cousin no harm. She has become dear to me."

Jennet returned his bow. "Thank you, sir knight, that relieves my mind." A small frown creased her brow. "How have you come here?"

Brendan glanced at me. "She carries my talisman. It calls me. But I haven't the strength to remain. Farewell, my friend," he said with a smile. "I look forward to our next meeting."

He vanished, and so did the measly little stream.

Jennet collapsed on the flower strewn grass. "Okay. That was weird."

"Was it?" I settled beside her. "I'm so glad he came. Now you've seen for yourself that he's not a bad guy."

"No," she said, "he's not a bad guy and he genuinely seems to like you, maybe even care about you." She shivered, sat a little straighter, and looked me square in the eye. "But you still have to be careful, Emma. Promise me you won't stray beyond Feyland. Not even to see him. Promise me you'll leave immediately if the mushrooms are red."

Her expression was so fierce that I licked my lips. I didn't want to lie to my cousin, and I didn't want to endanger myself or any of her Feyguard friends, but I didn't want to lose Brendan's friendship either. He was, after all, the first friend I'd ever had.

"Emma..."

I buried my hand in my tunic, crossed my fingers, and said, "Fine. Okay. I promise."

And I meant it. Sort of. At least for now. But I had an out if circumstances should ever require me to break that promise.

For now, I'd be content to play the game. To use Feyland to get to know Jennet better — and possibly my own father! — and I'd be happy with brief glimpses of Brendan. After all, it was more, so much more, than I'd ever had before.

But if a time ever came when Brendan needed my help, I'd act without a second thought. No one had ever needed anything from me before, and I'd never had anything to give, so if the opportunity arose, I promised myself I'd grab it and not let go.

"So," Jennet's voice broke into my slightly rebellious thoughts — something else I'd never had the capacity for, rebellion! — and I turned my attention to the here and now. "Do you want to, you know, actually play the game?"

I grinned and grabbed her hand. "You bet! Lead on, cousin. I want to learn everything there is to know about Feyland." *And maybe Faerie as well*, I added to myself. No need to let Jennet know just how rebellious I was prepared to become...

PART X

ON GUARD

DEB LOGAN

AUTHOR OF *FAERY UNEXPECTED*

ON GUARD

SPUN YARNS
A SHORT STORY

FROM ANTHEA SHARP'S WORLD OF *Feyland*

ON GUARD

WALLACE PADDED SOFTLY ACROSS the wooden floor, following his boy. He faltered slightly as they passed a puddle of golden sunlight streaming through a low window onto the flagstone entryway. His old bones creaked and he longed to rest in that sunny patch, allowing the warmth to soak into stiff muscles. But he followed the boy, mindful of his duty.

In his prime, Wallace had been a mighty hunter. The terror of small rodents. Field mice and rabbits still avoided his domain, though he was far from his kitten days. Old age stalked him as once he had stalked prey in the greenbelt behind his humans' dwelling.

But despite his advancing age and loss of fluid grace, he held to his duty. The female of his pair of bonded humans had given Wallace charge of the boy when he had been nothing more than a squirming bundle wrapped in blankets.

"Watch over him, Wallace," his female had said. "Guard him, always."

And Wallace had. No harm had ever befallen the boy while Wallace was on guard. He would not shirk his duty now for the physical relief of sun-warmed stone.

The boy continued downstairs, as Wallace had known he would, to the windowless cave the humans referred to as *The Game Room*. Wallace glanced toward the ceiling, thinking of that glorious pool of sunlight. Perhaps later, when the boy tired of sitting in that chair. Perhaps there would still be warm sun to bask in then.

He glanced around the room looking for the most comfortable spot to maintain his guard. In the center of the room two tiered rows of dark blue cushioned chairs faced a blank white screen. Off to one side sat a low stool surrounded by sparkly red metallic cylinders. The male of Wallace's bonded pair liked to sit on that stool and beat on those cylinders. Wallace could appreciate his human's need to express aggression, but just the thought of that noise made his head ache.

On the other side of the room was the object of the boy's attention. A massive black leather chair surrounded by boxes full of mechanical whirrs and whistles. The boy sat on the edge of the chair pulling on skin-tight gloves that sparkled in the room's low light. He touched one of the boxes and high frequency noise assaulted Wallace's sensitive ears. The boy pulled a sleek black helmet over his head, covering his eyes with a darkened visor and completely occluding his ears.

Wallace closed his eyes in a slow blink. Why would any intelligent creature choose to blind himself in the middle of the day? The boy spent hours in that chair, completely oblivious to the world around him. He saw nothing, heard nothing. Wallace knew. He'd tested the boy, cavorting around the room leaping lightly onto surfaces where he had no right to be, even sitting at the boy's feet and yowling until the female had raced down the stairs to see what was wrong. All for nothing. The boy had not emerged from his helmeted stupor.

With resignation, Wallace leapt onto the padded chair closest to his boy, circled three times and sat, tail curled around his paws. He watched the boy's hands twitch on the arms of the big black chair. Sometimes he spoke, nonsense words and phrases that had no bearing on reality. *Quest* and *Feyland* and *Thank you, kind sir* were uttered with some regularity, but Wallace had long since learned to ignore anything his boy said while wearing the helmet and gloves.

More disturbing were the moments when the boy thrashed in the chair, grunting and jabbing with gloved fists. At these times Wallace prowled around the chair, on guard against the foe his boy obviously fought. But nothing ever manifested, nothing a fierce Norwegian Forest cat could sink his claws and teeth into, and soon the boy would subside once more into twitchy somnolence.

Wallace's head drooped, and his eyes closed, his nose nearly touching the chair's pillow-soft fabric. A frisson of warning jerked him awake and he gathered his legs beneath him, ready to spring.

A dazzling light appeared over the boy's right shoulder. A lightning-shaped tear in the fabric of the world. A delicate, pale green hand appeared in the rent, then another, fingers scrabbling to widen the opening.

Wallace watched with narrowed eyes, crouched and ready.

A small head pushed through the tear, followed by a shoulder and one long arm. Another moment and wings appeared, followed by a female torso.

Wallace waited, confused. His previous experience hadn't prepared him for a winged creature to emerge from a crack in thin air. His duty was to protect his boy, his totally oblivious boy. But was this small winged female a danger? How could she be? She was hardly bigger than a squirrel, and Wallace subdued squirrels with ease.

The creature, fully emerged now, dropped lightly to the back of the boy's chair and knelt there, resting. What manner of being was she? Her skin was palest green, like the tender shoots of grass in the spring, her tunic the darker green of oak leaves, her hair petal pink and her wings merely an iridescent shimmer. She blinked solemnly at Wallace with large, liquid eyes the color of molten emeralds.

"Well met, friend cat," she said, her voice as soft as a mother's purr.

Wallace blinked and eyed her warily, casting his memory back, searching. Images and sensations whirled past his mind's eye. His tail twitched in agitation, powerful leg muscles ready for a predatory spring. He remembered the touch of his mother's rough tongue as she licked him at birth, encouraging his lungs into action. He remembered the peace of floating in a fluid-filled sac safe in his mother's womb.

Further back.

He entered the racial memories of his clan, the fierce northern forest cats of ancient days. He remembered creatures not seen by his clan in many lives of cats: gentle tomtens, deadly ogres, fierce trolls, and tricksy ice faeries.

He licked his lips in triumph. The creature was a faerie. Not an ice faerie of the far north, blue-skinned and adorned in ice crystals, but a faerie none the less.

"Why are you here, faerie?" he asked, allowing only a hint of a growl to color his words.

"I'm no threat to you, friend cat," she said. "I am in search of sustenance, but my food is not your food. I am not your competition."

She glanced hungrily at the back of his boy's neck and smiled, showing needle-sharp teeth.

Wallace rose to full height, arching his back, his fur spiking. He hissed a warning. "Not the boy," he said, his voice deadly calm. "My boy shall not be your prey."

"Your boy?" she asked, turning to face him once more. "What allegiance have cats to human boys?"

"This one is under my protection. Seek your sustenance elsewhere."

She swaggered along the back of the boy's chair—his *oblivious* boy's chair!—and surveyed the room.

"I see no other prey, friend cat, and my options are limited. I can only enter this realm where the walls are thin, and the walls only thin where a human willingly enters our realm through the game, Feyland." She gestured to the helmeted boy. "This human has self-selected. I need the sustenance of his hopes and dreams and vibrant emotions. I need his essence. *Faerie* needs his essence."

Wallace stepped closer to the faerie, placing his front paws on the arm of the cushioned chair. He judged the distance to the faerie on the back of his boy's chair to be less than six feet. An easy jump in his prime; more challenging now. But he could do it. He *would* do it. That creature would not harm his boy. Not while Wallace lived.

"Find other hunting grounds, faerie. This human and his parents are mine. I will not give them up." This time, Wallace allowed his growl full voice. The creature had been warned.

"Come now, cat," the faerie wheedled, her voice sweet as cream. "What's the difference between one human and another? This one is small and puny and fails to show you proper respect. You can do better. Besides, cats and faeries are natural allies. Our clans have always been friends. "Give me this scrawny human. You can do better."

Wallace's determination lagged, eased by the sweetness of her words. Tension flowed from his body and his eyes lost their focus and drifted closed.

A memory stirred in the deep recesses of his mind. Mesmer. Faerie mesmer. The clever green creature was hypnotizing him!

He shook himself free of her guile and sprang to his boy's defense, knocking against the back of the boy's helmet in the process and pinning the faerie to the leather with unsheathed claws. "He is mine!" he yowled. "You shall *not* harm my boy!"

The faerie shrieked and squirmed, but could not escape.

The boy yelled and scooted forward, turning a visor-blinded face to the struggle on the back of his chair.

Wallace lowered his muzzle to within a breath of the faerie's face and whispered, "Tell your clan and court. Warn them. Do not return to this dwelling. Wallace the Fierce guards these humans. They. Are. Not. Your. Prey."

Before his warning could die on the air, Wallace grabbed the faerie in careful jaws and tossed her back through the rent between the realms. As she vanished, so did the tear.

The boy, having finally managed to yank his helmet from his head, glared at Wallace. "What is wrong with you, cat?" he yelled. "Get off my chair! I don't know what you think you're doing, but you've ruined my game. Now I'll have to start that level all over again."

He shoved Wallace off his chair, jammed the helmet on his head and settled back into his game.

Wallace stalked around his boy's chair, head high, tail waving like a battle standard. Not only had he defeated the faerie and protected his boy, he'd held old age at bay. He still had it. He was still Wallace the Fierce!

After another circuit of the room, he leapt back up to his perch on the cushioned chair, kneaded the seat and then circled his bulk into a comfortable position. The faerie had said one true thing, his boy didn't show him proper respect. He yawned and rested his chin on his front paws. But what could he expect? His boy was only human, after all, and obviously in need of a Norwegian Forest cat's protection.

Fortunately for him, Wallace was on guard.

TEN STORIES BY DEBBIE MUMFORD

PART I

TRIAL ON THE TRAIL

DEBBIE MUMFORD

Trial on the Trail

A Yellowstone Adventure

1

Ah, Yellowstone! There's no place like it.

Nature in all its glory. The scenic beauty. The mountain grandeur. The geothermal features.

What's not to love about Yellowstone?

Animals in their native habitats.

Tourons—tourist morons—clad in baggy shorts and flip-flops, their cameras at the ready, stalking the majestic wildlife as though they were domesticated beasts of burden in a petting zoo... and occasionally getting gored in the process.

Park rangers working tirelessly to keep both tourists and animals safe.

People are crazy, and my family was no exception.

I'd worked as a park ranger in Yellowstone for nearly a year and was anxious to show off the park's natural beauty, so I'd invited my family to vacation here. They rented a home in Gardner, Montana, the northern gateway to the park, and I was in charge of their daily excursions. If it was a natural wonder, I was going to make sure my family experienced it.

And who exactly was this family I'd taken time off work to escort through the park?

My parents?

Sure. Theo and Rose Knowles. The academics who'd raised me and who tried not to show their disappointment when their second son had chosen to become a lowly park ranger.

My older brother?

Yep. The one and only Dr. Chester Knowles. My parents' dream son. The man I'd never live up to; the man who had everything. While I was tramping around in the woods keeping records of deer sign and how many beaver were building dams on the Gardner River, Chet was performing miraculous neurosurgical procedures and saving lives. When he wasn't busy at his prestigious hospital, he was fulfilling his duties as husband to Emmaline and father-of-the-year to their twin sons. James and John (not so fondly known as the holy terrors) were four year old know-it-alls and a general pain in everyone's butt. Though, of course, no one but me would admit it.

Wait! What about a sister?

Uh huh. Got one of those too. Gina Knowles. The baby of the family. No husband or kids yet, just a fashionista female who'd much rather be doing the club scene than tramping around the wilderness with the fam. The great outdoors is so... dirty. Don'cha know?

But they were all here now, and I was determined to show them just how amazing Yellowstone could be.

2

Everything went straight to hell on the third day.

We'd already done Old Faithful, the best known of the park's more than five hundred geysers, and the only one whose eruptions scientists have been able to predict for over a hundred and fifty years. Old Faithful is a park icon for a reason.

We'd wandered around Mammoth Hot Springs and been amazed by the broad terraces of travertine deposited by the continually flowing hot water. Even Chet had been dazzled by the display of colors. Yellow. Gold. Orange. All created by microscopic algae and bacteria that flourish in the extremely hot water.

We'd visited the Hayden Valley, that wide fertile valley dotted with herds of bison and elk. We'd even been lucky enough to spot a lone grizzly bear lumbering across the far side of the valley. Since no one wanted to encounter a grizzly close up, everyone had been thrilled to watch him through the binoculars I'd provided.

On the third day, we packed a picnic lunch of peanut butter sandwiches, apples, trail mix, and bottled water, tied on our best hiking boots, and headed for Dunraven Pass. I wanted Mom and Dad, and especially Chet, to see the views from the top of Mount Washburn. Actually, they were the only ones I wanted to guide up that trail. I'd hoped to leave Emmaline and the boys, and especially Gina, at the Canyon Visitor Education Center, a great place to while away the hours.

But no. Everyone insisted on making the trek up the mountain wearing backpacks containing their lunches and water bottles.

I explained that it was a six mile round trip hike and that four-year-old legs might not be happy with the distance or the elevation gain, but Chet overruled me. He knew his kids and his wife. His family was fit and healthy. Anything I could do, they could do.

I pointed out that I was acclimated to the altitude and the topography, they were visitors.

Chet was having none of it, and to my complete amazement, neither was Gina!

My fashionista sister was determined to make the hike as well. Gina! Whose sole prior hiking experience consisted of strolling through her favorite shopping mall.

So, we all grabbed our backpacks—mine filled with emergency supplies in addition to lunch—and with considerable trepidation I drove my family to Dunraven Pass, parked in the lot, and led the way to the Mount Washburn trailhead.

What. A. Mistake.

Make that a *colossal* mistake!

We'd barely covered the first mile when Gina started whining that her new, very stylish, hiking boots were chafing. She'd have blisters!

I bit my tongue to keep from reminding her, and everyone else, that I'd told them not to hike in new boots. They needed comfortable, well broken-in foot wear for a six mile hike. Especially since we'd be gaining elevation throughout the first three miles.

I offered Gina the keys to the range rover. "Why don't you head back down, Sis? You can wait for us in the car. Maybe take off your boots and apply some moleskin to the sore spots before you put them back on?"

She looked at me like she had in grade school when she thought I was about to pull a prank on her.

"Seriously, Gina. We've got another five miles to go. You're going to be miserable." I gave her my best compassionate expression, the one I used on *tourons* as I gently steered them away from danger.

She bit her lip, glanced at Mom, then grabbed the keys and said, "Whatever!" before turning and limping back down the trail.

I glanced at Emmaline and the twins. "Anyone else want to turn back?"

Emmaline looked tired and slightly sweaty, but she shook her head. "We're fine."

Chet tousled his sons' hair. "We're having a blast, right boys?"

James looked mutinous, but John elbowed him in the ribs and gave me his best cherubic smile. "This is great, Uncle Jed!"

Mom smiled. "Lead on, Ranger Knowles."

So I did.

To my relief, Mom and Dad were weathering the hike well. When I praised them for their endurance, Dad beamed.

"We took you advice," he said proudly. "Bought our hiking boots a couple of months ago and have been wearing them religiously on our daily walks through the neighborhood."

Mom nodded vigorously. "Once they stopped feeling awkward, we even drove out to a local park and hiked up a trail a few times." She glanced around at the tall pines we were walking through. "It was nothing like this, of course, but I'm sure it helped."

I grinned. "Great job getting in condition. You two are going to love the view from the top."

"What about us?" James asked, managing to sound whiny and belligerent at the same time.

I stifled the desire to roll my eyes and pasted a smile on my face. "You guys are champs. Isn't it great to be outside in the fresh air?"

James shrugged, then punched his brother and ran off down the trail.

"Don't get too far ahead," I called after them, amazed that *I* was the one acting the role of responsible parent.

Chet slapped me on the shoulder. "You worry too much. What could happen? They can't get lost. This trail is totally obvious."

I grimaced, but decided against reciting gruesome tales of things I'd seen happen to tourists in Yellowstone's backcountry. Of course, this well-established trail hardly counted as backcountry.

The trouble came when we completed the forested switchbacks and reached the last section, the part of the trail that traversed a rocky ridge and was devoid of vegetation. The views from the open ridge were amazing. Not as good as they would be at the summit, but still awesome.

"James. John," I called. "Watch your footing on the ridge."

Chet chuckled. "I swear, Jed. You're like an old mother hen."

"Call them back, Chet," Mom said, an edge of worry in her voice.

"John," Emmaline called, "come here. James, come. This instant!"

The boys had reached a particularly narrow point of the ridge. One where the land slid precipitously away on either side. The trail was wide enough not to be of concern for people who were minding their feet, but for two little boys caught up in a game of chase, it might as well have been a tightrope.

James shoved John, who elbowed him right back.

Both boys' stepped off the trail, one to either side, and both lost their footing as their feet slipped on the scree of loose rock.

The twins screamed and scrabbled with hands and feet as Chet and I dashed for them.

I dove for John, grabbed his hand and pulled him back to the safety of the trail. Emmaline ran to us and scooped the little boy into her arms.

I turned to help Chet pull James to safety, but...

...he wasn't there.

Neither father nor son remained in sight.

Mom and Dad huffed to join us, Mom hurrying to Emmaline and John.

"Where's Chet?" Dad demanded. "What happened to James?"

I motioned Dad back, then edged closer to where the scree covered hillside dropped away. James had come to a stop about twenty feet down the hill, but his father's greater weight had carried him much further. Chet might have continued his bruising slide, but he'd crashed into a scraggly pine about sixty yards down the slope.

James was on his stomach, crying and clutching a scrubby little bush, but he appeared to be uninjured.

Chet was conscious, moaning loudly, but his leg hung at an odd angle.

Great. Not only was the strongest member of our group, aside from me, down, but he was injured ... and unlikely to be of much help extricating himself from his situation.

"Mom," I said, dropping my backpack to the trail and unzipping it, "take Emmaline and John on to the top. There's a viewing deck sheltered by a fire tower as well as a bathroom. Wait there while Dad and I get James and Chet up that slope."

She nodded, then frowned at the edge of the trail where her son and grandson had disappeared. "Are you sure you don't want us to stay and help?"

I shook my head. "Honestly? You can help me most by keeping Emmaline and John out of my way." I yanked a hank of rope out of my backpack and glanced around. "Please, Mom. I need to know the rest of you are safe."

She touched my arm, nodded and chivvied the sobbing Emmaline and wailing John toward the summit.

Dad cocked his head, his eyebrows raised in question. "I wondered why you were toting that backpack along."

"Tools of the trade," I said. "Too many things can go wrong, even on a safe hike like this."

"Obviously," Dad said dryly.

"I never head out without supplies. Now, let's see about getting Chet and James back to the trail."

James wasn't a problem, once Dad cajoled him into a calmer state. He weighed next to nothing and wasn't that far downslope. I simply tied the rope around my waist, knotted the end into a loop, and tossed it down to him.

"You're doing fine, James," Dad called, his voice calm and steady. "Just grab the rope, son."

"That's the way," I said as James caught hold of the loop. "Now see if you can put the loop over your head. That's right, now get your arms through. Perfect."

I nodded to Dad and said quietly, "Get ready to grab him. I'll pull him up the slope. You lay down with just your arms over the edge. When he gets close enough, grab him, but don't slip over yourself."

Dad nodded and flattened himself on the trail.

"Okay, James," I called to the little boy. "I want you to hold onto the rope. I'm going to pull you up. It's going to scrape, but don't let go." I grinned down at him. "Everything is going to be fine."

Even at the distance, I could see his eyes go wide, but he didn't even sniffle as I started pulling him up the slope. Inch by miserable inch I pulled my four-year-old nephew up the rocky slope. He closed his eyes against the dust, but didn't cry out even though I knew the rocky scree had to be scraping his tender skin.

Finally, he was close enough to the top for Dad to grab his little hands where they held the rope tightly. Once the boy was in his arms, Dad rolled over onto his back, clutching his grandson to his chest.

I knelt beside them. "You're one tough kid, James. You're safe now. We've got you."

I met Dad's gaze. "Take James to his mom and brother."

"But..."

I shook my head and nodded at the boy. "Come back when you can. I've got some figuring to do." Reaching into my backpack, I pulled out two bottles of water. "Take these with you. I'm sure all of you could use some water."

Dad nodded and managed to get to his feet without releasing James. Holding the boy's hand firmly in one of his own, Dad accepted the water bottles with the other and guided James up the path.

I sat down on the edge of the trail and stared down at my injured brother. How was I going to get Chet up that rocky slope?

I pawed through my backpack as I considered my options.

There weren't many.

No trees to anchor the rope while I scrabbled down the slope to my brother.

Sure, I had a first aid kit and could get myself down to Chet, but then we'd both be stuck downslope waiting for rescue.

Chet was an adult. I could call down to him that I was taking his family to safety and would be back with reinforcements.

But I didn't want to do that. I didn't want to leave my big brother on the side of a mountain, alone and injured.

Emmaline and the twins would just have to tough it out until Chet was safe.

I pulled out my one and only viable option: my park issue two-way radio. Being a park ranger had its perks.

"Don't do anything rash, Jed," the dispatch operator said when I called the situation in. "You'll have reinforcements shortly."

"Thanks. We'll all be here." I said with a wry laugh. "Out."

4

Chet reclined in a hospital bed in Bozeman, Montana. His broken leg had required surgery, and was now swathed in white and suspended above the bed by a system of ropes and pulleys. Emmaline sat in a large leather chair beside him, both of their boys curled in next to her. Mom and Dad stood beside the bed, Mom gently stroking Chet's hair.

"We were all so worried about you," Mom said quietly. "I couldn't imagine how Jed was going to rescue you."

"Well, he didn't, did he?" Chet said with a grimace.

I stood quietly at the back of the room beside Gina, my shoulder braced against the wall. Trust Chet to find a way to downplay my involvement in his rescue.

Dad straightened to his full height. "Jed may not have done the actual rescue, but it was thanks to him that the park rangers on duty knew you were in trouble." He gave Chet a stern look. "I'll give you some leeway since I know you're still in pain, but you owe your brother your thanks. And you need to stop denigrating his career." Dad turned to face me. "We all do."

"Yes," Emmaline said quietly. "Thank you, Jed. You were right.

The boys and I should have gone to the education center. If we hadn't been along, none of this would have happened."

"Agreed," said Mom. "At the very least, we should have listened to Jed and kept the boys under control. He's the expert in the field, and we ignored his warnings."

"At least I went back to the car when he told me to," Gina added.

I put my hand over my mouth to hide a grin. Gina... my obedient sister. I nearly laughed out loud.

"Fine," Chet grumbled. "Jed's a hero, and park ranger is a noble profession."

Mom smiled at me. "We're so proud of both of our boys. Both of them saving lives." Chet spluttered indignantly, but Mom continued. "Chet in the operating room, and Jed saving people from their own mistakes in the Yellowstone backcountry."

My chest swelled with pride and gratitude... until I heard Gina mutter, "Great. Now *I'll* have to find a way to save people."

Family.

There's nothing like it.

Not even the grandeur of Yellowstone can compare.

PART II

JOLLY WELL DONE

DEBBIE MUMFORD

Jolly
Well Done

1

I stepped onto the Brewer's cedar plank deck and surveyed the backyard. What a paradise! Well-manicured flower gardens hugged the fence line on two sides. A softly splashing water feature complete with viewing bench rested under a huge spreading oak. Acres of lush green grass covered the center of the lot, and a vegetable and herb garden stood in neat rows just outside the kitchen door.

I inhaled deeply, enjoying the subtle fragrances of the late summer garden. Heavenly. And I was a woman who could appreciate the moment.

All in all, the footprint of the Brewer's house and garden was larger than my entire neighborhood! I was lucky to have met them at a local dog show. Lucky to have gotten the gig as their dog-walker, and this week, their dog-sitter.

And, oh my goodness! What a dog!

Prince Jolly Well Done, called *Jolly* by family and friends— including me— was an apricot standard Poodle, currently sporting a puppy cut since he had no upcoming shows. His fur was cut to an inch all over, except for his mustache— no self-respecting male

Poodle would be caught dead without a mustache— and a cute little ball of fluff on the tip of his tail.

Having attained Grand Champion status, Jolly was the toast of the Poodle breeding world. His services were called for on a regular basis, and his stud fees staggered my lower-middle-class mind.

Jolly was an exceptionally valuable dog.

And his owners trusted me to care for him while they were vacationing in the South of France.

It had been a nice gig. I liked Jolly and I loved staying in the Brewer's posh place. But my time in the upper class digs was just about over. The Brewers were due home late this afternoon.

Time to take Jolly for a nice long walk before giving him a good brushing out. Maybe even a bath, depending on what he'd been up to while in the backyard unsupervised.

Speaking of unsupervised... where was that dog hiding?

"Jolly," I called loudly, scanning the yard. The big apricot Poodle was nowhere to be seen. "Come on, boy. Time for a walk." I shook his collar and leash. That sound usually brought him to me at a run.

No Jolly. A sinking sensation hit my stomach.

He couldn't have escaped, could he?

I searched every inch of the backyard. Under bushes. Behind trees. Between the rows of string beans.

I walked the fence line. A six-foot high fence made of cedar planks to match the deck. Every plank was solid and in place.

But... I found evidence of digging in the far corner beneath an ornamental Japanese maple tree. Examining the hole closely, I couldn't imagine that as an escape route.

Jolly was a big dog.

Jolly wasn't a digger.

At least, if he was, no one had ever mentioned it to me.

But the dog wasn't in the yard.

The very valuable, Grand Champion stud dog wasn't in the yard.

He wasn't anywhere to be found.

I stared at the shallow hole beneath the fence, took my bearings, and ran for the house.

Time for search and rescue.

I had to find Jolly before the Brewers got home... or my dog-walking / dog-sitting career was over.

An even worse thought struck me. They couldn't sue me for the loss of the valuable animal, could they?

Oh, God! Did debtor's prisons still exist? 'Cause there was no way I could pay for a dog like Jolly!

2

Circling the Brewer estate, I found the shallow depression on the other side. The fence separated the manicured backyard from a nature preserve. A very wet, very marshy nature preserve. A natural area filled with wetland creatures.

Creatures I knew nothing about.

There were paths through the preserve— I often walked Jolly on those trails. Safely collared and leashed. But the depression under the fence was nowhere near one of our established walks.

"Jolly!" I called. I whistled. I sang his favorite walking tune.

No dog appeared.

I knew dogs, loved them, but I was no tracker. I had no idea how to tell which way he might have gone.

Yanking my cell phone out of my pocket, I called in the reserves. My brother Jeremy.

Jer was an Army Ranger. He'd know what to do.

"What's up, Sis?" he asked without preamble.

"I lost Jolly," I said, trying to keep the panic from my voice. "I think he's loose in the nature preserve that backs up to the Brewer place."

"And you're calling me because..."

"You're a Ranger," I huffed. "You know how to do things. You can track him, right?"

Jeremy laughed. "You're a riot, Jenny! You seriously think I trained to track a dog through a swamp?"

I glanced around at the marshy ground, the tangle of undergrowth, and the forbidding looking trees. "You'd be better at it than me." I took a deep breath. Begging my big brother for help wasn't something I liked to do. "Please, Jer? The Brewers are due back later today. I have to have Jolly safe and clean before they get here!"

He blew out a breath, which whistled through the cell connection. "Okay, okay. I'll be there in fifteen."

"I'll meet you in the preserve's parking lot." A heartbeat or two of silence passed before I added, "Thanks, Jer."

"Don't mention it," he said. "Seriously. Don't. Mention. It. The guys in my unit would razz me for weeks if they knew I was tracking a dog."

"A very valuable dog," I added before canceling the call.

3

Turns out Jer wasn't much better at tracking than I was.

Sure, he was more confident and not afraid to get his boots muddy tramping through the wetlands, but he didn't find a single paw print that we could attribute to Jolly.

We tramped around the edges of the marshy ground, calling and whistling, to no avail.

Jolly didn't answer.

He didn't come.

He didn't bark.

We didn't even hear a whine or a whimper.

"Okay," Jer said after a solid hour of tramping around. "Here's the plan: you head back to the house, then do your normal walk through the preserve. Maybe he found his way to the trail and is looking for you."

I nodded. "Great. What are you going to do?"

"I'm heading into the deeper swamp. Maybe he's gotten snagged on something and can't get away."

My heart raced. Jolly couldn't be injured. He just couldn't!

"You've got your cell phone, right?" Jer asked.

I pulled it out of my pocket and held it up.

"Call me if you find him. I'll do the same." He checked his watch. "Let's meet back at my Jeep at fourteen-hundred."

"That's two o'clock, right?

He rolled his eyes, but said, "Right."

We parted company and I ran to the trail Jolly and I walked regularly. I almost sighed with relief; it felt so good to be back on familiar ground.

But I didn't find Jolly.

I called. I whistled. I promised treats. But no big apricot Poodle appeared.

Where in the world had that dog disappeared to?

Back in the parking lot, I called Jer.

"Nothing," I said as soon as he answered. "Not a trace. You have any luck?"

"Maybe," he replied. "I found a..."

His voice caught and breath whooshed out loudly.

"Jer!" I cried. "Jeremy! What happened? Are you still there?"

Silence.

4

The line remained quiet. I was frantic. What to do?

The line was still open, so I didn't want to hang up on my brother. But I desperately wanted to call the police.

You don't call 9-1-1 when a dog goes missing, but a brother who suddenly goes silent on a phone call deserves a bit more attention.

I paced the empty parking lot, unsure what to do. I could run back to the Brewer's. They still had a landline. I could call the police from there. I certainly wasn't doing Jer any good here in the parking lot.

Just as I was heading toward the street that would lead me back to the Brewer's, a motorcycle pulled into the lot and parked. I ran over and nearly gave in to tears as the rider pulled his helmet off.

"Have you got a cell phone?" I gasped.

The guy— good looking, dark hair, blue eyes, dressed in black leathers with no insignia on his jacket— glanced at the phone in my hand and quirked an eyebrow.

"Collecting 'em?"

"My brother's hurt," I said, the words pouring out of my mouth. "He's dropped his phone, but the line is still active. I need to call 9-1-1, but I don't want to end this call."

The guy nodded once, pulled out his phone and punched in the emergency number. When dispatch answered, he said, "This is Detective Chambers, badge number five-oh-six-three. We have an emergency at the nature preserve off Lincoln Avenue. Send a search team, dogs, and a medical unit."

I sank onto the pavement and dissolved in tears.

Literally.

I didn't think that was a real thing... until it happened to me.

5

Detective Chambers— he asked me to call him Matt— stayed with me while the officers and their dogs started at the hole under the fence and moved into the preserve in a structured search pattern.

Fifteen minutes passed, then half an hour.

I don't know what I expected, but I guess it was immediate results.

Nearly an hour later, Detective... Matt's two-way radio crackled to life.

"We have them, Detective," a staticky voice reported. "Looks like the guy slipped on some moss and cracked his head on a rock. He's groggy, but coherent. His cell phone is about fifteen feet away."

My breath caught, and tears leaked from my eyes again, but I held it together.

"Any sign of Jolly?" I asked.

Matt's eyebrow quirked up again.

"The dog we were searching for. Standard Poodle, apricot in color, fur in an all-over puppy cut."

Matt relayed my question.

The officer on the other end laughed. "Yeah. The dog's here too.

Curled up next to the guy. He was licking the man's face when we found them."

I held out the leash and collar to Matt. "Think they'll need these?"

Matt laughed and shook his head. "Doubt it. The K-9 unit is prepared for stuff like this."

6

J olly was clean and bouncy and overjoyed to see his masters when the Brewers arrived home.

I was still a little shaky, but the dog showed no ill effects from his adventure. I was still deciding whether or not to own up to the experience, when the doorbell rang.

Mrs. Brewer glanced at her husband and then me, surprise written all over her face. "Were we expecting company?"

"Not that I know," Mr. Brewer said, stepping past her to open the door.

"Mr. Brewer? I'm Detective Matt Chambers. I just wanted to make sure Jenny and Jolly were recovered from the incident earlier this afternoon."

The Brewers turned to look at me.

Time to fess up.

Matt joined me as I walked my employers through Jolly's adventure.

"Well," said Mrs. Brewer. "This is unexpected. I've never known Jolly to dig holes before."

Mr. Brewer nodded. "We'll have to do some thinking about how to prevent a recurrence. Thank you for your perseverance, Jenny."

"Yes," agreed Mrs. Brewer. "You went above and beyond to insure our boy's safety." After a pause, she added, "Is your brother all right?"

"He's fine," Matt said before I could even manage to open my mouth. "The medics checked him out and said there was nothing to worry about. But they took him to the hospital anyway." He glanced at me, and smiled. "Just for observation."

Turning to the Brewers he added. "If Jenny is off duty, I'd like to take her to the hospital to see him now."

"Yes, of course," they said, very nearly in unison.

I grabbed my purse, gave Jolly a good rub behind the ears, and said, "No more escape attempts for you, buddy." Then I followed Matt to his motorcycle.

He handed me a helmet.

As I fastened it, I asked, "What are you really doing here?"

"Taking you to see your brother," he said. Then he grinned. The man had a wicked smile to go with the devastating good looks. "After all, a guy needs to get in good with a girl when he wants a date. Make that multiple dates."

My heart turned a few somersaults, but I managed to smile coyly and say, "Hmmm... we'll see."

PART III

A WALK WITH GEORGIA

DEBBIE MUMFORD

BESTSELLING AUTHOR OF *SORCHA'S HEART*

A Walk with Georgia

SPUN YARNS
A Short Story

1

Who knew that walking the dog could be perilous to my soul?

Georgia and I had just strolled around a curve in the duff covered path through a pine forest, when she stopped, gathered her haunches firmly beneath herself and prepared to attack. A low growl rumbled through her chest, filling the too quiet air.

I stopped by her side, puzzled. Georgia might be built like a tank — she's a very solid bull mastiff — but she's the gentlest, toasted-marshmallow gold giant in the dog world. She considers all children her playmates, and despite her size would happily climb into any willing adult's lap. And loyal ... words fail to describe the intensity of her devotion. Even on long walks through heavily wooded areas, she doesn't require a leash. She wouldn't dream of leaving my side, of leaving me unprotected.

Given her psychological make-up, this aggressive position deserved my attention. I didn't try to calm her. I scanned the trees for danger ... and immediately understood.

A visual anomaly hung in the air a few yards to our left. If Georgia hadn't reacted, I could have walked right past without noticing, but with my dog on alert the incongruity was impossible to overlook. The air shifted and trembled within a large oval that hung between two towering pines. Whatever it was, it wasn't connected to the earth, but floated a foot or two above the needle strewn forest floor. The edges wavered rhythmically, almost as though keeping time with a silent heartbeat, and while the center showed the grayed-out of a dusky woodland, the scene didn't match the forest where Georgia and I stood.

I could see huge lodgepole pines reaching for the sky behind the anomaly, but their massive trunks failed to bisect the throbbing oval that hung between me and them.

Time slowed. My pulse pounded, drowning out even Georgia's threatening growl. I wanted to reassure the dog, but words deserted me. Besides, my lips and throat were suddenly so dry I doubted I could even manage a croak. Primeval fear gripped my soul. The certain knowledge that death and the destruction of all I knew waited on the other side of an unknown that had suddenly become visible.

A shadow materialized in the center of the anomaly and my muscles unlocked. Adrenaline coursed through my veins; it was time to fight or fly, and I was no fighter.

"Georgia, come," I said, my voice harsh with fear. What if her instincts demanded that she fight? "Heel," I cried, and turned and ran.

She leapt forward with a threatening snap of her jaws, then turned obediently to chase me.

Too late.

I'd allowed my paralysis to last too long. I should've run when Georgia first brought the phenomenon to my attention. Our opportunity for escape had expired.

Wind whipped my hair as leaves and pine duff pelted my face. Saplings and undergrowth leaned precariously toward the strange oval. My leather jacket pulled me back as though some monster had grabbed me by its suede surface. I glanced behind me and saw that the shadow had become a vortex, the oval a dark maw, sucking my world into the unknown.

Georgia fought to stay beside me, the powerful claws I worked so hard to keep a reasonable length dug into the earth, creating furrows as she was inexorably drawn backwards. I grabbed a young pine, wrapping my arms around its trunk, gripping the rough bark with too soft fingers as my feet sought to lose contact with the ground. But what about Georgia? I couldn't let my dog be dragged into that maelstrom while I hugged a tree!

But what could I do? Even if I could reach her, my hold on her collar would be tenuous at best, and that single strap of leather about her neck might endanger her quite as much as the vortex that sought to pull us into who knew where. What if my attempts to save her snapped her neck? Why had I ever abandoned her harness and leash? With those I might have had a chance of tying her safely to a tree.

Her great brown eyes met mine and a piteous whine begged me to fix this. Me. Her source of food and shelter and love. Her world revolved around me. She looked to me with love and loyalty ... and lost her grip on our good solid earth.

"No!" I screamed as my faithful dog tumbled into that dark maw. Without a thought, I released the tree, my anchor to reality, and was sucked through the vortex which snapped shut behind me.

2

I woke to Georgia's warm breath wafting across my face. Thrilled though I might be to find we were both alive and together, her breath was ... doggy, in the extreme. Pushing her away from my face, I sat up, threw an arm across her broad back and surveyed our surroundings.

Her calm reinforced my own sense of no immediate threat. She sat quietly beside me, tongue lolling from the side of her mouth, ears forward, looking around with an air of serene contentment. I shook my head, amazed at the immediacy of a dog's life. She'd evidently put the horror of being dragged through a vortex behind her.

Too bad I couldn't do the same.

Clinging to my dog, the only familiar element in my current circumstance, I drew comfort from her nearness while trying not to infect her calm with my fear. Because I was terrified. I couldn't even say, "Where on earth am I?" because I was horrifyingly certain that the answer was, "Nowhere."

Wherever Georgia and I had landed, we weren't on earth. We sat in a small clearing surrounded by tall, well I don't know what they were, but they weren't trees, and whatever grew on the land around us, it wasn't grass. A deep purple creeper that might pass for some kind of succulent covered the ground, starred here and there with tiny white blossoms. The not-trees at the edge of the clearing were also colored in unearthly shades. Lilac roots and trunks blended into canopies of magenta, wine, and mauve.

Steeling myself, I raised my eyes to the sky. Instead of the cool blue scudded with fluffy white clouds of my home, I found a lemon yellow shell and two blazing discs, one a fiery orange, the second, and smaller, a juniper green so dark it bordered on black.

Suddenly feeling a deep kinship with Dorothy, I hugged my massive Toto and whispered, "We're not in Kansas anymore." Then I buried my face against Georgia's solid shoulder while I fought off the hysterical giggles that threatened to steal my breath, and very possibly my sanity.

When I felt a bit more in control, I straightened, accepted a loving swipe of Georgia's tongue, and stood, resting my hand on her head.

"Well," I said, "wherever we are, we're going to need food, water, and shelter, and I'm not at all sure we'll even recognize the first two if we find them." I glanced down at my dog. "I'm going to be relying on you, girl. Your instincts on what's edible or drinkable have got to be better than mine."

A happy "woof" answered me, and I stepped forward into an adventure I hadn't sought.

"On the bright side," I said aloud, more for my sake than Georgia's, "I'm dressed for walking and we'll get plenty of exercise." It had been a lovely fall day in the foothills of Colorado when Georgia and I left for our walk. She wore a red leather collar and I was dressed in layers. Jeans, warm socks and hiking boots covered my lower body, but my torso sported a black silk turtleneck, a dove grey T-shirt, and a green plaid flannel shirt, all topped by my chestnut brown suede bomber jacket. Except for a hat and gloves, I was in good shape for whatever weather this place might send our way.

We hiked through an unnatural stillness. No birds sang, no small creatures rustled through the undergrowth. Truth be told, there wasn't any undergrowth, just that deep purple succulent and the lilac not-trees. Georgia had marked the first not-tree we encountered when we stepped under the forest canopy. Evidently the odd colors didn't bother her. Of course, I wasn't really sure what she saw since humans and dogs perceive color so differently. But she was so nonchalant, I took a chance and ran my fingers over the not-tree's trunk.

I wasn't prepared for its silky smoothness, but I was even less prepared for its warmth, or the faint pulse I detected vibrating just below the surface.

Skin! Touching these not-trees was more like running my fingers over skin-covered flesh.

Jerking my hand away from what should have been rough bark, I urged Georgia forward. I suddenly felt less like a woman walking her dog through an oddly colored forest, and more like a small girl lost in a sea of strange men's legs.

The memory chilled me. I'd been about four, at church with my parents. Daddy had carried me into the vestibule after the service. He'd set me on my feet, instructing me to stand still while he helped Mother into her coat. I'd only wandered a few feet, but when I grabbed the pant leg of the man who stood beside me, I'd been startled to find a stranger's face looking down at me. The crowded room had suddenly seemed alien. All those legs clothed in dark suit pants, just like my dad's, but which of them was Daddy? I'd been on the brink of panic when Daddy's strong arms scooped me up and his wonderfully familiar voice said, "There you are! You're okay. Daddy's got you."

Remembered comfort flooded me, but departed just as quickly. I wasn't lost in a crowd of caring members of my church family; I was lost in an unknown place among who knew what these things that weren't trees were! If something leaned down and scooped me up, it wouldn't be into the arms of a loving father.

I picked up my pace, trying not to break into a panicked run—after all, I had no idea where I was going, but also trying not to allow so much as my jacket to graze any of the not-trees.

Gradually I calmed and began to take in the details of the not-tree forest. No undergrowth and the not-trees appeared to be very evenly spaced. Too evenly spaced. I stopped and turned a slow circle really looking at the rows of whatever they were around me. Rows. Evenly spaced. No undergrowth. These things ... these not-trees were being cultivated. Nothing grew wild with this kind of precision back home on earth, and I doubted that it did wherever the heck I was now.

Cultivation meant intelligent life.

Something farmed this land. And Georgia and I were trespassing.

3

Between the excessive exercise — Georgia and I had probably walked further today than we normally did in a week — and the bursts of adrenaline that had pumped through my body, I was sorely in need of water. I knew Georgia had to be thirsty as well, so I gave her her head and hoped she'd lead us to water. Or something that passed for water and would be safe for canine and human consumption.

At long last we came to the end of the not-tree farm. Georgia paced slowly, head down, tongue hanging out. I stumbled after her, barely managing to stay on my feet.

"Just one more step," I'd promise myself. "You can rest after one more step." I'd one-more-stepped myself to the edge of exhaustion. I was on the verge of collapse, when Georgia's head came up and her ears perked forward.

Forcing myself onward, I followed as she picked up her pace and trotted almost happily to a small clearing. This one was covered in pale silver creepers with bright gold flowers. So many flowers that the center of the clearing appeared to be a pool of molten gold.

Georgia trotted straight to the center and buried her snout in the golden flowers. When she raised her head and looked at me, petals dropped to the ground like beads of purest honey.

She barked once and buried her muzzled back into the pool of flowers.

A pool of flowers? My nerves sizzled and dehydrated neurons flared. Water! Georgia had found water! I stumbled after her, falling to my hands and knees by her side. The silver creepers seemed to emanate from the pool, their golden flowers covered the surface, floating like interlocked water lilies.

Georgia had indeed dripped flower petals, having destroyed a section of the plants in her haste to reach the liquid beneath, but the liquid itself had a slightly yellow tint as I cupped it in my hands.

To drink or not to drink? I couldn't survive long without water. Die of dehydration or die of ingesting a poisonous substance? Neither sounded appealing. I glanced at Georgia. She looked fine. If the liquid was a poison, it wasn't fast-acting.

"Good dog, Georgia," I said. "You found us something to drink, and I said I'd trust your instincts. Here's hoping we've both made good decisions."

I brought my cupped hands to my lips and sipped.

I'd never tasted anything so good in my life. Cool. Thirst-quenching. Life-sustaining. The liquid had a light, sweet flavor, reminiscent of watermelon on a hot summer day. I sipped slowly, and then lay down beside Georgia to allow my body to accept what it had been given before I attempted another handful.

I closed my eyes and ran my tongue over dry lips, almost able to perceive my cells plumping, my energy rising.

Having drunk her fill, Georgia rolled onto her back and accepted my homage of grateful belly rubs.

The sky was darkening to a deep burgundy by the time I was satiated. We had no shelter, but having seen no living creatures other than ground cover and not-trees that day, I decided not to worry about it. I curled up next to Georgia and hoped that the temperature drop would not be too drastic. I fell asleep wishing I'd thought to bring water bottles, dried jerky, a sleeping bag and maybe a small tent on our walk that morning. But who expects to be sucked into a vortex to another planet, or plane of existence, or alternate universe when they head out to walk the dog for twenty minutes?

Adventure has never been my thing, and this one was certainly not planned.

4

Sometime in the middle of the night I woke to Georgia's deep-throated growl. With no moon or stars visible, I was as blind as if I'd had no eyes. I oriented on Georgia by the sound of her growls and rested my hands on her back. Her hackles were up.

A soft, sibilant whisper sounded in the darkness to my left, barely audible over Georgia's growls. My stomach fluttered and my pulse roared in my ears, but I stroked Georgia's back and managed to say, "Hush, girl. We need to hear." She quieted, momentarily.

Something poked my arm and I jumped.

Maybe something poked Georgia too. She lunged forward with a full throated bell. Her jaws snapped and I heard a horrible sound like tearing flesh.

More sibilant whisperings and shuffling like many small feet retreating.

"Georgia! To me!" But I needn't have called. My lap was suddenly full of heavy, warm dog, licking my hands and face, and whimpering. I held her tightly and wished fervently for a flashlight. Georgia rarely licked and almost never whimpered.

"Good girl," I whispered. "Brave, girl." Whether I was praising

Georgia or admonishing myself, I'll never be sure. Sleep banished, I waited for a new day to dawn.

Morning revealed a small dusky green carcass. The creature had a squarish body with no discernable head, six appendages, three of which had multiple stick-like fingers. Georgia had torn one appendage off and mustard-yellow blood oozed from the damaged areas.

I assumed it was dead. It didn't move and I had no way of guessing as to its vital functions. I could vividly imagine one of those stick-like fingers poking me in the utterly lightless night.

"What do we do now, girl?" I asked Georgia. "We killed one of them, and we have no idea how many more there are, or even where they are." I pondered what I knew so far, which was abysmally little. "Do they not need light? Do they only come out at night? Are they the farmers, or just a small nocturnal species?"

I drank my fill, and considered whether or not the creature might be edible. But since Georgia had not gone near the body after killing it, I decided the odds were against that particular food source.

Cursing my lack of a container, I reluctantly left the pool. Surely we'd find another before our need was too great. Before we took off, I encouraged Georgia to sniff the remains.

"Find more, Georgia," I encouraged. "Find a settlement. We aren't going to find our way home alone, so we might as well look for more of these creatures."

She's not a hunting dog, but she's smart and she seemed to understand what I wanted.

We soon left the silver creeper behind and moved onto a plain of waist-high tubular plants. Deep plum color. Like leafless bamboo. If this plain had been planted, it had been sown by broadcasting the seed rather than planting in organized rows.

With no watch, no working smartphone, and no familiarity with this sky, I had no way to tell time, but we hadn't been walking long before Georgia's ear's perked up and her pace moved from slow plod to interested trot. I had just noticed a dark area on the plain when Georgia disappeared into it.

With a cry of alarm I hurried forward to discover that she had trotted down a gentle slope into a circular depression. From the rim, I watched as she moved to the center, circled once staring into what might have been entrances around the perimeter, and then settled to the ground and looked up at me, head cocked as if to say, "Why are you still up there?"

I sighed and made my way down the slope to join her. Whatever happened, we were a team.

I crouched down beside her and patted her head. "Good, girl. What have you found?" At regular intervals around the edge of the depression were what might have been entrances to fox dens or rabbit warrens. "Did you find a community?" I asked. "Are we right in the middle of the town square?"

She wagged her tail and sneezed.

"Well, if anyone wants to meet us," I said, sitting down. "They'll have to come out. I'm not crawling down a rabbit hole, and you don't look like you're exactly itching to explore either."

We sat quietly. Georgia rested her head on her front paws and closed her eyes. I leaned against her side, stroking her head or scratching behind her ears. After what seemed like eons, but was probably less than an hour, Georgia's ears perked forward and her eyes opened. No other movement signaled her change in alertness. I peered around, trying not to move my head, but anxious to detect what she'd heard.

I felt it before I saw or heard it.

A small tickle in the back of my brain. Not the back of my neck. Nothing touched me physically. No. I felt that tickle *inside* my skull.

My heart slammed against my ribs, my lungs seized. Terror clawed at my mind.

But Georgia remained calm. No raised hackles. No deep-throated growls. Just my dog, resting by my side, with her ears perked forward.

I'm not in physical danger, I told myself. *Georgia would know if I were being threatened.*

I breathed in deeply, forcing myself to calm.

Then I felt it again. More distinctly. Like a scratch inside my skull.

What? I thought. What is it?

Us, came the answer.

My hand stilled on Georgia's back. I closed my eyes and concentrated on my senses. On the feel of Georgia's fur beneath my fingers, the barest whisper of a breeze across my cheeks, the odd, sweet / salty / fecund smell of the plum-colored bamboo, the dryness of my mouth, and the emptiness of my stomach. I catalogued each sense and then moved past them into a part of my mind I'd never used. There I sensed a barely there thread of energy. A filament of thought not my own. I touched it.

And light blazed through my soul.

I saw them, the denizens of this world. Not a dead carcass that I couldn't tell what the pieces parts might be, but intelligent beings who understood their universe far better than I understood mine.

We communed. A true hive mind, they had no individual names or identities. Each organism functioned as the whole directed. They shared their world with me and drew out my understanding of my own. They called themselves Craylons.

They were curious about Georgia, what she was, her relationship to me, why they'd been unable to establish contact with her. Ahh. She was other than me. Not yet evolved, but cherished none the less.

Their mind was vast; their knowledge so much more than my single brain could comprehend. Even so, I understood. The Craylons only emerged after both suns had set. The combined radiation from the pair created a deadly peril for them. They had not developed eyes since they were never exposed to light.

But eyes or not, they were an inquisitive species, always seeking to increase their knowledge. Georgia and I had been pulled from our world during an experiment in one of their scientific facilities.

Forgive us, they said. *We did not intend you harm.*

I understand, I replied. *Forgive us as well. We were frightened. Georgia is a gentle dog and would never have killed except to protect me.*

The death of one is mourned, they said, *but the many continue. We will study the experiment and find a way to return you. Will you be content to wait?*

I smiled and hugged Georgia. What choice did we have? *Of course,* I replied. *We appreciate your hospitality.*

Darkness fell, but it held no terror. Creatures moved around us, but I held Georgia steady. Food and drink appeared and the light in my mind guided my fingers without the necessity of sight. Georgia and I ate and drank and slept in peace.

It might not be tomorrow, or even next week, but Georgia and I were going home. With all the Craylon knowledge my single human brain could carry.

PART IV

THE GHOST IN THE GLASS

DEBBIE MUMFORD

BESTSELLING AUTHOR OF *SORCHA'S HEART*

Red's Magick

SPUN YARNS
A Short Story Collection

1

Red swirled to the edge of his prison and peered through layers of bubble wrap and packing peanuts. Hands thrust the protective materials away and grasped the wrapped glass. Red recoiled in shock as his penitentiary jarred out of its dark womb into the diffused light of day. He blinked and squinted; the light grew brighter as the cushioning layers fell away.

"Don't drop that!" The tone of command assaulted Red's ears. He'd led a very sheltered life for the past couple of centuries. "The boss paid an arm and a leg for those panes of glass. You ask me, he's nuts. Who needs ancient crap when we manufacture the very best right here in the good old US of A?"

Red didn't understand all of the man's words, but he ruffled at being referred to as 'ancient crap.' He took careful aim and pushed his spell through the miring stasis of the imprisoning glass.

The overbearing speaker sneezed, sneezed again, and continued sneezing with emphatic regularity. Red's pane of glass settled partway back into the soft darkness of packing peanuts, forgotten while his unpackers rushed to the aid of his first American victim.

2

Maureen McBride watched with satisfaction as the workers set the panes of antique glass in the window openings between Mark Davidson's new sunroom and great room. She'd given her buyer in Dublin specific instructions about what she wanted, and he'd come through for her. The two-foot square panes had cost her a significant portion of her decorating budget, but the effect was exactly as she'd hoped. The green-tinged, slightly rippled glass mellowed the sunroom's brilliance and gave the great room an ethereal quality, which she intended to emphasize with paint and décor. This room would be fit for a queen, and Maureen fully intended to rule from it. She'd make Mark Davidson a fine wife; he just didn't know it yet.

"Be careful with that," she snapped when the dark-haired man's grasp faltered momentarily. "Those panes are irreplaceable. I'm incredibly lucky to have come up with four that match, as it is."

"Sorry, Ms. McBride," came the man's unexpectedly rich baritone, "I must've pinched a nerve. I got a shock when I touched this one."

Inside the pane of glass under discussion, Red peered at the figure across the room. A mortal female, and haughty; she reminded him unpleasantly of the Summer Queen. He ground his teeth and his blood boiled at the reminder of that humorless bitch. His temples throbbed with a centuries-old ache for revenge.

He settled to the bottom of the glass, despair washing over him. The Summer Queen existed far beyond his reach, safe from his small magicks.

But this mortal woman wasn't.

Red's spirits lifted, and he pressed his nose against his glass prison and stared hungrily across the room. Yes! The snooty female stood mere feet from him, making notes with a black stylus on a small tablet. Oh, she would do nicely. Tall for a female, she possessed delectable curves and flaming red hair. The hair settled his malicious intent. She wore it pulled back in a severe knot, but escaping tendrils confirmed his impression of long, riotous curls. The perfect scapegoat.

Now, he needed a man. He flowed to the right edge of his prison and inspected the fingers carefully pushing his glass into place. This one had felt Red's flame when his unprotected flesh touched the surface of Red's prison. He sniffed. Ah, of course, Celtic blood — and a connection already established. Red rolled across his glass in a series of exuberant somersaults, glad to be alive for the first time in ages.

3

The day's work complete, Sean Flynn's crew raced to pick up their tools and scatter to their individual lives. Most of the guys had homes to retreat to. Not Sean. Sure, he had an apartment, but home meant family, and Sean had no one in the Denver area.

He breathed a sigh of relief as he stepped away from the final piece of glass. No problems with the installation, but that unexplained shock when he grabbed the last piece worried him. He glanced at his hands — strong, capable, not a tremor to be seen. He considered extending a careful tendril of thought into the room, but noticed the red-headed interior designer walking toward him and thought better of it. Quickly, he knelt to gather his tools.

"Well," she said, running a finger across the still supple seal of the first window frame, "these frames look good. You seem to have mounted them without incident."

He ducked his head further, a roguish grin tugging at his lips. Her personality sucked, but still, he could happily mount *her* frame.

Facial features under control, he stood. "Yes, ma'am. Everything's looking good. You'll have to excuse me, it's Friday. I need to get ... "

Her questing finger reached the fourth and final pane of glass and a surge of lust raged through Sean's mind. God, those fingers! He needed those fingers to massage the erection that throbbed to life beneath his zipper. He throttled a hammer in his own fingers and forced himself to focus on the solidity of its wooden shaft.

She moved away from the glass, and the red haze faded, leaving Sean bewildered by the unexpected rush. He tried to pass it off as imaginary, but the painful hard-on shouted reality. The ocean roar left his ears, and he realized the job site was too quiet. His crew had disappeared. He and the McBride witch were alone in the nearly completed mansion.

"See you next week, Ms. McBride," he mumbled as he placed the hammer in his tool box, picked it up, and strode to the door.

"Next week? Won't your crew be working tomorrow?"

"Sure," he said turning to glance at the irritating woman. Man! Where did an obnoxious broad like her get off having a body like that? Even the mannish business suit couldn't hide her curves, and those legs! His erection surged against his jeans, and he glanced longingly at the door. "I just figured you'd have better things to do with your weekend than hang around a construction site."

"Oh," she said, "of course."

She moved toward him, and his world came unglued.

The door slammed shut, Sean lost his grip on his tool box, and the floor bucked, throwing Maureen into his arms.

"Get your hands off of me," she cried, slapping him so hard his eyes watered. "How dare you grab me like, like ... " she spluttered to a stop.

Sean backed away, stumbled over his forgotten tool box and landed hard on his butt on the floor's plywood subsurface.

Maureen McBride loomed above him, green eyes flashing, red hair pulling free of its tightly bound knot. "I'll report this," she said, the words barely escaping through clenched jaws. "Sexual harassment is a crime in this state."

Sean jumped to his feet and closed the distance between them. "I didn't do anything except keep you from falling." He noted with pleasure that she had to look up to meet his eyes. "It's not my fault you're so starved for physical attention that you intentionally stumble into men's arms."

Her face flushed scarlet, and she opened luscious red lips to scorch him with a rebuttal.

The floor heaved again. They fell into each other's arms, and Sean's tongue dove into her open mouth.

He wanted to struggle, wanted to get the hell away from this aggravating female, but the molten silk of her mouth tasted of honey ... and her tongue! It twisted coyly away from his and then pushed daringly past his teeth into his mouth. Oh, the soft, sensual pleasure of that dance of tongues.

Soft. Sensual. His hands finally reported their location to his brain, and he groaned into her mouth. His senses rapidly overloading, he moved his hands down her back and filled them with the ripe, firm, fullness of her buttocks. His erection leapt and demanded a closer inspection of the cleft pressed so tantalizingly near.

And then it ended, as quickly as it had begun.

She pulled away from his clutching fingers and backed up until she hit the far wall. Cold air shocked his senses, and he longed for her velvet warmth; all of it. No impeding cloth. Just skin caressing skin, and more. Oh, so much more!

"What's going on?" she asked her voice husky and raw. "I, I hardly know you."

I can remedy that, he thought. Aloud, he said, "I don't know. I may be nuts, but I swear the floor jumped." He stared at the dusty surface, anything to keep his eyes away from those enchanting, swollen lips. "Is Denver prone to earthquakes?"

She laughed, a nervous, throaty sound. "Not hardly. Aren't you from around here?"

He moved toward the door, careful not to get too close to her. The ludicrous thought baffled him, but she'd become a negative gravity well, whenever they got close .... Better to keep his distance.

"I'm from Illinois. Just moved out here a couple of months ago. You a native?"

She shook her head and the last clips holding her hair gave way.

His jaw dropped as the mass of shining red curls tumbled free of their restraint. The negative gravity pulled at his hands, and he fought to keep them at his sides. Damn, that hair would feel good sliding through his fingers, brushing across his bare chest, winding around ...

Enough! He turned to the door and forced his hand to reach for the knob.

"I wasn't born here, but I grew up in Longmont, went to college in Boulder." She laughed again, but this time the strained quality had evaporated. The sound danced through his mind. "I guess you could call me a native. What's wrong?"

Sean turned the knob. Nothing happened. He thumped the door near the knob and tried again. The knob turned, he felt the bolt shift, but the door remained immovable.

"The door won't open."

"That's ridiculous," she said, coming toward him.

He moved back and leaned against the wall. His body yearned to eliminate the space between them, but he willed himself to avoid her negative gravity effect.

She turned the knob and pulled against it. The door refused to budge. He watched her glance around the frame and smiled to himself. Maureen McBride knew the construction business.

"It doesn't look out of true," she murmured, her brow furrowed. "I don't see any reason for it to bind."

She turned her gaze on him, and Sean's breath caught. Consequences be damned, he'd gladly drown in those sparkling green depths.

He shook his head to clear his mind and said, "No, the door's set properly, and the knob is working. Something else is at work here."

"What? You think the house is haunted?" She snorted, and Sean knew he'd lost it. Even that unfeminine sound enticed him.

"This is brand new construction, remember? No ghosts here."

Sean felt a shift in the room's energy and held up his hand to silence her. He stilled his mind, consciously walled his physical urges away, and reached out with that unique ability he'd hidden from everyone but his mother.

"Never be ashamed of your heritage, boyo," she'd counseled, "but don't advertise it either."

He closed his eyes and followed the subtle power shift back to its source. Of course!

He opened his eyes and grinned at Maureen. "You've nailed it, Maureen," he said with a laugh. "We're dealing with a ghost, but not the kind you're thinking of!"

4

Maureen McBride blinked hard and stared at the attractive man who stood across the room laughing. She shivered, remembering the erotic kiss they'd shared and her gaze dipped below his belt. The erection she'd felt during their last embrace hadn't ebbed. Heat suffused her face and she turned her attention across the room.

"Pull yourself together, Mr ... um ... " Too late, she realized she didn't even know this contractor's name.

"Flynn," he supplied. "The name's Sean Flynn." He tucked his hands in his armpits, as if resisting the urge to offer her his hand.

"Right," she said, sliding her own hands behind her back. "Nice to meet you, Sean, but since we seem to be locked in a room together, I'd appreciate it if you didn't go crazy on me."

He laughed again, and Maureen relaxed. Sean Flynn's sexy baritone sounded well-grounded and totally sane.

"You can appreciate it or not, but we have a spirit here that we're going to have to deal with, and since it's your fault he's here, you'd better get on board fast."

"My fault? How do you figure that? And why should I believe there's a spirit here?"

He shrugged, but his blue eyes gleamed with humor. "You ordered the antique glass, so it's your ghost."

"The glass? You seriously think there's a ghost in the glass?"

"Yep. Look, I don't advertise it, and I don't care whether you believe me or not, but I'm psychic. It's a family thing — I got it from my mom. We're Celtic. Second sight, and all that shit. Anyway, there's a being in that last pane of glass. He's not a ghost, exactly, 'cause he's not dead. He's also not mortal."

Maureen inched further away from Sean and pulled frantically at the door. No go. It remained firmly sealed. She turned, leaned her back against the door and stared at the incredibly sexy lunatic watching her from the other wall.

"This is a joke, right? I mean, you don't look unhinged."

"Spending time locked in a room with you wasn't in my game plan for the night." He pushed away from the wall and walked to the newly installed antique glass. "Remember earlier when I almost dropped this pane?" He looked over his shoulder at her and pointed at the final piece of rippled, green-tinged glass. "He shocked me when I picked it up. I knew there was something there, but I let myself get, uh, distracted."

The look he gave her sent shivers down her spine. She stepped away from the door's support. Crazy or not, he pulled her, a magnetic force too powerful to resist. She glanced at the floor; not very comfortable looking, but that wouldn't matter if she rode him. She stopped moving, shook her head and tried to re-solidify her liquefied core.

"Okay. I don't know what's going on, but this is not normal." She licked her lips and locked her gaze with his. "Since I don't have a better answer, I'll accept that you're, whatever you are, and that there's something in the glass. What do we do about it?"

"Well, we could hit the floor and have mad, passionate sex, since that seems to be what he wants," Sean grinned, obviously enjoying her discomfort, "or we could try to communicate with him."

"What makes you think it's a him?"

"I can't explain it, but I'm definitely getting a male energy. Just like

I can't tell you how, but I know this guy isn't dead. He's trapped, but alive. And not mortal. Definitely not human. I'm guessing some kind of Fae."

"Fay?" Curious, she stepped closer to the glass. Unfortunately, that also brought her closer to Sean.

"Whoa," he said and backed away several paces. "If my mind is going to function, you need to keep your distance."

Warmth spread through her body, and she bit her lip. The thought of driving all rational thought from Sean's mind thrilled her. She closed her eyes, concentrated on their dilemma and tried again.

"What do you mean 'some kind of fay'?"

"You know, Faery."

"Fairy? Little naked people with wings? Give me a ... " She'd intended to say 'break,' but the sneezing fit hit her before the word made it out. She sneezed until she fell, and still the violent lung spasms continued. She lay on the floor writhing, unaware of anything except the need to pull oxygen into her lungs between frantic exhalations. When it stopped, she burst into tears, too tired and frightened to be concerned about Sean's arms cradling her body.

"It's over, Maureen. You're okay. Everything's going to be fine."

Gradually, she heard him crooning soothing comments over and over as he rocked her back and forth. She stopped crying and her breathing regulated. She relaxed and accepted the support and comfort of his strong arms.

"At least he's laying off the lust for a bit," Sean said, stroking her hair as he ceased to rock.

"How did you make him stop?"

"I reminded him you wouldn't be any fun dead." His dull tone sent a drift of snow through her veins.

"I'm okay," she said, struggling to sit up. "What do we do next?"

"Well, we start by remembering not to say, or even think, anything derogatory about the Fae." He glanced at the pane of glass. "I heard the General Contractor was hospitalized with a severe case of flu the other day. I wonder if our friend had anything to do with his sudden illness."

"Got it," she said. "The Fae are powerful, awesome folk. Check. What else?"

"I'm going to try to make contact with him. See if I can figure out what he wants."

A wave of fear raced through Maureen. "Have you ever done anything like this before?"

"Nope. Until today I thought the Fae were, well, you know, fairy tales. Okay, here goes." He gave her a feeble smile, stood, brushed the sawdust off his jeans and walked to the glass.

He stretched out his hand, placed it on the glass, fingertips first, and then, full palm. He took a deep breath and closed his eyes.

Maureen waited. She sat cross-legged in the middle of the floor, heedless of the dust or the unlady-like way her skirt hiked up around her thighs.

He's going to be fine, she told herself. *He's psychic; he knows what he's doing.*

She tried not to fidget, tried to clear her mind and think positive, happy thoughts about this man she'd just met. The man she'd had more lascivious thoughts about in the last hour than she'd had before in her entire life. The man who had quite probably saved her life.

Be strong, she thought. *Be safe. Get us out of here so I can get to know you without a fairy messing with my hormones. Be strong. Be safe.*

She closed her eyes and imagined herself and Sean hiking in the mountains, swimming at Boulder Reservoir, shopping at Cherry Creek. Her mind skipped forward, and she saw them skiing in Aspen, curled before a roaring fire, their bodies entwined on a rumpled bed in her Victorian home.

Her eyes flew open in time to see Sean turn, his hand still on the glass, a smile lighting his eyes. "I like the way you think, Maureen." His voice sounded husky and relaxed. "Red agrees."

Staring into Sean's clear blue eyes, Maureen forgot to be embarrassed. "His name is Red?"

"It'll do. His real name is beyond my ability to pronounce. He apologizes. He's been in isolation a long time. He confused you with the Faery Queen who cursed him into this glass."

Sean quieted and appeared to listen. "Red says you're nothing like the Summer Queen. You're capable of true love, and he's sorry he interfered except ... "

"What?" Maureen climbed to her feet and went to stand next to Sean, in front of the troublesome pane of glass. "You've heard my secret thoughts. What's he saying that you don't want to repeat?"

Sean's eyes slid away from hers, and a slight blush stained his high cheekbones. "He says Mr. Davidson wouldn't have suited you, that you're better off with me."

He snatched his hand away from the glass, ducked his head and stared at the floor. "I swear, he said that, not me!"

She reached out and took his hand, the one that had just been in contact with Red's glass. She lifted his knuckles to her lips and kissed them softly. "I believe you. Nobody knew I'd decided to make a play for Mark Davidson. I'd barely admitted it to myself."

He looked up, and she grinned. "Besides, I think Red might have just done me the biggest favor of my life. He introduced me to you." Maureen gazed into Sean's blue eyes and smiled. Mark Davidson would never know what he'd missed. Too bad for him. This unexpected contractor offered everything she needed and more ... a whole lot more.

"The door's unlocked now," Sean said, smiling back at her. "Can I take you out to dinner?"

"I'd like that," she said, her eyes never leaving his as she pulled him toward the now open door, "and for dessert, maybe we'll go back to my place and explore some of Red's, um, steamier suggestions."

Sean's eyes widened for an instant before settling into a gaze of smoldering intensity. "I've always subscribed to the theory that says, 'Life's short, enjoy dessert first!'"

Maureen laughed and raced Sean to the car.

PART V

RED'S BOWER

DEBBIE MUMFORD

BESTSELLING AUTHOR OF *SORCHA'S HEART*

Red's Magick

SPUN YARNS
A Short Story Collection

1

Raymond O'Connor swept into the Victorian bed and breakfast as though he owned the place. The dark-haired woman who opened the door fell back with a look of startled amazement on her face.

"Don't stand there gawking," he said, directing her attention to the man carrying his bags, "tell him where to put my things."

"Upstairs, first door on the left," she said, stealing a quick glance at Ray's well- known face.

"Upstairs? That's completely unacceptable. My cousin assured me she had a suite on the main floor."

"She does, I mean, there is," stammered the hostess, as frumpy a woman as Ray had ever encountered, "but it's only for special guests."

"Well, my dear," he said, giving her his best prince-charming smile, "they don't come any more 'special' than me. Now, where's the main floor suite?"

She motioned to a pair of curtained French doors at the end of the hall. Ray strode forward and swung the doors wide.

"Yes," he said, taking in the elegantly appointed king-size bed, comfortable seating area and private deck. He stalked across the room, opened a door to reveal a lavish bath, and then turned to stare through the vintage, green-tinged window to the immaculate rose garden beyond. "This will do nicely. I assume that's the closet?" He pointed to the only remaining door, and the woman nodded. "Fine," he nodded to the man, "stack my things over there."

Opening the door to the deck, he stepped out into the late afternoon sunlight and took a deep breath. He savored the Rocky Mountain air, even if it was tainted by a whiff of Denver's growing smog.

"The garden is lovely," he said over his shoulder to the hovering woman. "I'll take my breakfasts out here. Nine a.m. on the dot. I'll be in the bath from eight-forty-five to nine every morning. You may set up during that window of time." He stepped back into the bedroom. "Now, where is my cousin? I know she must be anxious to welcome me."

Good lord. The woman looked so pale he feared she might faint. Why in heaven's name was Maureen subjecting him to this person's star-struck gawking? Maureen knew he needed a hide-away, somewhere he could be alone, prepare for his Denver concert without having to worry about tripping over fans every time he stepped off an elevator. She had assured him that her entire bed and breakfast would be at his disposal; as well it might, considering what he was paying his cousin for his privacy.

"I'm sorry, Mr. O'Connor," the woman said, "Mr. and Mrs. Flynn are in Chicago. They had a family emergency. On Mr. Flynn's side," she added quickly.

"Chicago? You mean Maureen's not here?" He sank down on the loveseat, stunned by the unexpected news. "She knew I was coming, and she left? Who's going to see to my needs?"

"I'll be here, Mr. O'Connor. I live just down the street and I have a key. Maureen asked me to stop by every morning and fix your breakfast. It'll be no trouble at all."

"Stop by?" he repeated. "You don't work here?"

"Excuse me," said the man who'd been heaping luggage next to the closet door. "I need to get going. That'll be thirty-two fifty."

Ray jumped to his feet and reached for his wallet.

"Wait," said the woman. She turned to face Ray, and he saw that her eyes were bright with an emotion he couldn't identify. "I really think you should have this gentleman move your things upstairs to the room Maureen prepared for you." She took a step closer to Ray, glanced toward the deck, and lowered her voice. "This room has a, well, um, a reputation. They say it's haunted."

Ray stared at her for a moment, but failed to see the expected glint of laughter in her eyes. He glanced around the room and said, "Ridiculous. This is a perfectly lovely room and I have no intention of racing up and down stairs all day." He paid the cab driver and sent him on his way.

"Now, where were we? Oh, yes. Do you mean to say that you're not employed by my cousin?"

"No. Not really."

He must have looked as confused as he felt because she held out her hand and continued, "I'm Kathleen Mallory, Mr. O'Connor. It's a pleasure to meet you."

He took her hand and observed her closely for the first time. Dark hair, dark eyes, petite –- barely 5'2" he guessed -– and mature. Not a day under thirty. Very plain, with her hair pulled back in a pony tail and wearing that outdated skirt and blouse. Still, she had potential. If she made an effort, he thought she might be quite stunning. Those dark hazel eyes, definitely her best feature. Fathomless pools of empathy; a man could lose himself exploring those depths. She'd seen suffering. To his surprise, he found he cared.

He took a deep breath, held it for a moment, and let it out in a long sigh. "I'm sorry, Ms. Mallory," he said, "I'm accustomed to dealing with hotel staff; I assumed you were employed here."

"Not at all," she said, a frosty smile curved her lips, but didn't touch those lovely eyes. "Maureen Flynn is a friend. She's been very kind to me during a difficult time. I'm happy to help her out."

She turned and led him to the living room. Maureen, a former interior designer, had gone to some length to decorate her Victorian home in period. Ray found the room charming, with an old world air.

"Not to belabor the point," Kathleen said, "but are you sure I can't convince you to move upstairs?"

"You're serious, aren't you?"

"Yes. I know that Sean and Maureen never rent that particular room without first making the couple aware of its, um, eccentricities. I'm sorry, but I don't know the details. I just know that she prepared the Rose Room for you, not Red's Bower."

"Red's Bower? Now I'm really intrigued. Why would she call it that?"

Kathleen threw her hands in the air, an exasperated sigh escaping her lips. "Heaven only knows. I've never had occasion to stay in the suite, so I've never heard the briefing. I just know that Red's Bower is notorious, and that most of her clientele come because of curiosity about that room, whether they choose to stay in it or not."

"Well," he said, "if my cousin is brave enough to live in the same house with Red and his bower, I think I can brave sleeping there for a few nights."

"As you wish," she said. "I'm an early riser. Having your breakfast on the deck by nine won't be a problem." She turned and walked to the door. "I'll be off then," she said. "I left my phone number on the kitchen counter. Call if you need assistance. Good evening, Mr. O'Connor."

"Ms. Mallory," he said, reaching for the doorknob, "it's been a pleasure."

A thump sounded behind them, and their eyes met.

"Is anyone else in the house?" Ray asked.

Kathleen shook her head.

"A cat, perhaps?"

"Sean and Maureen don't keep pets. Too many people have allergies."

As if drawn by an invisible force, Ray and Kathleen turned simultaneously and walked down the hall. When they arrived at Red's Bower, they found the door closed.

"Odd," said Ray, his voice firm, but quiet, "I don't remember closing this door." He turned the handle and stepped into the room. Immediately, apprehension vanished, replaced by a sense of expectant well-being. He glanced over his shoulder, beckoned Kathleen to follow and strode to the window overlooking the garden. Placing his hand flat on the pane, he felt a zip of merry mischief dart across his mind. He turned, anticipatory delight thawing his heart and saw Kathleen framed in the French door.

Raw, ravening lust electrified his system. A goddess gazed at him from the threshold of this enchanted bower. He longed to loose those dark flowing locks, to run his hands through their lush richness. Her soft, hazel eyes, frightened now, like a doe ready to flee, but they would smolder when his caresses lit her soul on fire!

He allowed his gaze to worship the soft curves so modestly concealed from casual observation. But his inspection was far from casual. He fervently sought, and found, evidence of ripe fullness beneath the constricting fabric. He strode deliberately across the room, intent on worshipping her perfect form, communing with the divine in the depths of her silken temple.

Before he could reach her, his goddess launched herself into his arms, and they fell, a frenzied tangle of arms and legs, onto the billowy softness of the waiting bed.

2

Kathleen savored this heady new experience, a man's lips on her eyelids, her cheeks, her neck (Oh! Yes!), his tongue sliding along the upper slope of her breast. Too much cloth hampered his progress. Her deft fingers worked to unbutton, unzip, unfasten, while her mouth explored the outline of his ear, kissed the springy softness of carefully styled hair.

The moment he had stepped through the door, she'd felt it. The wave of desire, dragging carefully avoided emotions from their hiding places. The wave built as he touched the pane of antique Irish glass, pooling the power of her deepest fears and longings into its surging strength: her recent grief at her beloved father's passing; resentment of the need to dedicate her prime years to his care; guilt over that resentment; fear that she'd never find love, never experience marriage and children; deep, abiding yearning for sexual fulfillment. All these emotions, unacknowledged, compressed for a decade, crested when he turned those brilliant green eyes on her. When he strode toward her, she knew her wave must break upon his shore.

Now she lay panting under his glorious weight. Skin pressed to skin, they struggled together to break the bonds of individuality, to become one; a single, brilliant, pulsating entity, tingling with vibrant life. Sensations too exquisite to be contained rippled between them. The electric stimulation of senses rubbed raw. The intense compulsion to merge, to experience, to heave and surge, ebb and flow, give and take. The ceaseless, remorseless rhythm; push; squeeze; hold tight; and finally, when she could endure the supreme agony no longer –– release, glorious release! Her body quivered and contracted, intent on wringing every exhausted tribute he had to offer before heavenly lassitude carried her into sleep.

Kathleen drifted to consciousness on the wings of soul-deep contentment. She couldn't remember ever feeling so relaxed, so rejuvenated, so satisfied before. Indulging her senses, she kept her eyes closed and stretched, a whole-body yawn.

Her sense of well-being vanished when her outstretched arm encountered warm, naked flesh. Her eyes popped open, and Kathleen Rose Mallory sprang to a sitting position, sheet clutched protectively to her breast.

Ray O'Connor lay diagonally across the king-size bed, one forearm covered his eyes, but nothing could disguise the satisfied smile curving his lips.

Good God! What had she done? Indisputable evidence leered at her from every angle: naked, in a badly rumpled bed, next to one of the most famous classical musicians on the planet. And him Maureen Flynn's cousin! She'd never live this down. She'd be branded a wanton woman for the rest of her life. She might as well go downtown and choose a likely corner.

She huddled into a ball and scrunched her eyes tightly closed. She'd wondered what she would do with her life now that Dad was gone. The mortgage-free house belonged to her alone, her sole inheritance, but she had no marketable skills, having left college after her sophomore year to care for Dad. Well, perhaps she'd found her calling.

3

―――――

R ay woke, as he always did, with crystal clarity. One moment he slept; the next his mind engaged, fully functional. He removed his arm, opened his eyes and saw Kathleen sitting up, but pulled into a tight little ball.

Damnation, he'd done it again — let a love-struck fan finagle him into bed. He wondered what this little escapade would cost his career. He ought to strangle Maureen. She was supposed to protect him from this kind of shit. Well, too late now. He'd have to deal with the consequences.

His gaze traveled over Kathleen's curled body and lingered on her hands. Memory flashed, and his rod hardened. Those hands were gifted. He wondered idly if she played a stringed instrument. She'd certainly demonstrated deft finger control.

His erection throbbed, and he reached for her. Might as well get his money's worth, since he'd already plunged himself into fiscal liability.

He stroked her arm, and she jumped, eyes wide and frightened.

"Don't touch me," she cried.

"Aren't we a little past the nervous virgin stage?" He smiled, expecting a nervous giggle in return. Her reaction startled him.

With solemn dignity, she dropped the sheet, stepped from the bed and bent to gather her cast-off clothing. The view she offered as she sorted her things from his sent his blood pressure soaring. He wanted her under him, needed to slam into her velvet softness before his cock exploded.

"Kathleen," he croaked, barely able to push the name past gritted teeth.

She straightened and sailed from the room without sparing him a single backward glance.

He fell back on the bed, physical agony throbbing through his loins. And something else, an emotion he felt so rarely he almost didn't recognize it: shame. He swallowed hard, trying to avoid the truth, but couldn't. The expression in her eyes as she moved from the bed had been too clear. Kathleen Mallory was no star-struck fan. What in hell had happened in this room last night?

4

—————

"You did what? With *Kathleen*?" Maureen McBride Flynn closed her eyes and leaned her forehead against the wall of the gate at O'Hare International. The cell phone she held to her ear weighed a ton.

"What possessed you to stay in Red's Bower? Didn't Kathleen tell you I wanted you in the Rose Room?" She sighed and bit her lip, wondering how she could ever make this right with Kathleen. Ray didn't worry her; he'd had enough affairs to satisfy the most voracious gossip columnist. Although in all fairness, he'd cleaned up his act over the last eighteen months.

"We'll be home this afternoon. Don't do anything to make matters worse. Sean will explain everything when we get there." She paused to consider her next words and then blurted, "And Ray, take what you need and get out of Red's Bower. Stay away from that room 'til we get home."

She flipped the phone closed and walked back to her seat beside Sean. "I'm sorry, my love, but we've got a mess to clean up at home. Red's been playing with Ray. And Kathleen."

"Kathleen?" Sean groaned. "How in heaven's name did that

5

The hours dragged. Ray couldn't settle to anything. An uneasy guilt weighed on his mind. He took out his violin and tried to practice, but even the ingrained discipline of a lifetime of training failed him. At noon, he rummaged through the kitchen in search of food. Maureen's well-stocked pantry enticed him, until his eyes fell on the counter where the note with Kathleen's phone number taunted him.

Kathleen. He barely knew the woman, and yet she'd taken root in his psyche. He ached whenever he thought of the look in her eyes before she left Red's Bower. An entirely different ache wracked his body when he remembered the wildly passionate night they'd shared.

He reached for the phone, but stopped. Maureen's voice sounded in his mind, "Don't do anything to make matters worse." He grabbed the scrap of paper, shoved it into his jeans pocket, turned and stomped from the kitchen, his hunger forgotten.

At last, a car pulled into the driveway, and Ray pelted down the stairs to greet Sean and Maureen at the door.

"Am I glad to see you," he said. "I feel like I'm losing my mind."

Maureen hugged him, and Sean shook his hand.

"Believe me," Sean replied, "we're intimately familiar with the feeling." He waved at their luggage heaped by the door. "Let's ignore the unpacking for the time being and see if we can get this situation straightened out."

He led the way to Red's Bower, Ray following with obvious reluctance. Sean smiled. "Don't worry, Red and I have an understanding."

Ray stared at Sean. "You sound like there's someone in there."

Sean winked. "There is. He already knows you, as evidenced by your, um, unexpected night, but let me introduce you." He swung the door open and walked straight to the green-tinged glass. "Red, give Ray a glimmer so he'll know his cousin didn't marry a lunatic."

Ray watched in fascination as the glass fogged and a smiling, elfish face appeared. The glass cleared again, just as quickly. Ray blinked twice and remained standing despite his knees' strong desire to buckle.

"That was Red. As I understand it, he's a faery who was cursed into this pane of glass for playing inappropriate tricks on the Summer Queen." Sean grinned, a playful light dancing in his eyes. "I'm sure you can imagine her provocation, seeing as how you've experienced some of his tricks yourself."

This time, Ray's knees won. He stumbled to a chair and lowered his head into his hands. "This is all my fault. Kathleen tried to warn me, but I thought she was just spouting your marketing hype."

"Red's been a tremendous boon to our commercial success, I admit," Maureen said, coming to rest a hand on Ray's shoulder, "but we never allow anyone to stay in this room without first introducing them to Red and making sure they're aware of the kind of spells he's likely to cast. Those brave enough to stay usually become repeat customers."

"Oh, God," moaned Ray. "Does Kathleen know about this?"

Maureen shook her head. "She's heard the rumors, but she's never stayed in this room, so we've never had cause to introduce her."

"Well, she's certainly been initiated now."

"I know how you feel," Maureen sympathized.

"You can't possibly," whispered Ray.

"Actually, we can," said Sean. "Red introduced Maureen and me, in a house under construction, when I was setting his glass. He locked us in and, well," he stopped, glanced at his wife and smiled, "we've been together ever since."

"Wait a minute, how did he end up here?"

Maureen laughed. "The owner didn't believe me when I tried to tell him about Red. He fired me and used his influence to ruin my interior design business. Red took offense."

Sean picked up the story. "Let's just say that a few months later he contacted me and begged me to get that piece of glass out of his house."

Ray shook his head and then stood, resolution lining his face. "Okay. I'm fine, or at least, I will be, but what about Kathleen?"

Maureen patted her cousin's shoulder. "Don't worry. You concentrate on your music. Forget this ever happened. I'll explain things to Kathleen; find some way to apologize for the, um, misunderstanding. You don't ever need to see her again."

Ray nodded, more depressed than he'd ever been in his life. His mind accepted Maureen's solution, but his heart ached. He didn't know if he could survive without seeing Kathleen again.

6

Two months later, Ray arrived at Flynn's Bed and Breakfast unannounced. He presented his cousin with a bouquet of pink roses and her husband with a bottle of premium, aged scotch.

"Have you seen Kathleen recently?" he asked as Maureen arranged her roses in a sky-blue vase.

Maureen's hand stilled and she peered at Ray through the screen of petals. "She was over this morning. Why do you ask?"

"We've been corresponding ever since I went back to New York. She's finally agreed to see me again. I'm taking her to dinner and a concert tonight."

Maureen squealed and ran around the counter to hug him. "Ray, that's wonderful! I can't believe she didn't tell me. How long will you be here?"

"I'm staying for a week. If you have room, I'd love to stay here. If not, I'll get a hotel downtown."

"Of course you'll stay here! Oh, this is so exciting." She stopped bouncing and gave him a knowing smile. "Red certainly knows his romance."

Ray's breath caught, but then he grinned and said, "Yes, he does. I

PART VI

SEEING RED

DEBBIE MUMFORD

BESTSELLING AUTHOR OF *SORCHA'S HEART*

SEEING RED

SPUN YARNS
A *Red* Short Story

1

Evan Flynn leaned against the old-world mahogany bar and surveyed his domain. Flynn's Irish Bar was his dream-come-true. He'd designed every detail, from the painting of horses and hounds behind the bar to the softly glowing lamps on the scattered tables, but finding that bar in an abandoned restaurant scheduled for destruction ... well, that had been sheer luck.

He ran a hand over the smooth wood, lovingly restored by his older brother, Ben, rested a hiking-booted foot on the polished brass foot rail, and breathed in the scent of lemon oil and beeswax. The bar was his talisman. His good luck piece. He was Irish enough to believe in such things, as did the rest of his family. Grannie Flynn certainly had. She'd always insisted that Evan had inherited the family gift, that he had *the sight*, like his grandfather before him.

Evan shook his head and glanced over his shoulder to his grandparents' talisman, the pane of ancient Irish glass that had been the founding of his family. Without its intervention, his grandparents would never have met. It, or rather its inhabitant, had been the magic that had made their little bed and breakfast the destination of choice for couples seeking a romantic get-away in Colorado's Mile High City.

For nearly sixty-five years the family business had flourished in

Denver, first with Evan's grandparents and then his parents. Unfortunately, neither Evan nor Ben had been interested in continuing the tradition. Both young men had chosen the Pacific Northwest for their homes. Ben had settled in Seattle, but Evan had fallen in love with Portland.

After a long and successful run, Evan's parents had retired to Estes Park, Colorado, leaving the home that had housed the bed and breakfast unoccupied. But last year, when the city condemned the entire block where the house stood, Evan had returned to Denver long enough to rescue the pane of glass before a wrecking ball could shatter it.

He didn't have a clue what would happen to the inhabitant if the glass broke, but he wasn't interested in finding out. Red, as the inhabitant was known, was family. Grannie Flynn had always claimed that the fact that Evan could sense Red's presence, could sometimes even see him floating in the glass, was proof of Evan's gift.

Evan wasn't convinced he had *the sight*, but he did believe in Red's existence; he'd always felt Red's presence, right down to his very soul. The being in the glass might be insubstantial, and mischievous beyond belief, but as far as Evan was concerned he was also a Flynn, and no one would harm him while Evan lived.

Giving the mahogany bar a final pat, Evan straightened and headed for his office. Time to buckle down and get the monthly accounting done. As always, he paused beside Red's glass and placed the palm of his hand in the center of the two-foot square framed pane. His staff thought it odd that he'd framed a piece of blank glass and hung it beside his office door, but he didn't care. He liked having Red nearby, knowing that the little guy was keeping watch over the pub. A ghostly figure swam into view, somersaulted, and approached the surface. A slim, long-fingered hand stretched to meet Evan's and a pointed-eared head nodded in acknowledgement.

"Glad to see you too, Red," Evan murmured before opening the door and stepping into his office.

2
_____

K atie O'Malley stepped over the threshold of Flynn's Irish Pub and breathed a sigh of relief. She couldn't put her finger on the reason, but she always felt safe within these walls. The warmth she felt was an almost spiritual thing that seemed to emanate from the polished wood floor, the sturdy, unpretentious tables and chairs, the solidity of the gleaming bar. Even the odd piece of empty framed glass beside the office door seemed to welcome her.

And she needed to feel safe and welcomed somewhere in the world.

Breathing out a long sigh, she smoothed her slim black skirt and settled at her favorite table, in the shadows but with a clear view of the street outside the wide picture window. She liked to be able to keep watch without being seen.

A shadow, that was what she'd become. He'd driven her to wearing monochrome colors, to blending into the woodwork, to avoiding attention. Even here, in the warmth of this cozy pub filled with happy, chattering people, she clung to the shadows, lived an invisible life.

The waitress, a twenty-something woman whose nametag read

Peg, approached, flashed a friendly smile and said, "Nice to see you again. The usual, or are you up for something different tonight?"

Katie grinned. At least someone knew she existed. "The usual. Your Irish stew is too good to pass up."

Peg laughed. "I'll be sure to tell Evan you like it. It's his grandmother's recipe."

The pub's menu might be limited, but the food was hearty and homemade. Just what she needed; a touchstone to reality, to a life lived in the full light of day.

A life she'd left behind when she met Alex. Of course she hadn't realized she was entering an alternate reality when she accepted his invitation to dinner. He'd seemed like a nice man, charming and thoughtful. He'd remained so until the first time she'd entered his home. That was when the pleasant human had disappeared and the monster had emerged.

She'd been lucky, very lucky, to escape with her life.

Peg returned with a steaming bowl of stew, a platter of crusty bread and an aromatic mug of black coffee. Katie smiled and thanked her, as much for disrupting her morose thoughts as for the food.

Breaking off a piece of bread, Katie inhaled the mingled scents of her meal: yeast, herbs, savory meat, and the slightly bitter overlay of coffee. Mouth watering, she buttered the bread, watching the creamy smear melt into its fresh-baked warmth. Closing her eyes, she took a bite and chewed slowly, enjoying the flaky texture of the crust, the warm goodness of the buttered dough. The taste of the bread combined with the comforting aroma of coffee and stew transported her home. Back to the days when she'd lived with loving parents in the mid-west. Before she'd escaped to the Pacific Northwest and disappeared into a vigilant, invisible existence.

Vigilant.

Her eyes popped open and she glanced warily around the pub. She couldn't afford to be lulled into passivity by familiar food and a comfortable room. She had to remain on guard.

A dark-haired man exited the office, stroked the framed glass, and crossed to the bar. Peg approached him, smiled, spoke a few words with a nod in Katie's direction, and then moved off toward the kitchen. The man leaned back against the dark wood of the bar and turned his gaze on Katie.

She froze, her spoon suspended above the bowl of stew. He'd noticed her. He was looking right at her. She had no reason to fear this man—other than his gender, and she knew that to be an irrational fear which she fought to suppress—but her heart pounded and the fingers holding her spoon trembled.

She looked away from him, forced herself to dip the spoon into the stew and take a bite. The taste of ashes filled her mouth. All joy in her meal had vanished. Keeping her eyes downcast and thinking invisible thoughts, she continued her meal. Gradually the savory broth, tender-crisp carrots and potatoes and well-seasoned meat worked their magic and she relaxed. When her bowl was empty and the bread platter bore only crumbs, she sat back and sipped her coffee.

"Did you enjoy your meal?" The dark-haired man stood across the table from her, a pleasant expression on his face. He was taller than she'd realized, and very nicely proportioned. Clothed in a neat white shirt with narrow blue stripes and creased dark blue trousers, he looked ready for a casual business meeting. Only the well-worn hiking boots detracted from the look.

"Yes," she said. "The stew here is always good."

"You're a repeat customer then," he said with a smile. "I'm glad. I'm Evan Flynn, the owner."

Despite her fears, she was drawn to this man. So much so that she actually smiled back. "I'm pleased to meet you, Mr. Flynn. I like your pub very much."

He gestured to the chair opposite her. "Do you mind if I sit?"

She straightened, placed her coffee mug back on the table and glanced wildly around the room. Everything looked normal. The pub was full of people, every barstool occupied, all the other tables surrounded by couples and families. The room buzzed with conversation. She was safe.

Katie met Evan's eyes briefly, recognizing his puzzled expression before she looked away again. "Of course not," she murmured, hoping he wouldn't accept. But he did.

"Thanks," he said, pulling out the chair and folding his long frame onto it. "I'm glad to hear you like the stew. Grannie Flynn would be pleased to know the cook is doing right by her recipe."

3

—————

Evan studied the young woman across the table. Her dark hair held a touch of red and was pulled away from her face in a single French braid that fell halfway down her back. Stray wisps curled around her face, highlighting a wide brow, straight nose, and full lips untouched by cosmetics. But it was her eyes that drew him, clear and gray ... and frightened. She reminded him of a doe blinded by headlights, but wanting nothing more than to bound away.

She'd seemed comfortable before he approached. What had he done to frighten her?

"Do you live around here?" he asked, noting the tension in those lovely lips, the way her eyes widened and glanced around as if seeking help. "I don't think I've seen you in the neighborhood."

She drew a deep breath, then stilled and met his gaze. "I like to keep to myself."

He heard the dismissal in her words and was suddenly afraid she'd never enter his pub again. What had he done?

Perhaps nothing. Perhaps this frightened young woman needed help.

He sat back, surprised by this insight. Was his gift kicking in at last? He could almost see Grannie Flynn smiling and nodding.

Trusting his instincts, he leaned forward and placed a hand on the table, carefully avoiding touching hers. "Look," he said. "I know you don't know me and have no reason to trust me, but if you're in trouble, if you need help, I'm here."

She gasped, pushed back and stumbled to standing. "I ... I ..." but she got no further before another man joined them.

"Hello, Katie," the new arrival said. "Bet you didn't expect to see me in Portland."

"Alex," she whispered, her face so pale Evan was surprised she hadn't fainted. Terror rolled off the young woman in palpable waves. So this man was the cause of her fear, this Alex. Very likely her fear was legitimate if the menace Evan had detected in the man's words was any indication.

Standing, Evan stepped between them. "I'm sorry, sir, but this table is taken. May I find you seat at the bar?"

Alex turned his attention on Evan, causing him to straighten to his full six feet two inches. This dark man was dangerous, he'd need every inch and all his training to keep the situation under control.

Dark described the man well. Dark of hair and eye and demeanor and wrapped in a black calf-length duster over dark clothing. Menace poured from him, and Evan knew, *knew* that he intended grievous harm to Katie.

"Clear off," Alex growled. "Katie and I have business to discuss."

"I don't think so," Evan replied. Raising his voice he called to his waitress. "Peg, please call 9-1-1."

Alex swung a fist at him, but Evan evaded the blow and pushed Katie into the middle of the pub, toward the door to his office. If he could get Katie inside, he could guard the door until the police arrived. He might take a beating, but some of his regulars would likely come to his aid once they realized what was happening.

He was close to executing his plan when the unexpected happened. Katie lunged toward the door, but instead of escaping inside, she grabbed Evan's shoulder and planted her hand on Red's pane of glass.

The world dissolved around Evan and he felt himself drawn into

4

Katie didn't know what to do. She'd been so distracted by the man sitting across from her that she'd let her guard down, had forgotten to scan the street outside. Evan Flynn had surprised her with his perception, astounded her by his offer to help, and her a total stranger. She'd glanced up, noticed movement behind Evan and jumped to her feet.

Her worst nightmare had come true. Alex had found her. There he stood, in Evan's cheerful pub, leering at her. She was trapped. She had nowhere to hide.

And then Evan had stood up and moved in front of her.

This man she'd just met, had barely spoken to, seemed ready to defend her. And all she'd done to earn his help was compliment his grandmother's stew.

This couldn't be happening; the situation was too surreal for words.

He yelled for Peg to call the police, and Alex took a swing at him, but Evan managed to duck away. He pushed her further into the pub. Was he going to try to hide behind the bar? Maybe duck into his office, barricade the door and hope the police arrived in time?

She didn't know what to do, how to help. Panic clawed at her throat, drove her heart to triple time. She had to do something. She couldn't let Alex take her, and she couldn't let him harm a nice man whose only fault was being chivalrous. But what? What could she do?

As Evan pushed her closer to his office door, she felt it. An aura of power emanating from that odd empty frame. That piece of old glass, wavy and rippled and slightly green tinged, something about it called to her. What was it?

It didn't matter. Nothing could be worse than being captured by Alex again. Whatever the power behind that glass, it was benign compared to the evil that resided in the big man's soul. Besides, the closer she got to the glass, the calmer she felt. Her heartbeat regulated, her breathing eased. Rescue was at hand. All she had to do was touch the glass as she'd seen Evan do earlier.

Touch the glass ... but touch Evan first.

She grabbed Evan by the shoulder and laid her other palm flat on that two-foot square of old glass ... and felt reality melt away.

She closed her eyes and waited. Whatever would happen would do so without her further effort. She had made her choice.

Forces she didn't understand and couldn't name whipped and whirled around her, tried to drag Evan from her grasp, but she held on. Held on to the only bit of reality left to her, the man who had tried to save her.

At last the wild ride calmed and she felt steady on her feet again. She opened her eyes and found Evan staring at her over the shoulder she still held. They were in a large room that looked like it belonged in a medieval castle. Stone walls, slate floor strewn with rushes, and high narrow windows. Intricately worked tapestries hung on the walls and massive furniture, made of dark, heavy wood. A fire crackled merrily in a rock fireplace large enough for Evan to walk into without ducking.

"Where are we?" he asked. "What did you do?"

"I ... I'm not sure. That pane of glass by your office called me. I had to touch it, but I had to touch you, too."

Understanding lit his eyes. "Red? Are you here? Is this your doing?

"Red?" she asked.

He glanced at her with a veiled expression, then shrugged. "Well, you can hardly call me crazy since this is your doing. Red's a faery. He lives in that pane of glass. He's been in my family for generations."

Her eyes widened and she caught her breath. A *faery*? Was this guy for real? Of course, she had transported them from his pub to ... wherever the hell they were now, so she didn't have much room to cast aspersions on his sanity.

That was assuming they were really here. Wherever here was. For all she knew, she could be lying in some hospital bed in a coma. Or dying. Maybe Alex had killed her and this was her brain's way of avoiding obliteration.

"Actually, I don't *live* here, I'm incarcerated here. Biding my time until the Summer Queen relents and releases me."

A young man dressed like an elf in a *Lord of the Rings* movie appeared before the hearth. He had silver blonde hair clubbed at the base of his skull, pointed ears and cat-like green eyes that sparkled with amusement.

"Nice to meet you at last, Evan," he said, "though I had no idea you could transport." He turned his gaze on Katie. "And who is your charming companion?"

"This is Katie," Evan said, distractedly. "And I can't transport. Are you saying you didn't do this, either? You didn't pull us into your frame?"

Red's eyes widened and then his brows drew together in a thunderous frown. "I? Of course not! Do you think I would have spent all these centuries alone in this room if I could transport a mortal companion into my glass? Why, I've had to rely on voyeurism just to keep my sanity!"

"If you didn't do it," said Evan turning to look at Katie, "and I didn't do it – and I've touched your glass a million times over the years without being pulled inside – then it must have been you, Katie."

"Me?" she squeaked. "How could it have been me? I didn't even know Red existed."

"How fascinating," said Red, clapping his hands. "Let's not get all worked up, though. Come. Sit. Let me enjoy the first guests I've had in centuries!" He motioned them toward a set of heavy chairs grouped around the fireplace. "Have some refreshment. Tell me everything that happened. I've been napping; nothing exciting usually happens in the pub this early in the evening."

Evan and Katie moved closer to the faery and settled in chairs that were much more comfortable than they looked. Red conjured goblets of honey mead and a tray of small cakes. They smelled heavenly, like ripe strawberries and rich dark chocolate, but Evan eyed them with suspicion.

"Forgive me, Red, but isn't it unwise for humans to eat anything in faery?"

Red beamed at him. "Ahh ... you make me proud, boy! To think that in this day of disbelief a young man knows his faery lore."

Evan reddened, but narrowed his eyes at Red. "Just answer the question, please."

"Yes, you're absolutely correct. Humans should never eat or drink anything offered to them while underhill. However, you are quite safe here. My prison was removed from faery by a human knight at the command of the Summer Queen. We are not in faery, but in the mortal realm."

Evan nodded and accepted a goblet. "In that case, I thank you for your hospitality."

Red bowed. "And I thank you and your family for your companionship. Now that you've come into your gift, we shall be able to communicate more freely, even when you're not inside my pane of glass."

Evan took a sip of mead. "So I was right. Meeting Katie really did trigger my sight."

"Is that what did it?" Red turned to stare at Katie. "You must be a remarkable young woman," he said. "I've been aware of Evan's latent talent since his birth, but had despaired of it ever manifesting. How did you do it?"

Katie felt two sets of eyes boring into her. Each of them had power, different colors and scents, but power none the less. She threw a wall up in her mind and cowered behind it, afraid of what they might see.

Wait a minute! She could see and smell magic? She knew how to shield her thoughts? Where had that come from?

Taking a deep breath, she lowered her shields and looked at Red. "I don't have any idea how I've done any of this."

Red eyed her speculatively. "Tell me everything that's happened."

When Katie and Evan finally wound down after giving Red a very disjointed account of their meeting and Alex's untimely arrival, the faery stood and stalked around the room.

"You didn't say so," he said, stopping in front of Katie, "but I'm guessing you escaped an abusive relationship with Alex and you've been on the run ever since."

Her cheeks heated and she stared at the stone flags beneath her feet, but nodded.

"You needn't detail the abuse," he said, " but can you tell me how you escaped?"

She looked up, startled. "I ... well ... I don't actually know. I mean, he'd had me for several weeks ... horrible ... he did ..." she swallowed bile and stopped, her breath coming fast and shallow.

Red knelt before her and placed a hand on her head. "No," he murmured. "Don't think about that. Just think about your escape."

His touch calmed her, insulated her from those terrible memories. She closed her eyes and inhaled the sweet scent of freedom; fresh grasses, sunlit skies, and spring flowers. Red's gift of solace.

"Thank you," she murmured. "I honestly don't remember how I did it. I ... I just thought about how nice it would be to be invisible, to be able to walk past him when he opened the door to bring in supplies, and then ... I did it."

"Let me guess," he said. "You've been thinking invisible thoughts ever since."

"Well, yes. I've been concentrating on not being noticed, on blending in. I've been very lonely, but I've been safe." She glanced at Evan. "Except at Flynn's Irish Pub. I've always felt safe there, so I've often let down my guard. Peg's noticed me enough to remember my usual order. But I always sit in the shadows, at a table where I can watch traffic on the street outside."

Evan straightened in his chair. "So that's why I've never noticed you. I probably wouldn't have today if Peg hadn't called you to my attention."

Red nodded. "You, my dear, have faery blood. Judging from your abilities, I'd say some type of water sprite. You're very good at using shadows and letting others' attention flow over and around you. That's why you've been drawn to the pub, and why you're here. You felt my magic and it soothed you. Today, when you were threatened, you followed the connection between Evan and myself and allowed the stream of magic to carry you to my prison ... which is more of a refuge for you."

"I'm a faery?"

"No, no, child," Red said with a smile. "You have faery blood. You're fully human, but there's a faery hiding among the leaves somewhere in your family tree."

"Is my sight a remnant of faery blood, then?" Evan asked.

Red somersaulted through the air and landed beside Evan. "No, my boy. The sight is another matter entirely. Given by the elder gods to certain mortals to protect your race from my kind. Rarely needed these days, when the realms so rarely intersect."

Evan nodded. "Well, this has been great, and I'm glad we finally had the chance to meet, but how do Katie and I return to our world?"

Red shrugged. "No idea. I'm in prison, remember? I certainly can't free you."

Katie stood and straightened her shoulders. "Well, since I'm the one who brought us here, it must be up to me to get us back again." Her pulse quickened and she licked her lips. "But what do I do when we get there? How do I deal with Alex?"

Evan moved to stand beside her. "Don't worry, Katie. Remember, Peg called the police. He may already be in custody."

"And remember, my dear," added Red. "You have power. You are *not* a defenseless victim."

Katie glanced from Evan's serious but determined face to Red's enigmatic one. Human and faery, but both concerned for her safety. How very interesting.

She drew in a deep, steadying breath, clutched Evan's hand, and closed her eyes. Letting her senses range outward, she scented magic and turned in that direction. Opening her eyes, she saw a path sparkling in the dim light, mingled blue and green streams shimmered, like moonlight dancing on running water. The blue smelled of Evan, full of strength and determination and honor, while the green reminded her of Red, singing of mischief and love and age-old regret. The two streams were mingled by years of belief and acknowledgement and peaceful coexistence.

Pulling Evan along with her, Katie stepped into the blue-green stream.

5

Evan stumbled as he emerged from Red's pane, but clung resolutely to Katie's hand. He stepped in front of her before his senses stopped swirling enough to register what was happening in the room.

"Evan!" Peg cried, her voice shrill with alarm. "Where have you been?"

"What's happening, Peg?" he asked. "I pushed Katie into my office and we barricaded the door. Is everything all right?"

He glanced around his pub. Chairs and tables had been knocked askew, his patrons stood in silent, wide-eyed clumps against walls and near the door, a few sheltered behind the bar. A uniformed police officer stood with notepad in hand beside Peg, while another knelt beside Alex.

The big man glared at Evan from his position on the floor. He was flat on his belly, legs splayed and hands behind his back. Cuffed.

Evan relaxed and moved to the side so that Katie could see as well.

Peg rushed over, hugged Evan, then stepped back, wiping her eyes with a corner of her apron. "I didn't see where you went. It was like you disappeared, and then that guy went berserk. Thank heavens the police arrived when they did! He attacked them ... I mean, he attacked the police, yelling for Katie and swearing he'd kill you both, and the officers wrestled him to the ground and cuffed him."

She shuddered, and Evan grabbed a chair and guided her into it. "I'm so sorry you had to deal with all that, Peg. You did great. Thanks for calling 9-1-1. You're a real hero."

She smiled a bit wanly and glanced at Katie. "Are you okay, Katie?"

Katie nodded, her attention glued to the man on the floor. "I'm fine, thanks to Evan's quick thinking." She pulled her gaze away and turned to face Peg. "Thank you so much. For everything."

Peg blushed. "I didn't do anything," she said. "Not really."

Katie smiled, the first real smile Evan had seen and it changed everything. She glowed with happiness and a serenity that made him want to hold her close to his heart. His pulse quickened and he forced himself to look away. It wouldn't do to frighten her again. He intended to get to know Katie ... very well, but his instinct, his *gift*, told him he'd need to move very slowly.

"You noticed me," Katie said softly, "and that meant the world to me."

The policeman beside Alex rose and approached Evan and Katie. "We'll be taking him in for resisting arrest and striking an officer, but do either of you wish to press charges?"

"I do," said Evan without hesitation. "He didn't actually assault me, though he tried, but he's certainly caused some damage to my business and traumatized my customers. So whatever that's worth, yeah. Charge him."

The officer pulled out his notebook, jotted a few lines and turned to Katie. "And you, miss?"

She nodded and stepped closer to Evan. "Yes. I don't imagine you can do anything about what happened in Springfield, Illinois, but he followed me here and threatened me. I'll want a restraining order at the very least."

The officer nodded. "The city attorney will be able to advise you, but this is enough to hold him." After taking down Evan and Katie's contact information, he said, "A detective will be in touch to take your statements."

"Thanks for your quick response, officer," Evan said. "I have a feeling this could've been much worse."

With a final glance at Alex, Evan stepped to Red's pane. Brushing his fingers across the surface, he murmured, "Thank you."

My pleasure. Red's voice sounded within Evan's mind. *I'm looking forward to getting to know you and Katie better.*

Evan grinned, and taking Katie's hand led her to a seat at the bar. He was too, and his intuition told him that no matter how long it took for Katie to heal, their relationship would be worth the wait.

PART VII

SKYE DREAMS

DEBBIE MUMFORD

BESTSELLING AUTHOR OF *SORCHA'S HEART*

Skye
DREAMS

SPUN YARNS
A GOTHIC ROMANCE TALE

1

I dreamed of him again last night. The unbelievably handsome man with long black hair and eyes as dark as a winter night. I've dreamed of him many times in the eight years since my sixteenth birthday. Always the same dream. He smiles at me and tells me I am his destiny and he is mine... and that he waits for me in sky.

Not in *the* sky, but *in sky*. I've never understood what he meant by that odd phrase. How can he wait for me in the sky? When I was younger, I wondered if I should apply to train as an astronaut, but astrophysics and the science of flight never held any appeal. Instead, I majored in history. Celtic history, to be exact, and in my studies, I found a clue to this mysterious man's comment.

What if he wasn't speaking of the atmosphere above the earth, but of the Isle of Skye? Could the man of my dreams be waiting for me on an island off the coast of Scotland?

Last night he answered some of my questions. He told me that the time is near, that his name is Angus MacDubh and he waits for me in Skye, on the Trotternish peninsula at the table of the kwa-ring. I've no clue where that is (or even *what* it is), but a little Internet research should clear up the mystery.

I don't know whether or not it's a prudent choice, but I'm going to

Skye. After eight years of dreams, it's time to find out if Angus MacDubh is a real man or just a figment of my imagination. At least Skye is real. I've always wanted to travel and I can justify this trip to my family as part of my research for my doctoral thesis.

They don't know about my dream man... and I'm not about to tell them. At least, not yet.

2

———————

I rose and dressed quickly in tan walking shorts, red T-shirt, and the sturdy hiking boots I'd broken in on hikes around my Indiana home. Ready for the day's adventure, I strode into the common room of the bed and breakfast where I had rented a room just outside the village of Staffin on Scotland's Isle of Skye.

My journey here had been a dream-come-true. I was finally traveling abroad; seeing the sights in a foreign country. And not just any country, Scotland! The place where so many of the events I'd studied had taken place.

What an adventure! I'd flown from my home in Indianapolis to New York City's bustling JFK International Airport— an adventure in itself for a midwestern girl like me!— and then boarded a flight to Glasgow. After an exhausting day of sight-seeing in Scotland's most populous city, I took a train to Mallaig on the west coast of the Highlands. From there, I travelled "over the sea to Skye."

The whole time I was on that ferry, the words to the famous *Skye Boat Song* swirled through my head, commemorating Bonnie Prince Charlie's flight from the battlefield of Culloden. I was following the path of legend, and imagined myself to be Flora MacDonald spiriting the hunted prince from Scotland to my family's estates in Skye.

And then I set foot on the Isle of Skye... and felt at once that I had come home.

The village of Armadale, where the ferry docked, sat in a green, fertile valley surrounded by low hills and bordered by the sea. Though the village was quaint and lovely, it couldn't account for the emotion that welled in my soul when I stepped from the ferry onto the dock. The breeze swirled around me, cooling my face and caressing my hair, and I imagined a voice spoke to me— my dream man's voice— welcoming me home.

How odd. I'd never heard that my family was connected to Skye. If the dark-haired man hadn't begun visiting my dreams, I doubt I'd have chosen to study Celtic history. Everything I knew about Skye began and ended with a dream, and yet....

And yet I felt a connection to this place, to the very land beneath my feet.

Words whispered in my subconscious, *Don't delay. You are so close. Come to me, my heart!*

I raced to find the bus station and bought passage to the Trotternish town of Staffin, where I'd booked a room in a cozy little bed and breakfast.

"Are ye ready, then?" asked Mrs. Darrow, the B&B's owner.

I smiled and finished pulling my dark auburn hair into a messy bun atop my head where I could control it with a sun hat. "I am. I can't tell you how excited I am to see the Quirang, especially the Table."

"Well, I must say, I'd rest easier if ye'd let me call one of the local lads to guide ye on yer ramble."

Truth be told, I'd like that as well, but I shook my head. I didn't want any witnesses to what happened at the Table. If my dream man was there... well, I couldn't imagine how he could be, but just in case, I wanted privacy.

"Not to worry," I said brightly. "I have a great map and detailed instructions. Why, I even have pictures of the landmarks to guide me. I'll be fine... and besides, you know where I'm going."

"As ye wish." She sighed her concern, but gestured to the kitchen where a sturdy scrubbed oak table stood laden with food. "At least eat a hearty breakfast. Ye'll need yer energy for the climb."

While I loaded my plate with fried eggs, bacon, and a crusty oat scone, Mrs. Darrow bustled about her kitchen assembling food for my hike.

"Would ye like a thermos o' tea or coffee for the climb?" she asked as she packed a generous lunch into a brown paper bag.

"No thanks," I replied between bites of egg-soaked scone. "I think I'll stick with water. I'll fill my bottle before I go."

She continued to cluck over me and my preparations until I escaped out the door and down the narrow lane to the bus stop. The B&B was only about a mile from the trail head, but considering that the Quiraing walk was a loop of well over four miles, some of it through rough terrain, I decided to save my energy and take the bus.

A strange mixture of emotions boiled in my belly as I stared out the dusty bus window. Excitement, yes, but also a roiling coil of dread. Not quite fear, but an unease so deep I considered staying on the bus when it reached the drop off for the trail head.

If I were a superstitious woman, I'd've called that dread an omen.

Who was I kidding? I was a superstitious woman! Who but the superstitious would follow a dream all the way from Indiana to the Isle of Skye?

But my dream man had deserted me— my dreams had been innocuous since my arrival on the island— and a feeling of impending doom was strengthening with every turn of the bus's wheels.

I stared up at the high cliffs and shivered. They were simply a geological oddity, the result of a massive prehistoric landslip that had created impressive cliffs, hidden plateaus, and huge rock pinnacles. And yet, some unknown part of my mind insisted that they were more. My destiny was inextricably intertwined with those peaks and valleys.

My destiny... or my death.

3

The bus stopped at the car park that marked the start of the Quiraing walk. Summoning all my courage, I squashed the lingering unease and, concentrating on my excitement, climbed down from the bus. I settled my sun hat firmly atop my head, adjusted the straps of my backpack, and began my ascent of the Quiraing.

It was a beautiful, cloudless day. Blue sky above my head, rough dirt and rock path beneath my booted feet, the heady smell of earth and grass mixed with the salt tang of the not-too-distant sea. A steep grassy slope fell away to my right, while ancient cliffs towered above me on the left. I trudged on, glad for the hat that protected my head from the sun that baked the land.

After about a quarter of an hour, I came to my first real obstacle, a small stream running through a shallow, but rocky gorge. I scrambled down one side, hopped successfully across the water, and was scrambling back up the other side when a man's voice hailed me.

"Hello there," he said. "Need a hand?"

I glanced up from the rocky slope to see a man's hand extended in my direction. Without much thought, I accepted the offer and was boosted up the last few steps. Once on level footing, I pulled my hand back and studied my benefactor. Tall and blond, with sparkling blue eyes, the handsome stranger was dressed similarly to myself in khaki hiking shorts, cotton T-shirt, and a wide-brimmed flexible sun hat.

"Thanks," I said, reaching for the water bottle secured to the side of my pack.

"No problem. Nice to encounter a friendly face in this lonely place."

I glanced up in surprise, having just taken a sip of water. We were hardly alone. While the trail wasn't crowded, it wasn't deserted either. I could see four individuals moving along at a measured pace ahead of us, and if we stood still very long, the young couple behind me would join us.

Not sure quite how to respond, I asked, "Is this your first visit to the Quiraing?"

He grinned. "Definitely not. I've made this pilgrimage often during my life."

Pilgrimage. What an odd word choice.

I stowed my water bottle again and we continued up the trail.

"This is my first trip. It's certainly majestic."

He nodded. "That it is." We walked on a few paces before he glanced sideways at me and asked, "Do you mind company? If it's a solitary ramble you're after, I can drop back."

I smiled, but considered his question. Did I want company? Hadn't I declined Mrs. Darrow's offer to find a guide? But now that I was here, now that I was actually scrambling over this rough trail... maybe a knowledgeable companion would be nice. Especially one as personable and easy on the eyes as this man. I could always encourage him to continue alone when we reached the Table. If there seemed any need, that is.

After all, it was unlikely the man from my dreams would actually appear at the appointed place when he had no way of knowing when I would arrive.

Heck, I didn't even know when I would arrive.

"That's okay," I said before the pause became uncomfortable. "I'd like the company... if you don't mind pointing out the sights to me."

He grinned. "I'd be delighted. Always fun to see familiar sights through new eyes." He held out his hand. "I'm Eoin MacLeod, by the way."

I accepted his hand for the second time... and immediately felt my emotions spike, a heady mixture of attraction and something else. Anxiety. I released his hand as quickly as was politely possible. "Jane Allan."

We hiked on in silence, my unease growing with every step. I'd accepted his company, but I wasn't bound to the man. I could simply sit down on the trail and wait for the couple behind us to catch up.

Maybe I should do just that.

Maybe there was safety in numbers.

No. I was being ridiculous.

Eoin had done nothing but offer me his hand and his companionship. I had no reason to fear him. He was simply another hiker enjoying the same trail. And an experienced hiker at that.

But I'd given him my name.

Amazed, I realized that my increased anxiety at his touch had been a warning. My dream man had been warning me not to trust Eoin, not to give him my name. Well, if Angus wanted me to do, or not do, something, he was going to have to be a bit more explicit. Besides, how in the world could knowing my name hurt me?

And suddenly the answer burned in my mind: knowing a person's true name gives power over that person.

I had given Eoin power over me by telling him my name.

What a load of superstitious nonsense! The 'power of a name' thing was only true in fairy tales. Besides, I knew his name, too. We were on equal footing...

...but only if I knew what to do with the information, which I didn't.

I glanced at my hiking companion. A nice, normal (though provocatively handsome) man striding up the steep trail among the cliffs of the Quiraing. Nothing weird or uncanny about him. I shook my head. I was letting the legends and mysticism of my Celtic studies carry me away. Just because I was in Scotland didn't mean I'd left my twenty-first century pragmatism behind.

"Those cliffs up ahead," Eoin said, pulling me from my uncomfortable thoughts, "are known as The Prison."

I shook off my unease and answered. "I've read about those. They were called that because people thought they looked like fortress walls."

"Ah, you've done your homework. Good on you."

As I studied the formidable high cliffs, a question floated to the surface of my mind. What if they were called The Prison, because someone was imprisoned there?

Nonsense. If I could hike this loop, so could anyone else.

Not if they were cursed, came an imagined reply.

I shivered despite the sun's baking heat.

The trail narrowed and Eoin took the lead, striding a few paces ahead of me.

"When we round this next bend, you'll see some rather spectacular rock pinnacles," Eoin said over his shoulder. "The tallest is known as The Needle." I nodded, though he couldn't see me. I'd read about that on the Internet as well.

We hiked on for another hour, Eoin pointing out the occasional landmark as we scrambled over scree slopes, climbed stiles, and ducked under rock outcroppings. Once we came to a fork in the path marked with a cairn of stones. Eoin took the left-hand fork without hesitation, and I followed, pleased not to have to dig out my notes to refresh my memory.

We kept the main wall of cliffs on our left until we reached the cliff top, where the trail hugged the edge. The sheer drop was terrifying, but the view was amazing. Eoin pointed out the village of Staffin to the east, along with the islands of Raasay and Rona, and further across the water, the hills of Torridon on the mainland.

I felt like I could see forever... and my spirits soared.

When I'd soaked up the view, we continued on, moving away from the cliff edge and onto a worn path that soon became a series of turf steps.

Finally, we reached the summit... and my destination.

"Well," said Eoin, "we did it. This is the summit. Five hundred and forty meters, nearly eighteen hundred feet by your reckoning." He glanced at me and smiled. "You are American, aren't you? Your accent gave you away."

I returned his smile, warily. Now that we were here, my emotions were in turmoil. Intense excitement filtered by extreme anxiety made it hard for me to form a coherent thought.

"Yes," I managed to say. "I'm from Indiana, in the heartland of the USA." I walked to the cliff edge and stared down at a flat, grassy plateau surrounded by cliff walls and massive rock formations. "That's the Table, isn't it?"

Eoin joined me at the edge, and a frisson of fear zinged along my spine. "Yes. A rather austere and lonely place."

I stepped away from him, smiled, and held out my hand. "Well, I don't want to keep you. It's been a pleasure hiking with you, Eoin."

He glanced from my outstretched hand to my face, a little frown marring his countenance. He could hardly have missed my rather pointed dismissal. The briefest moment passed before he took my hand and pulled me close. "I'm in no hurry. I think I'll take my lunch on the Table. Appropriate, don't you think?"

He was too close. But he wasn't close enough! My emotions warred. He frightened me, here in this lonely, windswept place. But the pull of desire made me long to give in to his embrace, to raise my face to his and discover his taste in a kiss so passionate we might both burst into flames.

What was I thinking?

Where were the other hikers?

I glanced around, but no one was in sight. It was as if he and I were the only people left on the planet. I tried to step back, to pull my hand free of his, but it was like moving through molasses. My movements gained me nothing.

He laughed and released me, but I remained wrapped in a web of his power.

My instincts, my unease, had been correct. This was no ordinary hiker. Whatever he was, Eoin MacLeod was not a normal man.

I tried to speak. My jaw locked; no words came out.

"Tell me the truth, Jane. Why did you come to the Table?"

He released my jaw muscles, and I said, "I'm a scholar of Celtic history. I came to see the sights. I came to see the Table."

He scowled. "Then let's see it."

He waved his hands and a whirlwind formed. The air around me screamed and bits of sandy rock stung the bare skin of my arms and legs. My hat was torn from my head and my feet lost contact with the earth.

Be calm, said a voice in my mind. My dream man's voice. Angus' voice. *He canna harm ye if ye dinna give in to him.*

I held onto that promise, though I was certain my skin was being flailed from my body. After what felt like an eternity, the winds calmed and I found myself standing in the center of a large, grassy meadow surrounded by austere cliffs and majestic rock formations.

4

I was not alone. Two men stood a few feet away. One the epitome of the modern world, blond, blue-eyed, and dressed for a morning's hike; the other from a far distant time, long dark hair clubbed at the base of his neck, and clad in a linen shirt and blue and green plaid kilt.

Eoin MacLeod and Angus MacDubh.

It seemed the man of my dreams did exist. And, from the way they glared at each other, that he and my hiking companion were acquainted.

"Ye've no right to interfere," Angus said.

"And you've no way to stop me," Eoin replied.

My shaking legs betrayed me and I collapsed onto the grass of the Table. At least Eoin had spared me the treacherous climb down from the summit, though I doubted the scramble would have been as harrowing as the whirlwind he had called. Why was I here? Who were these men? What power did Eoin possess to be able to call the wind? For that matter, what power gave Angus the ability to invade my dreams?

And what did either of them want from me?

"Leave the lass out of this," Angus said, his voice quiet, but menacing.

Eoin's eye's flashed. "I tried to! Did I not send her forward in time? Did I not cause her soul to be reborn in a foreign land, far from the soil of Skye?"

He turned from Angus, strode a few steps closer to me, then whirled and returned to my dream man. "It was *you* who called her back; *you* who are the reason she is here... and in peril."

Peril? Anxiety clawed at the edges of my mind; I fought to calm it. What peril was I in other than feeling a bit topsy-turvy from Eoin's whirlwind?

"So I did," Angus retorted. "She is my life, my own... my destiny. Once she was reborn into this world, I could not but call her. And ye have no right to keep her from me."

"I can't let her join you," Eoin said. "You know I can't."

"Aye, I know." Angus sounded resigned. "And sorry I am that we canna exist peacefully in the world together, brother."

Brother? Did he mean that literally, or just as a figure of speech?

I rose from the Table's green grass and walked a bit unsteadily to the two men. It was past time for me to join this conversation. I stopped in front of Angus and held out my hand. "You must be Angus MacDubh," I said, proud of my steady tones. "I'm glad to finally meet you. I wasn't sure if you actually existed."

He reached for my hand, but Eoin slapped it away. "I'm sorry, Jane, but I can't allow Angus to touch you."

My eyebrows flew up and my mouth dropped open. "*You* can't allow? What gives you the right to make decisions about who I can and cannot touch?" By the time I finished the second question, my anger had flared, and with it a spark of fire sizzled from my fingertips in Eoin's direction.

I stared at my hand and staggered back, my heart racing.

Eoin cursed and nursed his own fingers.

Angus howled with laughter. "Think ye to control her now that she is a woman grown, Eoin? The more fool you!"

"What just happened?" I cried, no longer concerned with what either man thought. The tangle of my uncontrolled emotions was creating a ball of... something... in my chest. Something that threatened to burst out like the alien from that science fiction movie. I collapsed to the ground, pulling my knees to my chest in a fetal position. Somehow I had to hold it in... whatever *it* was!

"See what you've done?" cried Eoin. "She'll consume herself!"

"What *I've* done," roared Angus. "'Twas ye who made her angry!"

Both men dropped to their knees beside me, but it was Angus who stroked my hair, touched my cheek with gentle fingers, calmed my soul.

And this time Eoin who made no move to stop him.

"Hush now, lass," Angus crooned, his deep voice soothing the raging alien in my chest. "Ye need answers, and we need to give them, but first, ye must be at peace."

Eoin didn't touch me, but he joined Angus in the calming. "Rest, Jane. Let go. Let the power drain away into the good earth of the Quiraing. The Table will absorb the flow, as it has done for our clan for ages long gone."

Under the hypnotic influence of their voices, the *thing* in my chest dissolved, melting away. I could almost feel it seeping out my pores and into the grass that cradled me.

My mind collapsed under the weight of the unknown, and I fainted.

5

I woke in a stone chamber, bundled in woolen blankets and held securely in a man's strong arms. We sat in a throne-like chair before a roaring fire. The man's linen shirt was soft beneath my cheek and he smelled of heather and lichens. Angus, then. So much for Eoin's decree that my dream man should not touch me.

I stirred, and Angus placed a gentle hand on my head.

"Softly now," he said. "No one will harm ye here."

"I need to sit up," I said quietly. "I need to sit on my own."

"Aye," he said. "I understand."

Carefully, as though unwrapping a priceless piece of china, Angus drew back the blankets and helped me to my feet. My initial impression had been correct, we were in a large stone chamber, like something out of a medieval castle. Angus had been sitting in a large wooden chair, padded with sheepskins and bigger than any modern recliner. The floor was flagged and strewn with rushes. A log table large enough for ten men sat between me and the rough hewn double doors. A second chair, equally as large, sat on the other side of an immense fireplace where red-gold flames leapt and crackled, filling the air with the soft aroma of burning pine.

Eoin sat in the second chair, watching me with brooding eyes.

Angus stood, as though to offer me his seat, but Eoin waved him back. With a lazy flick of his fingers and a few muttered words, he created another chair, slightly smaller in scale, from nothing and settled it on the floor facing the fireplace, evenly spaced between Angus' chair and his own.

He bowed his head to me. "If you would join us, Lady Jane?"

I sat down on the sheepskin-padded chair, wondering if it would support my weight or disappear at my touch. It remained as solid as if it had existed from the beginning of time.

"Who are you people?" I asked. "And where are we now?"

Angus grimaced. "We are in my safehold within the Prison of the Quiraing, and glad I am to have your company." He turned a steely gaze on Eoin. "I've been alone far too long."

"Yes, yes," Eoin said querulously, "you've been hard done-by, and I'm the villain of the piece."

"Aye. Ye are."

"Would one of you please answer the question," I asked, more than a little exasperated. "Who are you people?"

"Why, we are *your* people, Jane," said Angus, as if that explained everything. "I am your match, your destiny, and he..." His voice trailed off. "Well, he..."

"Oh for heaven's sake, Angus," Eoin cried. "You're not explaining anything." He turned to face me. "Angus and I are brothers, twins to be exact. Our natures are opposite. Night," he gestured to Angus, "and day," he thumped his own chest. "We are born of a long-lived race that used to inhabit the Quiraing, but has long since fled this earth. We are born of magic and flame, and are immortal."

"Immortal?" I squeaked.

"More or less," said Eoin. "We can be killed, but it's not easy. Especially since we are also wizards."

"Wizards." This was getting better and better.

"Yes, or did you think you'd just failed to notice that chair you're sitting in?"

"Okay, you two are immortal wizards. What does that have to do with me?"

"You're an immortal wizard, too," Angus explained. "Or you would have been had my brother not interfered."

"Excuse me?"

"What he means is, you were prophesied to be his match. To complete Angus and make his power limitless. I prevented that."

"What?" I cried. "How?"

"He used his arts to bind me to this safehold, to keep me imprisoned in the Quiraing." Angus growled. "Then he..."

"Then I stole your soul from within your mother's womb and flung you into the future. I made sure that when you were born you'd have no memory of Angus, or our people, or the Isle of Skye. I made sure you'd be grounded in the heartland of a country that didn't even exist at the time when you were destined to come into being."

"You did what? How did you dare?" My anxiety returned like the whirlwind Eoin had conjured earlier. Swift and strong and untamable. So this was the reason the Isle of Skye felt so familiar. It was my ancestral home. This was the source of the alien that had felt like it would rip me to shreds earlier. It was the inheritance from my distant ancestors— who wouldn't have been so distant if I'd been born when I was supposed to be— my magical inheritance. A power I hadn't known existed and didn't have a clue how to control.

All because this man had interfered in the balance of my life. My life... and Angus'.

The thought of Angus calmed me, and the thing inside... my power... calmed as well. I turned to him. "Were we really destined to be together?"

He shrugged. "So the prophecy said. But ye were stolen before birth, so we never met in this world." He came and knelt before my chair, dark eyes searching my face, big hands enfolding mine. "I felt ye the moment ye entered the world, but I couldna come t' ye, bound as I am to this place, and I didna dare to touch the mind o' one so young. So I waited, and I watched, helpless to do aught else."

"But you did come to me," I said. "I've been dreaming of you for years."

"Aye, I did, but not before ye were of age. Then I entered your dreams and made myself known to ye, so that when the time came, ye would know me and come to me... just as ye have."

"Right," said Eoin, his voice breaking the spell like the rasp of a file on metal. "All very romantic. But did he ever tell you in those dreams what he intended to do with you?"

A blush heated my cheeks. "No, but he said we were destined for each other. I assumed..."

"You assumed that he wanted you romantically, as any naïve young girl would. You assumed he would marry you," he sneered, rising to his feet. "Well, you were wrong."

6

_____

I gasped.

Angus roared and lunged toward his brother. "Stay out of this, Eoin. Ye interfered once, and still she came to me. Of her own free will, she came. Ye canna keep her from me this time. She's a woman grown, with a will o' her own. This time the prophecy will be fulfilled."

"What prophecy?" I yelled.

Both men stilled and turned to face me.

"The one that says ye are my destiny, and I am yours," crooned Angus.

"The one that says that you will come to him willingly and sacrifice your life to ensure his ascendency," said Eoin, his voice thick with disgust. "Don't you see, Jane? He'll kill you to attain ultimate power over me."

The room stilled around me. Neither man moved. It was as if time had stopped while I pondered their words. While I tried to wrap my mind around what each was saying. Tried to pry beneath the surface to find the truth.

Not their truth. _My_ truth.

Who was I?

What was I?

Angus wanted me, that was evident. But for what purpose? Was he the man of my dreams? The love I'd subconsciously waited for? I hadn't dated much in high school or college. Why should I? I knew my love waited for me in Skye. I just didn't know what that meant.

I hadn't seen any overt magical powers from Angus, but he hadn't denied having them. Had he ensorcelled me from afar? Had he entered my dreams to ensure my cooperation with his scheme, this so-called prophecy? Had I come to Skye of my own free will... or had Angus planted that desire and nurtured it over the years until I had no choice but to come when he called?

And Eoin, what was his game plan? I knew nothing of Eoin except what I'd learned on the trail to the Table, and I had no way of knowing if anything he'd said to me was true.

Of course, the same could be said of Angus.

Angus wanted me to believe we were destined to be lovers... at least, that had always been my understanding.

Eoin wanted me to believe that Angus intended to sacrifice me to gain power over him.

But Eoin had admitted to binding Angus to the Quiraing and flinging my soul through time and space. All to thwart his brother.

And what of me? What did I believe?

I released the spell I hadn't known I'd cast and studied Eoin. He was less familiar to me, not having been in my dreams for years, and yet he'd been kind on our hike, and I'd been attracted to him as we climbed. If he'd displaced me in time and space in the belief that he was saving my life...

"What of you, Eoin?" I asked. "What is it that you want from me?"

He lowered his eyes and spoke to the flagged floor. "I want your freedom, Lady. I want you to make your choices without compulsion, to do as you see fit with the life you have been given."

"The life you stole from her," Angus growled. "She should have come into this world centuries ago, when the world was younger."

"When she would've had less choice," snapped Eoin. "When she would've obeyed simply because you were male and she female."

"Our destiny was prophesied…"

"I don't believe in prophesies," I interrupted, causing both men to stare at me. I had made my decision. I knew what I believed, and it wasn't in the power of prophecy.

"Eoin, why do you continue to hold Angus bound to this place?"

"To ensure your safety, Lady."

I nodded.

"Angus, what will you do if Eoin releases you?"

"I will follow you to the ends of the earth, my love, until I convince you that I am your destiny."

"And what does that mean to you, Angus? Do you intend to marry me and give me children?"

"Well, no, I mean, the prophecy…"

"I see. You have my leave to try to convince me to give you what power I may or may not possess, but let me tell you right now, if that means giving up my life, your efforts will not be rewarded. I repeat, I do not believe in prophecies."

I turned back to my hiking companion. "Eoin, I am no longer a child, and while I have no clue how to use any power I may or may not have, I don't believe Angus is a danger to me. I am no longer a naïve young woman. If I ask it, will you release your binding?"

"I will, my lady." He stepped toward me and extended his hand. I hesitated for a moment and then placed mine in his. Our fingers interlocked as if by their own accord. "If I may, I would ask a boon."

I nodded.

"Will you allow me to mentor you in your magic, Jane?" He stared deep into my eyes and I saw within a soul longing for connection, to belong to someone in this world. "And perhaps, one day, to court you?"

My smile reflected the warm glow his words kindled in my core. "I will."

Angus exploded. "Now wait a minute, the prophecy says…"

Eoin and I laughed, gazing into each other's eyes, and answered in unison. "We don't believe in prophecy!"

PART VIII

REALITY BITES!

DEBBIE MUMFORD

BESTSELLING AUTHOR OF *SORCHA'S HEART*

Reality Bites!

SPUN YARNS
A *Supernatural Yellowstone* Story

1
─────

The view from the ridge was killer, but the girl in my arms eclipsed its splendor.

I leaned my forehead against hers, closing my eyes and breathing in the scent of her: lavender and sage and the enticing muskiness of her sweat. I was a goner and I knew it; even Jenny's sweat was alluring. She angled her head, bringing those perfect lips to mine and Yellowstone's backcountry ceased to exist. Jenny filled my senses. The feel of her lithe, well-toned body in my arms, her intoxicating taste ... so sweet, but overlaid with a spicy wildness that set my senses on fire.

Time stood still. The wilderness around us evaporated. Primal emotions roared for fulfillment and I deepened the kiss. Our tongues danced a preview of the mating I hoped would follow.

Jenny stiffened, then tore herself from my embrace, leaving me weak-kneed, dizzy, and totally confused.

"Wha..." I opened my eyes, stumbled, and waited for my conscious self to catch up. Evidently my subconscious was still on duty, for the hairs on my forearms stood at attention and the back of my neck prickled with unease. Danger lurked nearby.

The world snapped into focus. Jenny stood facing away from me, arms outflung. She was magnificent, a fierce young mother protecting a child too slow-witted to recognize his peril.

Only she wasn't a mother and I wasn't a child.

I stepped to her side and grabbed her hand. "What is it, Jenny?"

She shook me off, adjusting her backpack and tightening its belt around her waist. "Not now, Ethan."

That's when I noticed the eyes. Dozens of amber eyes glowing from the underbrush. I sucked in a breath and took an involuntary step backward as wolves crept forward into the clearing where we'd stopped to enjoy that killer view.

They slunk forward on silent paws, bodies low, eyes fixed on their prey. Us. A rough semicircle formed as a dozen wolves emerged. Charcoal grey, nut-brown, silver grey, chestnut, every shade of pelt I'd ever imagined, even a black wolf.

We were surrounded. Behind us the ridge dropped away in a steep incline to the Hayden Valley far below. Just minutes before, I'd remarked that we were so high that the bison herds in valley looked like so many beetles. No escape in that direction.

Our only hope lay in the tall lodgepole pine a few steps to our right. I adjusted my backpack to ensure it would stay on during a climb. We'd need the provisions if we were treed for very long.

"Jenny," I whispered, grabbing her hand again, my voice ragged with fear. "We've got to get into that tree. I'll distract them while you climb. Get read..."

She shook off my hand. Again.

"No. You climb. I'll deal with this."

My jaw dropped.

The wolves crept closer. All except the black one in the middle. He sat on his haunches, tongue lolling out, staring at Jenny.

"Cut it out, Kam," she said, looking for all the world like she was talking to the black wolf. "This isn't funny."

I closed my eyes and breathed deeply, inhaling the scents of pine and sage and rangy wolf. Jenny had lost it. Stress had pushed her mind over the edge. We would die here on this ridge. Side by side. I wished I had a gun. I was a lousy shot, but at least I could've put Jenny down rather than allow her to be torn to shreds by the pack.

Opening my eyes, I squared my shoulders and stood beside the woman I loved. No way would I climb a tree and desert her, even if she had retreated into La-La Land.

"Kam's not here, Jenny," I said quietly, placing a hand on her shoulder. "It's just you and me against these wolves."

She glanced at me with pity in her eyes before turning her attention back to the black wolf.

Why was she fixated on Kam Jacobs? Especially now? The guy was scum. Sure, he was tall, dark and handsome, not to mention muscled like Atlas, but his personality sucked. He lorded it over the rest of the summer interns like he was the god of Yellowstone. All because he and Jenny lived here year round, their families being full-time forestry service employees. He might be more familiar with the terrain, but that didn't give him the right to make life miserable for those of us who had scraped and saved and prayed for the opportunity to work in this glorious wilderness for a summer.

And the way he treated Jenny ... like she was his by right. Just last week I'd had to pull him off her when he'd cornered her at a bonfire party on the beach at Yellowstone Lake. He'd knocked me flat, but at least he'd left Jenny alone.

"Ethan, please, you don't have a clue what's happening here," Jenny said, her voice firm and in control. "Just stay out of my way, okay?"

I removed my hand from her shoulder and held both up. "You're right," I said. "I don't understand, but I'm not leaving you." I turned my attention to the wolves, wondering how many I could keep off of her. I was in decent shape, but wrestle a dozen wolves into submission? Not bloody likely.

"Come on, Kam. You've had your fun," Jenny said to the black wolf. "What do you want?"

I glanced sideways at Jenny, stifling an exasperated sigh. I didn't want her to die thinking I doubted her, even if she had dropped off the edge of reality.

Whining wolves combined with scrabbling in the underbrush forced my attention back to the wolves. The pack was slinking away from the black one, tails between their legs. The big black writhed on the ground, but not in pain — he didn't yelp or whine, just spasmed in silence.

Was he diseased? I wracked my brain trying to remember how rabies presented.

Jenny watched with quiet passivity. The wolf's odd behavior didn't seem to concern her. Of course, I wasn't sure she was still viewing the same world I was.

The wolf's spasms increased, his limbs stretched and bent at odd angles. His pack mates whined and averted their gazes from the distressed animal.

Bile rose in my throat and I forced myself to swallow, to maintain. I didn't have a clue what was happening to that animal, but I knew it wasn't normal. Wasn't part of the natural world I inhabited. Sweat beaded my forehead and made my hands slick. I rubbed them on my jeans, but it didn't help.

In front of me, the black wolf melted. Fur puddled on the creature's flanks and was absorbed. Claws liquefied and retracted into misshapen hands. Jaws and teeth oozed, reformed, and congealed.

I longed to look away, to unsee the gruesome scene, but horror held me paralyzed. The transmogrification glued my muscles in place, as though every cell in my body had declared its stability in reaction to the absolute wrongness, the utter instability of what transpired on the forest floor.

Jenny stood her ground, stoic and silent, arms folded across her chest.

Kam Jacobs rose from the ground, naked and aroused. He shook back his shoulder-length black hair, glanced at the cowering wolves around him, and growled. All went belly up before turning over and laying flat against the ground, as if begging Mother Earth to shield them from the monster in their midst.

"What are you?" I murmured, fighting the blackness that gnawed at the edges of my vision. I desperately wanted to crouch on the ground and put my head between my knees until the dizziness passed, until the nightmare ended and reality reasserted control. But I wasn't asleep, I wasn't high on a hallucinogenic, and like it or not, my perception of reality had changed.

I held it together. Whatever else he was, Kam Jacobs was dangerous, and I refused to give him the satisfaction of watching me cower.

And to think I'd been worried about a pack of wolves.

2

———————

Jenny accepted Kam's transformation without a blink. She strode across the clearing and slapped him so hard the air rang with the sound.

"What the hell do you think you're doing?" she asked. "You have no business transforming in front of Ethan."

He wiped a trickle of blood from his lip and grinned. "Your fault, Jenny. You asked me a question. You know I can't answer while I'm wearing my wolf skin."

"That's not what I meant and you know it," she said turning on her heel and pacing back to me. "Why were you following us? Why did you bring the pack here?"

"What? You thought I'd just sit by and let Riley romance you out of my life?" He scowled at me, but kept his distance from Jenny's barely contained rage. "You're mine, Jenny. Always have been, always will be."

Jenny closed her eyes and took several deep, calming breaths. Her hands unclenched and her shoulders relaxed. I wanted to put my arms around her, to hold her close and rest my chin on her soft dark hair, but I knew I was out of my league. Until I understood what was happening, I'd keep my hands and my thoughts to myself.

"No, Kam," Jenny said, folding her arms across her chest again. "I'm not yours. I am not some dog to be owned and ordered about. I am my own person and I'll make my own choices about who I spend time with."

She stepped closer to me and wrapped an arm around my waist. I didn't need further invitation; I draped an arm across her shoulders and hugged her tight.

"And right now, I choose Ethan."

Kam's head snapped back as though she'd slapped him again. Rage lit his eyes and he dropped to all fours. He raised his head and his gaze met mine. "You're dead, Riley," he growled, and the transformation took him.

"Come on," shouted Jenny, propelling me forward with the arm around my waist.

"What about the pack?" I asked as we sprinted from the clearing.

"They won't leave him. We've only got a minute's head start, now run!"

Like that was going to do us any good. Once Kam was in wolf form again the pack would be after us, and no matter how fast we ran we didn't stand a snowflake's chance in hell of outrunning wolves.

But this was Jenny's world, not mine, and I still didn't have a clue about what was really going on. So I ran.

We careened down the trail, adrenaline fueling our flight. I skipped over roots, avoided rocks, and leapt fallen limbs, until Jenny grabbed my hand and led me off the trail and up an incline through thick underbrush. Brambles snagged my shirt sleeves and twigs scratched my face and neck. The terrain was rough, but Jenny didn't slow the pace and I worked to keep up.

My heart was hammering too loudly for me to tell if we were being followed and sweat blurred my vision, so maybe I can be excused for not questioning when we emerged on a rocky slope and ran into a cave. I knew better than to enter a cave without first checking for signs of occupation, but these were desperate circumstances.

I leaned against the rough wall, gasping like a fish just reeled from a stream. Jenny collapsed on the dirt beside me, sides heaving from our mad dash.

Pulling my water bottle from my the side pocket of my backpack, I sipped the lukewarm liquid and wiped sweat from my eyes. "This won't work, you know," I said. "They'll just follow our scent."

As soon as the words left my lips, I noticed a ripe, feral stink. I don't care how scared we were, neither Jenny nor I could ever produce an odor that pungent. I stared into the gloom of the cave's depth and my breath caught. Hell, my heart seized. I nudged Jenny with my hiking boot. "Jen? We've got to get out of here. This cave is occupied."

She swatted my foot and sat up. "I know, and Kam and his pack won't dare to follow us in here." She reached up, grabbed my hand and yanked. "Sit down. You're making Zell nervous."

A huge silver-tipped grizzly rose onto her haunches and snuffled in our direction.

My knees buckled and I joined Jenny on the ground. "Zell?" I squeaked. I wasn't proud of the sound, but it was all I could manage at the moment.

Jenny patted my knee and then crawled across the cave to sit beside the massive bear. She scratched behind the animal's ears before turning a radiant smile in my direction. "Isn't she the most magnificent grizzly you've ever seen?"

Since the sum of my grizzly experiences were taxidermied museum exhibits and glimpses across the Hayden Valley, I just nodded, speechless.

"Zell, this is Ethan. He's part of the family now. Protect him as you would me." Jenny stared into the animal's eyes for a moment and then stroked her thick fur. Glancing at me she grinned. "This day hasn't exactly turned out the way you'd hoped, has it?"

"Not exactly, no," I said, clutching my water bottle. A momentary vision of Jenny and me naked on a blanket beneath a canopy of aspen leaves floated across my mind. "I had something more mundane in mind. Not werewolves and pet grizzly bears."

She giggled and patted the space beside herself. "Come on over. I promise, neither Zell nor I will bite you. Well, if you're nice, I might."

I grinned weakly, stowed the water bottle, and, moving carefully and gingerly, joined her beside the bear. Zell stretched and laid a massive paw across my legs. I managed not to scream. Her claws were as long as my hand, the pads as thick and rough as an iron file.

Jenny took my hand and gazed into my eyes. "You've been very calm, Ethan. I think you're the bravest man I've ever met." She glanced down at our entwined fingers. "I'm sorry. I never intended for you to find out like this. I would've told you eventually, if it looked like things were getting serious, but, well, Kam…"

Zell growled low in her throat and stood, careful not to mash my legs into the dust. She moved to the entrance of the cave and roared. I covered my ears as the sound reverberated around the small space, bouncing off the walls.

"Kam's here," said Jenny, as if a friend had just rung the doorbell.

3

Jenny strode to the cave entrance and wedged herself into the small space between the rock wall and Zell's bulk. I wanted to see out too, but there wasn't room beside Jenny. I stepped sideways and realized I could match Jenny's position on Zell's other flank. Was I brave enough to squeeze between a grizzly and a rock the way Jenny had? Scylla and Charybdis had nothing on this bizarre situation.

What the hell? I'd already lived longer than I'd thought possible since the appearance of the wolves.

I pushed into the small space with feigned confidence. Most animals sense fear, so I tried to keep mine at bay. The bear's fur was coarse, more like spines than hair, but as my hand worked its way deeper into the shaggy pile, the texture softened to downy warmth. A muscle twitched beneath my fingers and Zell swung her massive head in my direction.

I scratched the skin beneath the downy fur and she snorted softly and turned her attention back to the action outside the cave. Reassured, I wriggled forward and peered under her chin.

Kam stood just outside the cave, wearing black sweat pants and a stained tee shirt with the sleeves torn off. Nice to see him wearing something besides a massive erection, but where had he found clothes? And more importantly, where was his wolf pack?

Jenny's disembodied voice sounded from the far side of the bear. "Thanks for stopping by one of your stashes," she said. "I'm not really in the mood to swoon over your muscles."

"Come on out, Jenny. Let's talk this through."

"What's to talk about, Kam? You blew it. You let your jealousy run wild and revealed things to an outsider that should've remained secret."

Kam's face darkened and his fists clenched, but he glanced at Zell and shook it off. "What are you going to do with him, Jen?" he asked. I could hear the strain in his voice as he tried to sound calm and reasonable.

"Well, I'm not giving him to you and your pack," Jenny retorted, not bothering to hide her anger. "Is that what you thought? That I'd just stand by and watch you kill a man I care about?"

Kam widened his stance and folded muscled arms across his chest. "We can't just let him walk away, Jenny. He knows too much."

"You don't know me at all, do you, Kam?"

I could imagine Jenny shaking her head, could hear the sorrow in her voice.

"Go back to your wolves, Kam. I'll take care of Ethan."

Kam dropped his arms and stepped toward the cave. Zell growled a warning — a sound I felt vibrating through her muscled body. Kam stopped.

"Jenny?" he whimpered.

"We're through, Kam. This is the last mess I clean up for you."

I shuddered at the steel in her voice and wondered how the woman I loved intended to take care of me. I closed my eyes, leaned against the rock wall, and breathed in the fetid stench of grizzly. I'd been a dead man since Kam interrupted that glorious kiss. At least now I knew that Jenny would be safe, and that was all I'd really wanted. I would meet my fate like the brave man Jenny thought I was.

Fresh air wafted across my face as Zell lumbered back into the cave. I opened my eyes and searched the slope. Kam had gone. No wolves were evident. Jenny stood across the entrance watching me with a worried expression.

I put on a feeble smile. This would be hard enough for her, I had no intention of making it tougher.

"Are you okay, Ethan?" she asked. "You look a little green around the gills."

I straightened away from the rock. "I'm fine," I said, my gaze dropping to the dirt at my feet. "What's next? How do you clean up this mess?"

"Oh, Ethan," she cried. The next thing I knew she was in my arms, her head tucked beneath my chin. "Do you really think I'd let anyone hurt you?" Tears seeped through my flannel shirt and a sob wracked her body. I hugged her tight and rubbed my cheek across her hair. The scent of lavender and sage rolled across my senses and my own eyes moistened.

She sniffled and pulled back so that she could gaze into my eyes. "I'm taking you home to meet my parents."

My heart stuttered and then leapt into overdrive. Her parents? Blood drained from my face and the edges of my vision darkened. Again. I sure as hell hadn't seen that one coming.

4

Jenny explained as we walked, Zell pacing beside us. Kam wasn't a werewolf, and Zell wasn't a pet.

Kam and Jenny belonged to a supernatural community that protected the Yellowstone valley. Their unusual abilities were fed by ley lines of magical power that coalesced and knotted in and around the geothermal features. Just as Yellowstone was unique in geophysical terms, it was also unique magically.

Jenny's family bonded with animals in the Yellowstone ecosystem. The animals were also effected by the magic, being larger and more intelligent than their normal cousins.

Kam's heritage was shape-shifter, or skin walker to borrow a Native American term. His family could change shape at will. As children, the skin walkers experimented with many animal shapes, but at puberty they had to choose just one. Kam had chosen a wolf. His father had settled on a mountain lion. Kam's mother was mundane, like me.

When we came to the edge of a clearing with a neat log cabin in the middle, I stopped beneath a white-barked aspen and hunkered down to take in the sight. The cabin was built of native pine, evident in the varying sizes of the logs. Gray chinking alternated with red-brown wood, resting on a thick foundation of large rocks, rounded and smooth from a river's action. The roof was shake-shingled and smoke curled from a river-rock chimney. A wide porch fronted the cabin, complete with a matching pair of log chairs. A paddock in the back abutted a sturdy shelter for several horses. The clearing looked homey and comfortable. A picturesque homage to the American West.

Jenny walked on a few paces before noting my absence. She turned and looked back at me, head cocked to one side, a small furrow between her eyebrows.

"Ethan? Is anything wrong?"

Hysterical laughter bubbled up inside, but I managed to choke it back. Seriously? Was anything wrong? Let me think about that. I'd been stalked by a pack of wolves, discovered that shape-shifters exist, found out that my girlfriend is bonded to a grizzly bear, and was now facing an imminent introduction to her parents, who had god-only-knew-what unnatural skills and lived in a picture-perfect log cabin.

"No," I said, holding onto my sanity by sheer determination. "Nothing's wrong. I just realized that I'm filthy and sweaty and I'd really like a shower and clean clothes before I meet your parents." I straightened, readjusted my backpack and stepped to her side. "But that's not going to happen, so I'll just hope for the best."

She placed a hand on my arm and smiled at me. "Don't worry, Ethan. They're going to love you."

Zell chose that moment to charge into the clearing roaring what I hoped was a greeting. A golden eagle appeared in the sky and flew to the bear. After circling Zell a few times and screaming its own greeting, the magnificent bird perched on a limb that stuck out from one of the logs supporting the porch roof.

The front door of the cabin swung open and a man and woman emerged. He wore a red plaid flannel shirt, faded blue jeans, and well-worn waffle stompers. His salt-and-pepper hair was in need of a trim and his chin and cheeks were stubbled with several days growth of beard.

Jenny's mother was an older version of my love. Her hair was long and dark, her temples streaked with gray. Like her husband, she wore flannel and jeans, though on her they looked comfortable rather than scruffy.

Mother and daughter ran to embrace, while her father and I hung back, measuring the situation. When they broke apart, Jenny and her mother each held out a hand — Jenny to me, her mother to her husband. He stepped off the porch and claimed his wife's hand. I stepped to Jenny's side, but didn't touch her. She curled her fingers and let her hand drop.

"Mom, Dad," she said, "I'd like you to meet Ethan Riley. Ethan, these are my parents, Jed and Linda Leigh."

Her mother spoke first. Disentangling herself from husband and daughter, she stepped to me and held out her hand. "We're thrilled you're here, Ethan. Welcome to the family."

I frowned, a little confused, but took her hand. Calloused fingers. Strong grip. This was a working woman, and not in the sense of a cubicle jungle. "Uhm ... thanks." Not exactly gracious on my part, but it had been a weird day.

Jenny burst into tears, and Zell whined and clawed the ground.

My mouth dropped open. Of all the things I'd thought might happen, that hadn't even crossed my mind. Jenny had faced down a wolf pack, dragged my sorry ass on a flight through the forest, sent Kam packing, and explained the unexplainable, and *now* she was crying?

Her mother gathered Jenny into her arms and whispered soothing words in her ear while stroking her hair.

I glanced at Jed Leigh, completely bewildered.

Jenny sobbed out the words, "It ... it's not ... what ... you think! Kam ruined everything."

Jed moved to my side, took my arm and propelled me toward the cabin. "Come on in, son," he said. "I can tell there's a story to be told."

I glanced over my shoulder to see Linda escorting Jenny inside as well, so I allowed myself to be led. The living room was every bit as homey as I'd expected. Dark leather sofa and chairs, solid plank flooring, a river-rock hearth with a banked fire. Jed led me to one of the leather chairs and nudged me into it. He settled in another. Jenny and Linda cuddled together on the sofa. Glancing out the front window, I saw Zell curl up beneath the eagle, preening on its perch.

"Now," said Jed. "Tell us what's going on. You're neither one looking too fresh and sprightly."

I shrugged out of my backpack, setting it to one side, and leaned forward, elbows on knees. Did I really want to try to put the day's events into words? With people I didn't know? On the other hand, these were Jenny's parents. If anyone should understand, it'd be them.

In halting sentences, I outlined our day. How we'd gone for a hike, been set upon by wolves; how Jenny had recognized Kam and everything that had happened since.

"What I don't understand," I said as my story wound down, "is why Jenny is crying now? She's been amazing all day. She's saved my life repeatedly." I turned my attention to the only person in the room who mattered to me, "So why are you crying now? When we're both safe and everything is over?"

Jenny just hiccoughed and buried her face in her hands.

"I think I can explain that, son," said her father. I turned my puzzled gaze on him. "In our family, we don't reveal our nature and bring anyone home to the folks until we're sure of acceptance."

I frowned. "Acceptance?"

He sighed. "Think of it like this, a guy wants to marry a girl. He'd be a fool to buy a ring and propose, especially in public, if he wasn't damned sure of his girl's response."

I fidgeted in my chair and let my gaze drop.

"Jenny isn't sure of your answer," he continued. "She wasn't ready to ask for your commitment. Kam forced her hand." He turned to his daughter. "Am I right, baby?"

Jenny straightened away from her mother, wiped her eyes, bit her lip, and nodded.

I stared from one to another of them, feeling very thick. My eyes met Jenny's and the pleading in their depth nearly broke my heart. I slid from my chair and knelt on the floor at her feet. Taking her hand,

I asked my question. "So, your dad is saying that by revealing your nature and bringing me home to meet your parents, you'd be asking me to marry you?"

Her eyes brimmed with tears, but she nodded.

"And we ... you weren't ready to make that decision, but Kam screwed everything up?"

Another silent nod. Her cheeks pinked and her gaze slid away from me.

I held her hand so tightly I could feel her bones move beneath her skin. "What about now, Jenny? Do you want to marry me? Because I've never wanted anything so much in my whole life!"

Her eyes widened and her lips formed an 'O'. She stared into my eyes and cried, "Truly? Oh, Ethan!" And then she was on the floor beside me and I was kissing her tears away.

We never even noticed when her parents slipped from the room.

After a few minutes, we caught our breath and she settled into my arms, her head resting on my chest.

"Just one question," I said, closing my eyes and stroking her hair. I'd never felt so content and relaxed in my entire life. Jenny loved me, and I would spend my life in Yellowstone. Not only had I survived the day, but all my dreams had come true. "When we have kids," I asked with a lazy smile, "they won't be grizzly cubs or anything, will they?"

Jenny giggled and punched me in the ribs. "No, but they may bond with bears ... or wolves ... or something."

I kissed the top of her head and inhaled her sweet fragrance of lavender and sage. "I can live with that," I whispered. And I could. Happily. Ever after.

PART IX

THE CAT LADY OF YELLOWSTONE

DEBBIE MUMFORD

BESTSELLING AUTHOR OF *SORCHA'S HEART*

The Cat Lady of Yellowstone

SPUN YARNS

A *Supernatural Yellowstone* Story

1

The world as we knew it ended on a Friday afternoon in July, during the height of tourist season. But since we live off the grid in a secluded mountain valley in Yellowstone National Park, we weren't aware of the devastation until Sunday morning.

Our homestead consisted of two log cabins, built of native pine logs of varying sizes with chinking made from local clay, sand, and good old Yellowstone mud. Both homes rested on thick foundations of large river rocks. The roofs were shake-shingled and the chimneys were also fashioned from smooth, rounded river rocks. A wide porch fronted the original cabin, and boasted a matching pair of log chairs. A wrap-around porch graced the newer cabin, built when Jason and I married. We had a sturdy porch swing on the front and two willow rockers on the side facing the forest.

A paddock in the back abutted a sturdy shelter for our horses, and a weathered barn with long, low rooflines stood guard over the rest of our livestock: six goats, a dozen chickens, and a few ducks. We'd had cows and pigs at one point, but had lost them to predators and hadn't yet replaced them.

Our gardens were in full bloom. A herb garden outside the kitchen door of the original cabin lent gentle fragrances of rosemary, thyme, and oregano to the sweetness of the flower beds lining the walkways between the cabins. A large vegetable garden teemed with life. Squash, beans, and potatoes crowded up against tomatoes, carrots, lettuce, and celery, while asparagus and marigolds guarded the borders.

On that fateful Sunday, Jason and I saddled our favorite horses and made the two hour ride from our home near Mary Lake on Yellowstone's Central Plateau to the Visitor Center at Fishing Bridge on the north shore of Yellowstone Lake. We had made this ride every Sunday since our daughter, Ruth, left home to study veterinary medicine at Colorado State University. Now that she had taken a job at the Denver Zoo, the tradition continued.

Thanks to long years of friendship between my family and the park rangers, we were allowed to use the computer equipment at the Visitor Center for a video call with Ruth on Sunday mornings; our only form of communication with our daughter.

As I said, our homestead was off the grid. We had no modern conveniences: no phones, computers, television, or any other form of electrical appliances. But we had everything we needed. And thanks the generosity of Yellowstone National Park, we had weekly contact with Ruth.

Maybe I should tell you a little about how we came to live in Yellowstone, but not be employees of the park service.

My family, as well as a few others, have lived in what is now known as Yellowstone National Park since before recorded history. When men of European descent first came to this region, we simply melted into the forests. They were unaware of our existence.

The local tribes, the Crow, Blackfeet, Shoshone, and Bannocks, knew of us... and feared us. They considered us demons and avoided our lands.

But when Yellowstone became the first National Park, our forefathers came out of the wilds and *persuaded* the authorities to grant us our homesteads, to *grandfather* us in, as it were. It is well that the authorities acceded to their wishes; the park would not exist otherwise.

You see, the tribes were correct when they named us demons. Those of my bloodline, and of the lines of the other families included in that arrangement, are not strictly human.

We are a supernatural community that calls the Yellowstone region home... and protects it ferociously. Our unusual abilities have been fed for generations by ley lines of magical power that coalesce and knot in and around Yellowstone's geothermal features. Just as the region is unique in geophysical terms, it is also unique magically.

The women in my family form lifelong psychic bonds with animals. My bond-mate is a cougar known as Faithful Huntress, or Faith. My mother formed a bond with grizzly bear named Zell. So far, Ruth had avoided forming a bond. She wanted to leave the valley and go to university. Someday she'll return, and when she does, she will form a permanent bond.

Other families have different abilities. The men of the Jacobs clan are shifters, *skin walkers* in the old vernacular. My dad's rival for Mom's affection, Kam Jacobs, shifted into a black wolf and played alpha to a pack of normal gray wolves. Kam's jealousy forced Mom to reveal our nature to Dad prematurely, but... well, I'm living proof that their tale ended well.

Anyway, on that Sunday morning when we reached the populated area of the park near Fishing Bridge, we discovered that something had gone dreadfully wrong. The normal hustle and bustle of weekend tourist traffic was missing. Oh, we saw cars and trucks and SUVs, but none of them moved. The paved roads, the bridge over the Yellowstone River, looked like long, narrow parking lots. Ones where the vehicles had simply been abandoned.

We rode cautiously between the stranded cars, noting the people wandering dazed and aimless between the rental cottages and the beach. We reined our horses in, glancing at each other.

"Should we turn around?" I asked.

Jason nodded, his gaze sweeping the area. "Probably, but I'd like to know what's happening." His gaze returned to mine. "This is anything but normal."

"Agreed." I scanned the people, noting their interest in us... and our horses. "Let's go back to the forest and settle the horses. I'll ask Faith to guard them for us."

"Good idea. I wouldn't want to lose them," Jason said, turning his bay gelding, Sorkie, and moving back toward the tall timber, "especially to city folk who wouldn't know how to care for them."

My roan mare, Jezzie, followed with almost no prodding from me. While we ambled back to cover, I contacted my cougar. Like all bond animals, Faith was larger and stronger than others of her species. She was also exceptionally long-lived. We had bonded when I was just fifteen, more than thirty years ago. The usual life span of a cougar topped out at fifteen years, but Faith remained healthy and strong.

What do you require, She Who Walks With Strength and Grace.

A wave of love swept through me, and I smiled. Faith delighted in using the full form of my name. Everyone else just called me Grace. In fact, most people thought Grace *was* my full name.

We're near Fishing Bridge, I told her, *something is wrong and we need to investigate, but we don't want to leave the horses unguarded. Will you protect them?*

Of course, she said, her thoughts as calm and unruffled as a lake on a windless day. *I am not far. The forests and meadows are unusually quiet today, and the humans I have seen seem nervous and on edge.*

Thank you for coming. We have seen the same. We'd like to try to find out what's happening.

A few moments later, Faith appeared beside Jezzie. The two animals touched noses in greeting before Faith moved on to Sorkie. Our horses had long since accepted my cougar as part of the family. While another predator would spook them, Faith's scent caused no distress.

Jason and I dismounted and walked toward the visitor center, secure in the knowledge that Faith wouldn't allow anyone to approach Jezzie and Sorkie. Before we reached the bridge—the visitor center lay on the far side—we found David Andresson, a long-time park ranger and a friend.

"David," Jason said, extending his hand.

"Jason," David replied, shaking my husband's hand. "Grace. I was wondering if you two would venture down today."

As he spoke, he led us into a sheltered spot near the bridge abutment.

"Why wouldn't we?" I asked, puzzled.

David studied my face before nodding. "That's right," he said. "You're place is off the grid. You wouldn't have any way of knowing what's happened."

Jason shook his head. "No idea," he agreed, "but it's obvious something is wrong. Nothing is moving and from the sound of things, nothing mechanical is working."

He was right. We could hear the river singing and gentle waves lapping the shore of the lake. A buzz of voices reached our ears, but the hum of refrigeration units, air conditioners, motors, all the normal sounds of a populated area were missing.

"Whatever it was," David said, taking off his hat and wiping his forehead on his shirt sleeve, "happened on Friday afternoon. The first we knew was when all the lights went out in the Visitor Center. Gradually we've discovered that everything electrical ceased to function at the same time." He leaned closer, as if to avoid being overheard, though no one was near us. "Management thinks we've suffered an EMP." He caught our uncomprehending expressions and clarified, "Electromagnetic pulse. Knocks out technology."

"Oh," I said, stupidly.

"And that made the cars quit?" Jason asked.

David nodded. "Everything with computer chips and electrical starting systems. There are a few old, purely mechanical pick-ups around the park, but most of those are in disrepair. Still, we're trying to get them running. We've got tourists stranded in bear country. We need to get as many as we can find into the bigger park enclaves: Mammoth, Canyon, Old Faithful, here at Lake. Even Madison and Roosevelt will be packed."

"How can we help?" Jason asked.

David replaced his hat, tapping it firmly in place. "Head on back to your place. If you find stragglers, bring them down to us. I don't have any idea how long this outage will last, but we've got a good supply of food, fresh water, and we can cram people tight into the lodge and rental cabins. We'll hold out until help arrives."

"We can do that," I said, while David and Jason shook hands. "Good luck."

As Jason and I trudged back to our horses, I said, "I wonder if the outage extends all the way to Denver?"

Jason put an arm around my shoulders as we stepped beneath the trees. "I don't know, but Ruth is a smart girl, surrounded by animals she loves. She'll be fine."

"I wish we'd been able to talk to her," I murmured, my heart suddenly feeling very heavy. "I wish she was here with us, where Faith could keep an eye on her."

"I know," he said, squeezing my shoulders. "We're lucky to live where we do, to be as prepared as we are. We'll be fine."

I hoped he was right.

2

David's optimism was misplaced. No help arrived. No trucks or busses came to ferry tourists out of the park. No planes flew overhead to air-drop supplies into the overcrowded enclaves. Those who were able made their way out of the back country and down to the visitor centers. A few hardy souls shouldered backpacks and trekked out of the park and back to civilization.

David and the other rangers wished them well... and prayed that when they made it out, civilization would still exist.

Jason and Faith and I did what we could. Jason guided stragglers off the plateau and down to the rangers. Faith and I hunted, supplying David with game as often as we could.

At first, people were content to wait for the lights to come back on, for their cars to start, for life to return to normal. But when it became obvious that wasn't going to happen, and that the National Guard wasn't going to swoop in and rescue them, things got dicey.

Gangs formed.

The rangers did their best to establish strongholds and protect the non-violent from those who devolved into human predators, but they weren't trained or prepared for such circumstances.

Why would they be?

They were naturalists who, though they might be excellent marksmen, had never aimed at human targets. They were good men and women who wanted to do the right thing, and expected everyone else to play by the rules as well.

But the rules had changed, and the park service personnel needed to change as well.

Some were able to make the transition. Some weren't.

Good people died, both rangers and tourists.

Too many ruthless people survived.

On his last trip to Fishing Bridge, Jason led a family of five to what he still thought was the safety of the Visitor Center. Unfortunately, David and his charges had been overwhelmed by a group of desperate men who had allowed their savage natures to get the upper hand.

My husband, Ruth's father, died defending the family he had shepherded out of the wilderness.

The world as men knew it may have ended on a Friday in July, but my world ended on the Tuesday in September when Faith's cougar kin reported the slaughter of my husband and the people he'd been trying to save.

3
_____

A month after David's murder, Faith pushed me out of bed. I landed in a heap of filthy linens on a wooden floor littered with discarded clothes, dirty dishes, and dust bunnies the size of baseballs.

Enough, Faith growled. *Jason is dead. You are not. Bestir yourself and act like a woman again.*

My eyes filled with tears at her callous mention of Jason's name. "You don't understand."

She sat on her haunches before me as I struggled upright, pushing strings of matted hair out of my eyes and behind my ears. Cocking her head, she gazed into my eyes.

I do not understand death? she asked. *I, who deal it out to prey with regularity? Who has fed you this last month? Who fed the people David protected for months before that?*

"Not the same thing," I said, shaking my head and pulling the dirty sheets closer around my shoulders. "Jason is dead. My mate. The only man I've ever loved. How would you feel if I died?"

I would follow you into the summer country, she purred, *for it is only my bond with you that holds me in this world.*

I stared at her. Faith had never spoken to me of her belief in what lies beyond this life.

You are my world, She Who Walks With Strength and Grace, but there is more to your world than just me. You must get up and live. For Ruth. For me. For the youngling my kin herded to this cabin. She needs your protection.

"A youngling," I cried. "What youngling?"

A child's face appeared at the edge of my bedroom door. "Are you talking to me?"

A little girl, no more than eight, stepped into view, eyeing Faith warily and glancing curiously at me. The child's hair was easily as dirty as mine. It might have been blonde, then again, it might have been a light brown. Her jeans were caked with mud and torn at the knees. Her tee shirt might have been pink once; now it was too stained with grass and dirt to be sure. The jeans jacket she wore was too lightweight for October in Yellowstone, and her sneakers were little better than nothing. She'd clearly been wearing that outfit for far too long.

I stood as quickly as I could, which wasn't very fast considered how tightly the sheets were wrapped around my legs.

"Who are you and where did you come from?" I asked, rather stupidly, clutching my sheet and stepping past Faith so that I stood between her and the child.

"I'm Lacey. Who are you?"

"I'm Grace. I live here."

She leaned sideways, trying to see around me to Faith.

"Why is that big cat in here?"

"She's a cougar and she lives here," I said. "Her name is Faith."

"You have a pet cougar?" she asked, her brown eyes widening. "That's weird."

"She's not a pet, she's my friend," I said, a bit too sharply. I closed my eyes, took a deep breath, exhaled completely, and tried again, making an effort to sound calm and friendly... like unknown children appeared in my filthy cabin every day. "You didn't tell me where you came from."

Her eyes clouded with tears and she bit her lower lip, sniffling.

"Never mind," I said, dropping my sheet and striding toward her. I held out my hand. "You can tell me later. Right now, let's get you something to eat."

After that, you should both take a bath, Faith murmured behind me. *You reek.*

I didn't turn around and stick out my tongue, but it was very tempting.

Between them, Faith and Lacey brought me back to life. Caring for the child gave me a purpose again.

By the time we'd eaten, bathed, picked up and washed all the dirty dishes, and generally made the cabin livable again, I was feeling almost normal.

"Come along, Lacey," I said. "You can't wear that old tee forever."

After her bath, I'd pulled one of Jason's tee shirts over her head. It hit her mid-calf and the neckline threatened to fall off her shoulders. Totally unacceptable for long-term use, but her clothes were unsalvageable rags. No point in even washing them. Fortunately, I had options.

"Where are we going?" she asked, grabbing my hand and holding it tightly. "There are bad men out there."

I glanced at her. She was shaking so hard my arm tingled. Poor little mite. She still hadn't told me her story, but that would come.

"Just to the other cabin," I said, reassuringly, "and Faith will protect us. She might purr for you and me, but she can be ferocious if she needs to."

Lacey nodded and followed me onto the porch. I hesitated, then swung her up into my arms for the short walk to what had been my parents' cabin. The child was barefoot, and while we didn't have snow yet, the stone path would be freezing beneath her little feet.

"Ready? Here we go!" I raced across the porch, down the steps, over the path, and up onto the older cabin's porch.

Lacey giggled as I deposited her onto her own two feet again. "That was fun!" Her face shone, and I wondered how long it had been since she'd had reason to smile.

I pushed the door open and ushered her inside. The house was cold, having been unoccupied since my mother died two years ago. Jason and I had made a point of keeping it clean and pest free, but no fire had been lit in the hearth in the month since his death. He'd laid a fire the morning he'd taken the family to Fishing Bridge, but I'd never struck the match.

I did so now.

Lacey huddled on the hearth rug in her inadequate tee shirt, waiting for the flames to warm the room. Faith laid down behind her, providing a back rest and additional warmth. To my surprise, the little girl leaned back into the big cat, accepting the offering of friendship and security.

She likes you, I said to Faith alone.

Of course, my cougar purred in reply. *I am very likable... and trustworthy.* After a moment, she met my gaze. *She reminds of Ruth, when she was a kitten. It is good that my kin brought her here.*

I nodded. "Stay with Faith, Lacey. I'll just be in the other room, rummaging around in some old boxes."

The child nodded, then curled up on the rug beside the cougar and closed her eyes. The poor little thing was undoubtedly exhausted. I'd had a month of nothing but rest... if existing in a dazed stupor can be said to be restful... and the morning's activity had tired me out. No telling how long it had been since the little girl had been fed and warm and safe enough to sleep soundly.

Faith would protect her. Time to get on with my search. I strode down the hall to what had once been my bedroom. The double wedding ring quilt on the queen-size log bed was dusty, but the room was as neat as it had been since Jason and I had moved into the second cabin. Hurrying to the closet, I unstacked boxes of out-of-season and outgrown clothing. The boxes were neatly labeled in magic marker, so I had no trouble finding the clothes I'd set aside from Ruth's childhood. I also found a box of toys. Rag dolls my mother had made, little cars and trains Dad had carved from bits of deadwood, and some wooden puzzles and games that dated to Mom's childhood.

Returning to the living room with my treasures, I found Lacey still fast asleep, Faith purring beside her. I rummaged through the first box of clothes, found a pair of underwear, jeans and a long-sleeved red plaid flannel shirt that I judged would fit, then opened other boxes until I had socks, boots, and a down jacket as well.

Hefting a couple of boxes, I headed for the door. *I'm going to take all this stuff home,* I told Faith. *Call me if she wakes.*

I will do so.

After several trips between the cabins, I not only had everything transferred, I also had Ruth's bedroom set up for Lacey. The bedding had been aired, clothes tucked away in the chest of drawers Dad had built for my daughter, and toys lovingly stowed in the toy chest. One calico bear, a favorite of Ruth's, rested on the pillow, ready to be snuggled by a little girl who'd lived through too much, too young.

Pleased with my progress, and more at ease in my skin than I'd been since... well, best not to think about that just now... I returned to my parents' cabin to wake Lacey and help her dress.

4

Our homestead soon became an orphanage of sorts.

Faith informed me that her cougar kin and Zell's grizzly kin reported many children wandering lost and alone in the back country.

Many had lost their parents to marauding gangs looking to rape and steal, others were orphaned through accident or attacks from predators not part of Faith and Zell's network. For though Zell had died when my mother did, her kin remembered our family as part of their own and continued to watch over our homestead.

Through the efforts of the cougars and grizzlies who claimed us, children appeared at the border where our homestead met the forest. Some were old enough to expect death from the large predators who herded them, and arrived terrified. Others were too young to walk the distance and were carried by their clothing, as if they were cubs or kittens.

However they arrived, Faith and Lacey and I welcomed them.

That first winter was hard. I'd been in deep mourning when I should have been harvesting and storing vegetables from the garden. By the time Lacey arrived to bring me back to reality, the garden was suffering. We managed to salvage a good amount of the produce, but not as much as we should have harvested. Fortunately, my family had been putting food by for years. Our pantry and root cellar were well stocked... even with all the extra mouths to feed, we would make it through the winter.

We were far better off than most.

The deep snows of December put an end to new children arriving. The bears were in hibernation, and the cougars no longer found living children. Our population stabilized at twenty-four: one adult, twenty-two children, and one cougar.

Besides being traumatized by events since that fateful Friday, our little tribe had some communication issues. Yellowstone had been an international vacation destination. Tourists came from all over the world... and so did the children who appeared at the homestead. Not all of them spoke English, but they all responded to food, warmth, and kindness.

Fortunately, a few of the kids were old enough to be of help. Lacey, though only nine, was serious beyond her years. Hiding under a bush while big, strong men beat your father to death and raped and murdered your mother will do that to a child.

Sam was our eldest at thirteen. He'd managed to save not only himself, but his ten-year-old brother, Jessie. Jamie and Ellen were twelve and a huge help with the younger children, as were Davey, Lynn, and Robbie, our eleven-year-olds.

The rest of our tribe ranged from nine to... well, I had no idea how old Caleb was. He was our baby, and I guessed he was around eighteen months. No name, of course. I'd dubbed him Caleb.

He was the last to arrive, just before Christmas. One of Faith's cougar-kin brought him in, a large male, who was unwilling to release the child.

Grace, Faith called, her mind-voice less calm than was usual. *Join us.*

I dropped the sheets I was folding and scanned the room for one of the older children. Spotting a dark-haired girl, I said, "Ellen, I have to go out for a minute. You're in charge."

The pretty little brunette glanced up, met my gaze, and nodded solemnly. All of these children were solemn. I wondered if they would ever be anything else?

Shrugging into my down jacket and pulling a knit cap over my ears, I stepped outside and looked around until I found my cougar. Faith sat at the edge of the forest on the far side of my parents' cabin. Another cougar, almost as large as Faith paced just beyond a dark bundle in the snow.

The bundle moved.

I ran to join them, slowing my pace before I arrived to avoid alarming the big cat.

My kin-brother has brought us another child, Faith said, as I stopped beside her, *but he wishes for assurances.*

I met the strange cougar's gaze, trying to ignore the child moving lethargically between us. *What is your request?*

This human is small and weak, he answered, *and I have kittens to feed. If the prey fails to live, I claim the meat.*

I inhaled sharply. I'd never liked thinking of humans as prey, but our world had changed, and the cougars had been incredibly helpful to all of us. I glanced at the child and my heart lurched. He was so tiny... at least I thought it was a boy. Too young to speak. Starving and dehydrated, the baby was too weak to even cry. I had to get him into the house and care for him.

I met the male cougar's gaze once more and nodded. *I accept your terms. If this small one dies, Faith will bring the carcass to your den.* I looked at Faith. *If she agrees.*

My cougar closed her beautiful tawny eyes, then opened them slowly. *It is agreed. If this one lives, I will help you find other meat for your kittens.*

Very well. I leave this small one with you. And he melted into the snowy forest.

W̲e survived the winter. All of us. Even Caleb.

When I first carried Caleb into the cabin, I'd despaired of saving him. His little belly was bloated and distended, his arms and legs little more than fragile sticks. He showed no interest in sucking the rag I'd dipped in warm water, and his eyes were crusted closed. Sam and Lacey milked one of the goats, while Ellen and I bathed him and swaddled him in soft flannel. Warm and dry and cuddled close, he suckled earnestly when I put the milk soaked rag to his lips. He'd turned the corner. The baby had decided to live.

After that, he improved rapidly. I kept him close, wearing him wrapped close to my heart while I tended to the other children and the myriad chores of keeping our homestead running. Before the winter was over, Caleb was toddling around the cabin with the other little ones.

Faith kept her promise to her cougar kin. She hunted for us weekly, but also made time to help her cousins keep their families fed.

I worried that we'd be vulnerable when the snows melted. While the winter had been hard, spring and summer would present a danger the snow had prevented: attack by roving gangs of desperate men.

The homestead was well supplied with rifles and ammunition, and I was an excellent shot. But I was only one woman, and I couldn't afford to waste ammunition teaching Sam or Ellen or Jamie to shoot.

Rather than worry the children, I shared my thoughts with Faith... and found her unconcerned.

You worry needlessly, she told me when I expressed my concern.

Needlessly? I was shocked by her seeming indifference. *Have you forgotten how Jason died? We have twenty-two children to protect!*

She stuck a back leg in the air and licked herself. I closed my eyes in exasperation.

I forget nothing, she purred. *You forget who and where you are.*

Excuse me!

She sat up on her haunches, wrapped her tail around her feet, and gazed into my eyes. *You are bound to me. Your mother was bound to Zell, a grizzly bear. Her mother before her was bound to Arend, a golden eagle. You live on the land your ancestors have occupied since time began. All the clans who have ever been bonded to your family guard this homestead.*

She switched her tail in irritation.

Did you think we, who have benefitted from your people's protection for generations, would abandon you in your time of need?

Tears filled my eyes and I swiped them away. *Forgive me. I did not mean to insult you and your kin and all the others who have protected my family through the ages. I didn't think.*

She flopped onto her belly and rested her head in my lap. *Of course you didn't. Who could be expected to think with all these kittens underfoot? That is why I am here.*

Love and relief filled my heart... and I laughed. For the first time in many weeks.

Spring slid into summer bringing warm days filled with sunshine and cloudless skies. The children ran around the meadow jumping and chasing and playing games only they understood. I watched them with quiet pride. They were survivors, yes, but better still, they were remembering what it was to be children. And Faith and I, and the animals who had brought them here, had made that possible.

I wished Jason were here to see what we had accomplished. He would have loved seeing the homestead filled with life.

I wished Ruth were here, safe on the land of her ancestors. I prayed that wherever she was, she was safe... and as happy as my little charges.

I put away my longing for my lost loved ones. There was work to be done. Always.

Calling the children together, I laid out my plan. Now that warm weather had arrived we had no need to huddle together in one cabin. It was time to make use of both of our homes. Sam and Jamie would be in charge of my parents' cabin and the boys who would occupy it.

Privately, I shuddered at the thought of the damage a dozen little boys could do to the building, but we needed the space and there was only one of me. Besides, these weren't normal little boys. These were boys who had survived terrors and truly appreciated the warmth and security the homestead provided.

The nine girls and I would remain in the cabin Jason and Ruth and I had made our own. Caleb would also stay with me.

We divvied up the tasks and went to work cleaning the cabin that had stood unused through the winter, assigning personal space to each inhabitant in both cabins, and moving meager belongings into place.

Once everything was in place, we held a family council and reviewed work assignments for the maintenance of our home. Sam took notes, and when everything was decided, he and Ellen made charts to hang in their respective cabins.

Our tribe was not only organized, we were, if not exactly happy, content.

I was working in the vegetable garden with Robbie, Lacey, Kamiko, and Sven, when Faith yowled a warning. I dropped my hoe and raced to the front of the cabin.

What? I cried to her. *What's wrong?*

Strangers! she yowled, her vocal cry melding with her mind voice.

A strange cat approaches. One whose kind I don't recognize. And a human comes with the cat!

I stopped dead, scanning the trail leading to the cabins. At the edge of the forest, a single figure approached. A big cat accompanied the person. A very unhappy cat judging by its slink, the closeness of its belly to the ground.

Children crowded around me, alerted by Faith's yowl. I waved them back.

"Go inside," I said firmly. "Stay out of sight until I know what we're dealing with."

They melted away without argument, though I was aware of somber eyes watching from the cabins' windows.

Who is it? I asked my cougar. *Why did the guardians allow this person to pass?*

Faith didn't answer. She paced back and forth across the trail a few yards in front of me, tail switching, a low growl emanating from her throat. She was far more concerned with the unknown cat than with the human that accompanied it.

Suddenly, Faith froze. Nose in the air, ears pricked forward. She screamed and raced toward the strangers, her lean body low and sleek.

My mind overflowed with her joy!

She's home! She Who Loves with Purity and Truth is home!

I gasped, unable to catch my breath. My knees threatened to buckle, but I refused to allow it. I needed them to function. I needed to run!

My daughter was home! Against all odds, and who knew what hardships, Ruth had made it home from Denver.

Ruth, who my cougar had just announced using her full name.

She saw me coming and ran to meet me. We met in the middle of the trail with an impact that would've knocked us off our feet if we hadn't grabbed each other and hugged tightly.

I closed my eyes and wept, holding my precious daughter in my arms.

"You made it," I cried. "You're home."

"Oh, Mom," she whispered. "I never thought I'd see you and Dad again."

My throat closed, too choked by joy and grief to allow speech. Time enough to tell of Jason. Right now, I savored the fact that Ruth was safe in my arms.

At last, we broke our hold and gazed, grinning, into each other's tear-filled eyes. I looked past her to the strange cat. She looked beyond me to the children now lining the cabins' porches.

"Who..." we both said at the same time, then burst out laughing.

Faith purred and rubbed Ruth's leg. She reached down absently and scratched my cougar behind the ears.

The other cat growled.

"Hush, Snowball," Ruth said aloud, for my benefit. She turned to the big cat and said, "This is Faith. She's bonded to my mother and helped raise me. You will treat her with respect." Turning her gaze on Faith, she continued, "Faith, this is my bond-mate, Lady of Ice and Snow. You may call her Snowball. She is still young and has had no cat to teach her. Will you guide her?"

Faith purred her assent and asked, *What manner of cat is my new sister?*

"You've formed a bond," I said quietly, pride filling my heart. Then, more loudly, "Faith wants to know Snowball's breed. Is she a snow leopard?"

Ruth nodded. "She was one of my charges at the zoo. When the EMP hit, everything was chaos. Her mother was killed. I managed to save her... and we formed a bond in the process." She stroked Snowball's sleek head, and the black and white cat closed her eyes and purred. "She's saved my life more times than I can count on our journey home."

The children were leaving the safety of the porches, sidling by twos and threes closer and closer to us. Ruth cocked her head and nodded in their direction.

"Looks like you've had adventures too."

I laughed. "That's an understatement. Let's go inside." I gestured for the children to join us. "Come on, everyone," I called. "I want you to meet my daughter, Ruth, and her friend Snowball."

They started forward, but stopped, all eyes on the snow leopard.

Ruth turned to me. "They're used to Faith, right?"

I nodded.

"It's all right," Ruth said encouragingly. "Snowball is like Faith. She won't hurt you, but please don't crowd her. She'll want to meet you one at a time."

And so, nearly a year after the end of the world, our tribe increased by two. We were now two adults, twenty-two children, a cougar, and a snow leopard. All protected by the wildlife of Yellowstone.

PART X

THE TIE THAT BINDS

1

Cameron McClellan dropped to his knees, instinctively shielding himself from the aftermath of a bomb blast in Iraq — half a world away from his Denver boardroom. A red haze of pain paralyzed his senses. The dry erase marker he'd been wielding at the white board dropped from nerveless fingers. His skull ached with the intensity of Kyle's anguished screams.

Shock and concern from startled colleagues registered in a diminishing corner of his mind, but the searing agony of Kyle's wound prevented Cameron from responding to their questions. Cameron's breathing mirrored Kyle's panting gasps. His arms and legs echoed Kyle's desperate attempt to drag his shattered body away from the fiery remains of the humvee, to shelter beneath the inadequate branches of a roadside shrub. Cameron's eyes closed with Kyle's, but he didn't see concern on friendly faces; blood-soaked dirt, hellfire, and mind- numbing pain filled his brain as he followed his twin into oblivion.

2

Cameron woke to the smell of antiseptic and the feel of crisp sheets tucked securely around his body. A blinding headache made him reluctant to open his eyes, but soft breathing and warm fingers stroking his arm encouraged him. With a fortifying inhalation, and moving his head as little as possible, he peered at his surroundings. Institutional white walls, curtained room divider, narrow, railed bed, and Sophie. His wife's warm brown eyes studied him with concern, their lids swollen and puffy. Her heart-shaped face, reddened and blotchy from crying, testified mutely to an overwhelming grief.

"Oh, Cameron," she whispered, her voice thick with yet more tears, "I'm so sorry."

"No," he said. The word emerged with more force than he'd imagined he could produce.

"The rear detachment officer called." She glanced away from him, bit her trembling lip, and continued, "Kyle died in a roadside bombing. Probably about the time you collapsed at the office."

Her gaze slid back to his face before dropping to the hand now clutching his arm. "You felt him die, didn't you? That's what caused your collapse. He contacted you when he died."

"Yes...no." Cameron closed his eyes and took a deep, steadying breath. He opened his eyes and caught Sophie's gaze. "Yes, Kyle opened the link and dragged me into his pain, but he's not dead." He turned his arm under her hand and grasped her trembling fingers. "Sophie, I'd know if he were dead. Kyle is alive."

Tears spilled from her eyes and followed well-established tracks across her cheeks to drip from her chin. "I'm so sorry," she repeated.

He opened his mouth to protest, but she laid a quelling finger against his lips. "Hush, my love. Don't...don't think about it now. Just rest. Once you're home, you can talk to the Rear D, yourself. Hear his account directly."

Cameron closed his eyes and touched the psychic link he'd shared with Kyle their whole lives. Nothing. The link lay dormant in the back of his mind, a frighteningly blank place that should have been vibrant with Kyle's zest for life.

He wasn't dead. Cameron would know if Kyle.... He wasn't dead.

For the first time in his life, Cameron McClellan experienced separation anxiety.

3

Through the doctor's jovial pronouncement that Cameron was healthy as an ox and ought not to be taking up space a truly sick person might need, through the signing of release papers and the indignity of a stocky male nurse wheeling him to the hospital entrance like a decrepit old man, and through the silent drive back to his comfortable Cherry Creek home, the link remained blank, tormenting Cameron with the lack of access to his twin. Sophie insisted on driving, though her grief-stricken face and rough breathing testified to her own heightened distress.

"I've made an appointment for Major Schmidt to call you first thing in the morning," she said, pulling the Lexus sedan into their well-ordered garage. "It was the first opening he had. Twelve men lost their lives in that explosion."

"Eleven," Cameron said, not meeting her gaze.

She sighed, but let the comment pass. She punched the remote, closing the garage door, and they climbed out of the car.

Halfway to the door into the house, Cameron paused.

"Toss me the keys, Sophie." She glanced at him, eyebrows raised.

"I'm fine," he said, "but I'll go nuts if I go inside and try to read a book or watch TV. I need to figure this out."

"What are you going to do?"

"I think I'll go to church. Maybe Reverend Andrews will be able to help me sort this out."

She nodded. "Are you sure you're up to driving? I could take you."

He smiled, closed the gap between them and drew her into his arms. "You're as broken up over this as I should be," he said and kissed her gently. "I can drive. You get some rest before the kids get home from school."

She leaned heavily against him for a moment and then drew herself upright. "If you're sure you're okay...you're right. I could use a nap."

He slipped the keys from her hand and nodded to the door. "Go. Get some rest. Reverend Andrews can keep an eye on me for a while."

Sophie smiled, stroked her hand across his cheek and said, "I love you, Cameron."

He caught her hand and kissed it. "I know."

Cameron prodded the link yet again when he pulled the door to the sanctuary open and strode the length of the center aisle. The increasingly familiar blankness curdled his stomach. He fell to his knees and leaned heavily on the sturdy oak communion rail. Kyle couldn't be dead, but if he lived, why couldn't Cameron detect his presence?

"Cameron!" Reverend Andrews's friendly voice boomed in the early afternoon silence. "What brings you to the Lord's house in the middle of the day?"

Cameron lurched upright, the weight of his expectations making him reel.

"Hello, Reverend Andrews." He'd come for this man's advice, but now that his pastor stood before him, awkward thoughts filled Cameron's brain. He remembered practicing sleight-of-hand with the collection plate. He pushed the thought away. They'd been twelve at the time, and he and Kyle had paid for their crime. At thirty-five, he didn't need to cower before his spiritual advisor.

"I know you're busy," he said, pushing both hands deep into his pants pockets, "but I need to talk something out. Do you have a few minutes?"

Reverend Andrews placed a hand on Cameron's shoulder and gestured toward the pews. "All the time in the world," he said with a smile. "How can I be of service?"

They moved toward the pews, the aged wood so dark it appeared black. Cameron balked when Reverend Andrews moved to sit. The long, maroon cushions padding the hard seats conjured images of congealed blood. He closed his eyes, seeking the peace that usually permeated this place, but the sanctuary's silence only highlighted the disturbing blankness of Kyle's link.

"I'm sorry, sir," he said. "It's too quiet in here." He gave the pastor a wry grin. "I'm not myself today. Would you mind if we took a walk?"

The aging man halted in the act of seating himself, hung suspended for a moment, then stood and readjusted his belted, black trousers.

"Of course, Cameron," he said, gesturing toward the door with his right arm. "Wherever you're most comfortable."

The gesture captured Cameron's attention and he noticed how feeble Reverend Andrews's arm appeared, sticking out of his short-sleeved white shirt. When had God's representative grown frail? This man had towered over Cameron's life — physically at first, then spiritually.

They stepped through the oversized, carved oak doors and into the afternoon sunlight. Cameron took a deep breath, and his shoulders relaxed. They strolled down the tree-lined city street.

Reverend Andrews remained quiet until the silence compelled Cameron to speak. He hung his head and addressed the sidewalk in low, husky tones.

"I'm worried about Kyle and concerned about my own grip on reality."

"Tell me what's troubling you."

Cameron sucked in a deep breath, and words tumbled out. "You remember me and Kyle as kids, don't you? All the trouble we got into?" He glanced sideways. A smile twitched across his pastor's lips.

"Certainly. What you boys didn't think up, no one would." He draped an arm across Cameron's shoulder. "How is Kyle? What has you worried? I know he's in Iraq, but I'm assuming it's more than his posting."

Anguish clawed at Cameron's gut. He closed his eyes and allowed himself to be guided by the older man's touch. When he pulled himself under control, he opened his eyes.

"Something happened this morning," he said. "The rear detachment officer called to tell us Kyle died, but...."

"No!" Reverend Andrews interrupted. He stopped walking, fought visibly for control, and tried again. "Tell me what happened."

"I experienced his pain and blacked out; ended up in the hospital myself, but he's not dead. I know he's not dead." Cameron sighed, scrubbed his face with his hand, and forced himself to meet the pastor's startled gaze. "Didn't you know that we, that Kyle and I, well, we have a psychic bond?"

"I've heard of such things with twins," Reverend Andrews said, starting to walk again, "but no, I had no idea."

"We've never advertised it," Cameron said with a shrug. "We learned early that it made people nervous. But it's real."

He stopped walking again and turned to face the older man, who quickly adjusted to the change in momentum.

"That's how I know he's alive. The army is mistaken. Kyle isn't dead. But the problem, the reason I came to you, is that our link isn't functioning. It's...well, it's just kind of blank."

Compassion suffused the pastor's face. "I'm so sorry, Cameron. This must be so difficult for you." Reverend Andrews stood in the bright sunshine of a May afternoon and reached for Cameron's hands. "Son, if you say you and Kyle had a unique bond, I can accept that." He paused and stared deep into Cameron's eyes. "But if your, uh, link, isn't functioning, and you've been notified of his death, then you must accept the reality of that awful truth. I'm so sorry for your loss. You have to hold onto the knowledge that you'll meet again in a better place."

The thin arm reached out and gently turned Cameron back the

way they had come. "Let's go back to my office," Reverend Andrews continued, "There are arrangements to be made."

Cameron sighed and accompanied his pastor back to the church. He'd have to find his own answers. He'd known he would, but he'd hoped Reverend Andrews could advise him, help him decide on a course of action. Funeral arrangements would not help Kyle survive the attack.

4

Cameron spent the morning buried in his den trying to convince the military they'd made a mistake. The rear detachment officer assured him in a calm, soothing voice — the kind Cameron imagined he'd use with a deranged killer holding a gun — that there had been no mistake. Twelve men had been assigned to the humvee, and twelve bodies had been recovered. He admitted that the remains had been too badly mangled to allow for visual identification, but the numbers matched the duty roster, and Kyle's tags had been discovered. Decisive identification would follow in a few days.

In desperation, Cameron called Lieutenant Colonel Douglas Avery, Kyle's long-time friend. Doug understood Kyle and Cameron's unique connection.

"Doug, you don't understand," Cameron said, exasperation coloring his voice. "If everyone thinks he's dead, no one's going to look for him."

"I'm sorry, Cameron, but from what I've been told, there just isn't any chance Kyle survived. You know I'd be out there beating the bushes myself if I thought the possibility existed."

"How can I convince you I'm not just refusing to face his death? Doug, he's alive. Kyle is alive and he needs our help."

Cameron heard muffled voices on the other end of the line. He waited.

Doug sighed and said, "I've got to go, Cameron, but I'll ask to see the final identification reports. In the meantime, if you get any concrete evidence, call me."

They disconnected, and Cameron slammed his hand on the smooth surface of his polished oak desk. The resultant stinging grounded him in the here and now. He needed answers, and Kyle was the only one who could give them to him. He leaned back in his chair and steepled his fingers. Who could he consult about a malfunctioning psychic connection?

He smiled grimly, remembering the time he and Kyle had visited a local psychic. They'd thought it would be a kick to exchange information with someone who understood their unusual abilities. Unfortunately, the woman had turned out to be a fake.

The only person who'd ever accepted their psychic link had been that research assistant from the University of Colorado Twin Study.

Cameron sat up. The research assistant. He hadn't thought of the man in years. He wondered where the grad student was now. Surely not still with the university? What was his name? Adam...Ed...Edgar...Ewan.... No, Evan! Evan Langstrom. He remembered because Kyle had found the name amusing for some unknown reason.

A few minutes' Internet research determined that an Evan Langstrom currently practiced psychiatry in Denver's LoDo district. Smiling, Cameron picked up the phone.

Dr. Evan Langstrom stood when his receptionist ushered Cameron into his office. The men shook hands and sized each other up. The young researcher Cameron remembered had matured into a medium height, wiry man who carried himself with assurance. Langstrom delivered his handshake with a firm, decisive grip, and his eyes, behind their shield of thick glasses, glittered with lively intelligence.

"Nice to meet you, Mr. McClellan," the doctor said. "I hope I can be of service."

"Thanks for working me in so soon, Doctor," Cameron replied. "I doubt you remember, but we've met before."

Dr. Langstrom's eyebrows arched. "Really? Refresh my memory."

"You did some research at the University of Colorado some twenty or twenty- five years back. I was one of your subjects."

The doctor frowned. "How interesting. Actually, I participated in several studies. Can you be more specific?"

"I'm an identical twin. My brother Kyle and I visited with you several times." Cameron hesitated. "You made an impression, and when my current difficulty came up, well, I remembered you."

"Cameron and Kyle McClellan. Of course." Dr. Langstrom smiled and led Cameron across the office to a comfortable sitting area comprised of a matching leather couch and chair and a sturdy maple rocker. "Now I know why your name sounded familiar. Since we're old friends, why don't we dispense with the formal titles? You call me Evan, and I'll call you Cameron. Deal?"

"Fine by me." Cameron relaxed into the overstuffed chair.

Evan plucked a yellow notepad from a side table and settled into the rocking chair, its seat and arms shiny from constant use. "How is Kyle, by the way?" he asked.

"That's actually why I'm here. I remembered that you seemed to believe us about our psychic connection, and I'm desperately in need of someone who will take me seriously."

Evan rocked back. "I'm listening."

Cameron leaned forward, elbows on knees, and told Evan about his confusion over the last few days. How, despite his inability to contact Kyle, he remained convinced that Kyle hadn't died in the explosion. His thoughts digressed, and he found himself describing growing up as a twin, reminding Evan about the special link Cameron and Kyle enjoyed and the myriad ways they'd used that connection to confuse and confound the adults in their lives.

"Eventually," he said, the corners of his mouth twitching with memory, "we learned to shut each other out. I mean, togetherness is great, but I didn't want him leering in the background when I went out with Sophie."

"A reasonable response," Evan agreed. "What happened when you reached adulthood? I assume you went in different directions after the study ended?"

"Yes. We both went to college, but I studied business and finance, while Kyle joined ROTC and followed an engineering track." Cameron met Evan's gaze through a gathering haze of unshed tears. "Kyle had a knight-in-shining-armor complex. I never understood it, and I couldn't talk him out of it. He lived and breathed career military."

Evan nodded. "Some people seem to be born with a calling. Did your bond remain strong?"

Cameron leaned back, letting the chair envelope and support him, and blinked back his tears. "Yes and no. When we bothered to use it, the link was strong — and distance didn't seem to matter — but most of the time, we were too caught up in our own lives to use it." His chest tightened, and his breath came in quick, shallow pants at the thought of all those lost opportunities. He curled forward in an effort to contain his pain.

Evan reacted to the change. He rocked forward and placed a hand on Cameron's hunched shoulder. "Relax, Cameron. You're safe. Close your eyes and concentrate on breathing deeply."

With a shudder, Cameron did as instructed. He felt Evan's hand leave his shoulder and heard the rocker creak as the man shifted his balance. The leather scent of the overstuffed chair gave him something to focus on — other than the pain in his chest. He concentrated on drawing that fragrance deep into his lungs until his muscles unclenched. When he opened his eyes, he straightened and met Evan's steady gaze.

"Kyle's in Iraq. He was involved in a roadside bombing yesterday morning," he said without preamble. "I experienced his pain, the disorientation and trauma of the explosion. 10:05 a.m. Central Standard Time. I know it sounds crazy, but I lived through it with him. The problem is the army believes he's dead, and I can't contact him." He collapsed forward, head hanging, hands dangling between his knees. "Something happened to our link. I don't know whether his injuries are so severe I can't reach him, or whether he's unconscious, or whether the blast broke our connection, but I know he's alive." His eyes flew open, and he raised his head to fix his gaze on Evan's face. "My brother is alive and injured ... and no one is looking for him."

"And no one in authority will take you seriously," Evan said. He nodded, his gaze never wavering from Cameron's. "I believe you. Let's see if I can help you jump start your connection."

Cameron slouched back in the chair, leaned his head against the padded leather back, and closed his eyes. Relief flooded his mind.

"The psychic element wasn't part of the university sanctioned study," Evan said, "but it came up often enough that I've done a bit a

research on my own over the years. Let's try some relaxation tech-
niques and see if you can get past whatever is blocking your access."

A few minutes later, Cameron reclined in peaceful bliss, listening
to Evan's quiet instructions.

"You're doing great, Cameron. Now, think about Kyle. Ignore the
link. Just concentrate on Kyle, his essence, the Kyle no one knows but
you. Relax. Picture him at ease and happy."

Cameron's lips curved upward, and he pictured Kyle in the
hammock they used to fight over at Red Feather Lake. His brother
dozed in dappled shade, a light breeze ruffling his dark brown hair.

"When you're ready, reach out to him. Gently."

Cameron stepped into his own mental image and laid a hand on
Kyle's shoulder. *Wake up, buddy. I need to talk to you.*

Kyle's eyelids fluttered open. *Where've you been? I've been waiting
for you.*

Never mind. I'm here now. Where are you?

Confusion flickered across Kyle's features. *Right here. Where else
would I be?*

Cameron bit back a sarcastic retort and knelt beside his brother
so their eyes were level. *Think, bro. If you open your eyes in the real
world, what will you see?*

The real world? Aren't we at the lake?

Cameron shook his head. *Mom and Dad sold this place years ago. I
live in Cherry Creek now, remember? With Sophie and the kids.*

Sophie's name triggered something behind Kyle's eyes. He sat up,
swinging his legs over the edge of the hammock.

*And I'm a major in the army. Stationed in Iraq. What are we doing
here? What's happening, Cam?*

*That's what I'm here to find out. You were injured, Kyle. I haven't been
able to reach you. The army thinks you're dead. You've got to help me,
buddy. I don't know how to find you.*

Kyle's brows pulled together in a straight line. He jumped up and
stalked around the hammock. When he reached the water's edge, he
bent, picked up a stone, and skipped it across the quiet surface of the
lake.

The humvee was destroyed. The pain.... He licked his lips and stared across the expanse of water with unseeing eyes. *I could barely move, but I managed to drag myself under a bush.* He stopped and turned to face Cameron. *That's all I remember until you woke me here.*

Cameron nodded. *You're unconscious, have been since you crawled under that bush. Kyle, you've got to wake up. You've got to figure out where you are and tell me. If I can tell Doug exactly where to look, he'll find you. I know he will, but you've got to help me, bro. I can't do this alone.*

Kyle shuddered, but determination tightened his features. He nodded and held out his hand.

Cameron grabbed it and savored the strength of his twin's grip.

I can do this. Kyle smiled, but a certain macabre grimness lit his eyes. *Stand down, Cam. This is my operation now. I'll get back to you as soon as I can.*

Cameron jackknifed to a sitting position and stared wildly around Evan's office. He reoriented himself and swung his feet to the floor. Facing Evan, he nodded.

"Thanks. It worked."

Evan clapped him on the shoulder before rocking back in his chair. "I'm glad. He's alive then?"

"Yes. He's been unconscious. I woke him to our link, and now he's attempting to regain consciousness in the physical world. He'll let me know where he is, if...."

"If he manages to pull himself out of the coma," Evan finished the sentence Cameron had been unwilling to voice.

Evan stood and gestured for Cameron to do the same. The men walked to the office door in silence. Evan paused with his hand on the knob. "Keep me informed, Cameron. I want to know how this turns out."

Cameron nodded without meeting the psychiatrist's eyes.

"And Cameron...."

He glanced up and met the older man's compassionate gaze. "You've done everything you could to save your brother. Far more than ninety-five percent of the people on this planet could have managed. If he doesn't make it, it won't be because of any failure on your part."

"Thanks," Cameron murmured, his vision blurring momentarily. "I think he told me the same thing."

Evan cocked his head inquisitively.

"When he ordered me to 'stand down.' I think he was taking responsibility for his own fate."

"Yes," Evan agreed. "A man doesn't reach the rank of major without understanding personal responsibility."

"Thanks again, Evan. For taking me seriously and for helping me reach him."

"You're welcome, Cameron. I'm glad I could help." Evan opened the office door and stepped into the reception area with Cameron. "Alice," he said to his receptionist, "please make a note: there will be no charge for this session. Mr. McClellan came in to follow up on a research project." He turned to Cameron. "It's been an honor, Mr. McClellan, and please, keep me posted."

Cameron shook the doctor's outstretched hand and then turned and strode from Evan Langstrom's office.

Cameron and Sophie sat at the table in the window nook of their tidy kitchen. The debris of the evening meal had been cleared away, and the kids deposited in the family room to enjoy a rare weeknight video. The adults required time to talk.

"I was right, Sophie. He's alive."

The uncertainty in Sophie's brown eyes irritated Cameron. He didn't want her pity or compassion; he craved her whole-hearted belief.

"You really think you contacted him?"

"Why is this so hard for you to accept?" He kept his voice quiet to avoid alarming the children in the next room, but he longed to vent his frustration in unrestrained accusation. "You know we're connected. You've known it since we were dating."

"I know," she whispered, dropping her gaze, "and I want to believe you. It's just that Major Schmidt seems so certain, and, well..."

"And you think I'm in denial," he finished with a sigh. "It's a good thing I found Dr. Langstrom. At least he believes me."

"That's another thing," she said, warming to the subject. "Don't you think it's a little convenient? You remembering this man's name after all these years? And finding him so easily? Are you sure he's a real doctor?"

"For God's sake, Sophie! What do you take me for? A complete idiot?" Cameron jumped to his feet and paced the length of the kitchen, spitting his words with quiet force. "Kyle and I spent a lot of Saturday afternoons with Evan Langstrom. Yes. It was a long time ago, but you don't forget an experience like that. You don't forget the only adult who ever believed you had a psychic connection."

He reeled back to the table and stood clutching the back of his chair. "I wracked my brain and remembered his name, okay? Then I Googled him. What's so strange about a man setting up his practice near the university where he trained?"

"The point is: Kyle's alive! If he can manage to figure out where he is, we might have a chance of rescuing him."

Sophie met his gaze, tears welling in her eyes. "I believe you, Cameron. I guess I'm trying to protect you in my own warped and terrified way. It seems such a long shot, such a remote possibility that you'll be able to convince anyone to do anything."

She stood, rounded the table, and pulled Cameron into a tight embrace. "Guard yourself, Cameron. Promise me you won't follow Kyle to the grave."

Insight hit like a physical slap, and Cameron hugged Sophie close. He'd frightened her. He'd been so tightly connected to his twin during the attack that he'd ended up in the hospital himself. Sophie had imagined the worst, still feared for his safety.

"I'm not going anywhere, Sophie. Kyle's my brother, and I've got to help him, if I can." He kissed the top of her head and squeezed her ribs as hard as he dared. "But you and the kids are my world. I won't leave you. Not until I'm forced from this life."

A deep sigh escaped her, and she relaxed in his arms. "Okay," she whispered. "What can I do to help?"

"Believe in me," he said.

"I always have."

Later that night, Cameron returned to the bedroom after his stint in the bathroom to find Sophie seated on the edge of their bed studying a photograph of himself and Kyle. She made a pretty picture, sitting there in her white cotton nightgown, her long, dark hair braided for sleep. Her serious expression tugged at his heart and made him anxious to find the answer to this puzzle. He crossed the room and sat beside her, noting the vivid contrast between his dark blue pajamas and the whiteness of her gown.

"Everything will be alright," he said. "Dr. Langstrom already spoke to me about the limits of my responsibility."

She smiled, a hesitant little smile that didn't quite reach her eyes. "I'm glad. Do you think Kyle will contact you tonight?"

He shrugged. "If he can. If he can't, well, I might have to accept that the communication we shared this afternoon was our last." A shiver ran down his spine, though he did his best to disguise it from Sophie. The link's continuing blankness frightened him. He'd expected Kyle to rouse himself the moment they broke contact in Evan's office. Each hour the link remained dark weakened Cameron's hope for Kyle's recovery.

"He'll contact you," she said.

"I hope so." He kissed her and crossed to his side of the bed. "I hope a lot of things."

7

Cameron visited the cabin at Red Feather Lake again in his dreams. He pushed through the screen door to the enclosed porch and raced to the hammock. The breath he hadn't known he was holding exploded in relieved laughter when he saw Kyle's recumbent form.

You scared me, Kyle. I thought I'd lost you.

He reached his twin's side and gasped. Kyle's eyes and cheeks were sunken, his flesh torn and mangled. Fear clutched Cameron's heart.

Kyle! Oh, God, Kyle. I'm so sorry... Tears stung his eyes, and he dropped to his knees beside the hammock.

I did it, Cam, Kyle whispered. *I woke up. That's why I look like this. The pain...well, the coma was the only way I had to deal with it.*

Oh, God, Cameron repeated, tears tracing his cheeks. *I'm so sorry.*

Nonsense. Had to be done. Listen. I'm in a farmhouse just north of Chamchamal. I can see goats, and when the door opens, I can see the outside. It's painted red, the door.

Does...does it hurt to talk? Can you answer a few questions?

Ask, Kyle commanded through tight lips.

How did you get there? Doug will ask.

The farmer ... on his way home from market ... put me in his wagon.

Why didn't he take you back to the post?

Afraid. A compassionate man, but he's seen too much...

They recovered twelve bodies. That's why no one is looking for you. Do you know who the twelfth victim is?

Kyle nodded and licked emaciated lips. *Reporter. Paul Doven.*

The one who's been missing?

Yes. We found him on patrol that evening, were taking him back to post.

Okay. That's enough. I'll call Doug. We're coming to get you, Kyle. Hang on. Don't you dare die on me! You hear me, Kyle?

A wan smile curved Kyle's lips. *Tell Doug to hurry.*

EPILOGUE

Cameron McClellan strode through the halls of the army hospital at Landstuhl, Germany, a man on a mission. He'd purchased the ticket as soon as he disconnected from the call to Lieutenant Colonel Douglas Avery. He never doubted Doug's ability to retrieve Kyle, not after Cameron had told him exactly where to look.

A white-coated doctor stood in the doorway of the room Cameron had been told was Kyle's. The man glanced up at Cameron's approach, noted his visitor's identification badge, and nodded.

"You must be Major McClellan's brother," he said with a smile.

Cameron breathed a sigh of relief. Kyle must be much improved if the resemblance was that notable. They hadn't looked anything like twins in the last Red Feather vision.

"Yes, I'm his brother, Cameron McClellan. How's he doing?"

"Lieutenant Colonel Avery found him in time. He's had a rough go of it, but he's healing nicely." A slight frown crossed his face. "I wouldn't normally consider this relevant, but you two are identical twins, I believe?"

Cameron nodded.

"Well, he's sustained some facial scarring that will require plastic surgery. I didn't want his appearance to be too much of a shock."

"I've seen him," Cameron answered. "He's alive. That's all that counts."

The doctor looked a puzzled, but Cameron chose not to enlighten him.

"May I go in?"

"Yes, yes. Of course."

Cameron stepped past the man and walked soft-footed to his brother's bedside. Kyle's eyes were closed, his face and limbs heavily bandaged, but his breathing was steady and easy. Cameron bowed his head and fought back tears.

"Where've you been?" asked a raspy voice. "I've been waiting for you."

Tears leaked from the edges of his eyes as Cameron met his brother's gaze. "Never mind. I'm here now."

Kyle raised a hand made awkward by bandages and IVs and gripped Cameron's strong, healthy one. "Thanks, Cam. Thanks for pushing the link, for waking me up."

"You're welcome," he said, his voice rough with tears. "I'm glad you're back. Don't ever make me face that blank link again."

"Deal," Kyle said. "Have you heard from Doug?"

Cameron shook his head.

"He sent me an email. The nurse printed it out and read it to me. Said he's buying that Iraqi farmer a whole herd of goats."

"That sounds like Doug," Cameron said with a laugh.

They fell silent for a moment, and then Kyle whispered, "When I get back to The States, when I'm better, what do you say we introduce your kids to Red Feather Lake?"

Cameron grinned and squeezed his brother's hand. "Whatever you want, Kyle. Whatever you want."

ALSO BY DEB LOGAN

Children's Stories and Chapter Books:

Cinnamon Chou Files:

- THE CASE OF THE MISSING INARIAN
- THE CASE OF THE GLITTERING HOARD
- THE CASE OF THE RECREATIONAL THIEF
- THE CASE OF THE VANISHING PUPPY
- THE CASE OF THE MISSING MERCHANDISE

Prentiss Twins Novels:

- THUNDERBIRD
- COYOTE
- WHITE BUFFALO
- THE TWELVE DAYS OF TRICKSTERS (SHORT STORY)
- A TRICKSTER HALLOWEEN (SHORT STORY)

"Read-to-Me" Stories:

- CHATTERMASTER
- DEIRDRE'S DRAGON
- THE FOX AND THE FLEAS
- MOM'S HELPER
- READ-TO-ME STORIES (COLLECTION)

Short Story Collections:

- GALACTIC CADETS: KIDS IN SPACE
- READ-TO-ME STORIES

Short Stories:

- ANGELIC VOICES
- LILAH'S GHOST

Young Adult Stories and Novels:

Dani Erickson Stories:

- DEMON DAZE
- SCHOOL DAZE
- FAMILY DAZE
- CHALLENGING DAZE
- DANGEROUS DAZE
- DANI'S DEMONS (COLLECTION)

Faery Chronicles:

- FAERY UNEXPECTED (NOVEL)
- FAERY BEAUTIFUL (SHORT STORY)
- FAERY UNPREDICTABLE (NOVELETTE)
- LEXIE'S CHOICE (SHORT STORY)
- OF DRAGONS AND CENTAURS (SHORT STORY)
- FAERY COLLECTIBLE (COLLECTION)

Feyland Tie-Ins:

- EMMA: A FEYLAND DRYAD
- ON GUARD: A FEYLAND STORY

Seer Chronicles:

- THE SEER CHRONICLES: VOLUME I (COLLECTION)
- TERRORS (SHORT STORY)
- TO HAVE...AND TO HOLD (SHORT STORY)
- SELKIES IN PARADISE (SHORT STORY)

- The Journal (short story)
- Paladin Shield (short story)

Siren Tales:

- Salt Water
- Siren Surf

Short Story Collections:

- Ghosts and Ghoulies
- More Ghosts and Ghoulies

Short Fiction:

- Amelia Fox: Spy in Training
- Beauty or Butterface?
- Flutterbies and French Toast
- Rush!
- That Lake House Summer

"WDM Presents" Anthologies:

- Spun Yarns Unwound, Vol. 1
- Tales of Mystery & Mayhem
- 2016: A Year of Short Fiction
- 2017: A Year of Short Fiction
- WDM Presents: Short Fiction from 2018
- WDM Presents: Short Fiction from 2019
- WDM Presents: Short Fiction from 2020
- WDM Presents: Short Fiction from 2021

ABOUT DEB LOGAN

Deb Logan specializes in tales for the young – and the young at heart! Author of the popular Faery Chronicles series, Deb loves the unknown, whether it's the lure of space or earthbound mythology. She writes about demon hunters, thunderbirds, and everyday life on a space station for tweens, teens, and anyone who enjoys young adult fiction. Her work has been published in multiple volumes of *Fiction River*, as well as in *2017 Young Explorer's Adventure Guide*, *Feyland Tales*, and other popular anthologies.

Sign up for Deb's newsletter and receive a FREE story!

To learn more, visit Deb at:
debloganwrites.com
Or send her an email at:
debloganwrites@gmail.com

ALSO BY DEBBIE MUMFORD

Kristi Lundrigan Mysteries:

- DELECTABLE MOUNTAIN QUILTING (NOVEL)
- IN A PICKLE (NOVEL)
- FOOL'S PUZZLE (SHORT STORY)
- WILDFIRE! (SHORT STORY)

Gus and Ghost Short Story Series:

- SEVENTH
- SEVENTH: FIRST FRUITS
- DEATH OF AN ALCHEMIST (UNCOLLECTED ANTHOLOGY)
- SEVENTH: THE SAMHAIN DILEMMA
- DARK OF THE MOON (UNCOLLECTED ANTHOLOGY)

Logans of Lastalrig Series:

- HER HIGHLAND LAIRD (NOVELLA)
- HER HIGHLAND YULE (SHORT STORY)

Red's Series:

- RED'S MAGICK (SHORT STORY COLLECTION)
- SEEING RED (SHORT STORY)

Signs of the Prophecy Novels:

- YOUNGEST
- SEEKER
- CHOSEN (COMING SOON!)

Sorcha's Children Series:

- Sorcha's Children (Omnibus Edition)
- Sorcha's Heart (Novella)
- Dragons' Choice (Novel)
- Dragons' Flight (Novel)
- Dragons' Desire (Novel)
- Dragons' Destiny (Novel)

Supernatural Yellowstone Short Story Series:

- Reality Bites
- The Cat Lady of Yellowstone

Uncollected Anthology Short Stories:

- Death of an Alchemist (UA Alchemy)
- The Wedding Cake (UA Magical Arts)
- Dark of the Moon (UA Paranormal Pirates)
- In the Banyan Copse (UA Unexpected Histories)
- Old One (UA Magical Quests)

Universal Star League Short Story Series:

- Voyages Into The Black (Collection)
- The Warbirds of Absaroka
- Awakening the Warrior
- Incident on the Odyssey
- The Queen's Captive
- The Lost Colony
- Freighter Families in Space

Witchling Short Story Series:

- Witchling

- THE SOLITARY SORCERESS
- TO PROTECT A PRINCESS

Stand Alone Novels:

- SECOND SIGHT

Historical Fiction:

- HER HIGHLAND LAIRD (NOVELLA)
- HER HIGHLAND YULE
- INCIDENT ON THE HIGH LINE
- MISS BAINBRIDGE'S SUMMER ADVENTURE
- MISS BAINBRIDGE'S CHRISTMAS PARTY
- SISTERS IN SUFFRAGE
- THE TRAIL WHERE WE CRIED
- THE WHITE DRAGON AND THE RED

Short Story Collections:

- LOVE IN A FLASH
- TALES OF BYGONE DAYS
- TALES OF LOVE & MAGICK
- TALES OF THE UNEXPECTED
- TALES OF TOMORROW
- TALES OF DISASTROUS DEEDS

Short Fiction:

- A GROVE OF MOUNTAIN ASH
- A WALK WITH GEORGIA
- AN ALIEN ADVENTURE
- ASTROMANCER
- BECAUSE OF THE CHRISTMAS STROLL
- BENEATH AND BEYOND

"WDM Presents" Anthologies:

ABOUT DEBBIE MUMFORD

Debbie Mumford specializes in speculative fiction (fantasy, paranormal romance, and science fiction) as well as mystery and historical fiction. Author of the popular *Sorcha's Children* series, Debbie loves the unknown, whether it's the lure of space or earthbound mythology. Her work has been published in multiple volumes of *Fiction River*, as well as in *Heart's Kiss Magazine*, *Amazing Monster Tales*, and many other popular anthologies. She writes about dragon-shifters, time-traveling lovers, and detectives—whether amateur or professional—for adults as Debbie Mumford, and science fiction and fantasy for tweens and young adults as Deb Logan.

Join Debbie's special announcement newsletter list and receive a FREE story!

To learn more, visit Debbie at:
debbiemumford.com/
Or send her an email at:
deborah.mumford@gmail.com

facebook.com/DebbieMumfordWrites
amazon.com/author/debbiemumford
bookbub.com/authors/debbie-mumford
twitter.com/deborah_mumford

www.ingramcontent.com/pod-product-compliance
Lightning Source LLC
Chambersburg PA
CBHW030848030726
47495CB00005B/1420